Race Traitors

TO
ROSE
Best
Wishes
always
Mark [illegible]
11 NOV 06

Race Traitors

Mark Davis

iUniverse, Inc.
New York Lincoln Shanghai

Race Traitors

iUniverse books may be ordered through booksellers or by contacting:

iUniverse
2021 Pine Lake Road, Suite 100
Lincoln, NE 68512
www.iuniverse.com
1-800-Authors (1-800-288-4677)

Book cover design by
Julius Burrell and Mark Davis

Edited by:
Lori Chapman
Rachel Davis
Joanne Partipillo
Dr. Julian Williams

ISBN: 0-595-32167-4 (pbk)

ISBN: 0-595-66483-0 (cloth)

Printed in the United States of America

To Ted and Frances Davis

"I miss you so much!"

"When a brother kills another brother, he becomes a traitor to his race."

—Terry Callier

"Race Traitors is a moniker given to any person who murders another member of the same race."

—Mark Davis

Acknowledgments

I cannot begin to mention all the people and all of the resources consulted in the preparation of this manuscript. There just is not enough that can be said to express my indebtedness. However, I would like to mention the names of some people who have contributed immensely toward the success of this novel.

Paris Patton, Julius Jones, James Tullos and Michael Orr spent countless hours reviewing and recalling the events that occurred during that era. BSerenity and Pbenesh. Authorassist reviewed the original manuscript and made welcomed suggestions that enhanced the clarity of the manuscript. Their careful evaluation of the contents of this novel and their suggestions were deeply appreciated.

Bennie L. Crane, was meticulous in his efforts to guide me through the writing and publishing of this work. I cannot express my appreciation to him. Finally, I would like to give special recognition to Dr. Julian L. Williams, who completed the final edit and made significant recommendations toward the development of the characters.

I would like to sincerely thank these wonderful people for their contribution. I hope they will be proud of the role they played in the development of this novel.

Prologue

"In these bloody days and frightful nights when the urban warrior can find no face more despicable than his own, no ammunition more deadly than self hate and no target more deserving of his true aim than his brother, we must wonder how we came so late and lonely to this place."

—Maya Angelou

In 1974, the city of Chicago experienced a historical increase in the number of homicides; as a result of this violence, 970 human beings lost their lives. Murder trended up from 1965 through 1976, increasing 169 percent. Young Black males between the ages of fifteen and twenty-four represented the majority of those numbers, creating a new wave of anxiety and despair in the hearts of mothers whose children were amongst that age group. As a result, the Chicago Police Department was over-burdened with murder investigations and unable to accurately address the rising homicide rate.

At this juncture in Chicago's savage history, the city recorded 4,071 aggravated assaults with a firearm. There were two local street gangs waging gang warfare, creating a corridor of death and desolation in neighborhoods throughout the city. The Blackstone Rangers and the Devils Disciples terrorized the Woodlawn and Englewood communities, leaving in their wake the bitter reality that hundreds of Black male children would die before this cultural cataclysm was recorded.

During this time, drugs, guns, greed, murder, and misfortune all clustered together to create a period of brutality and death. Interestingly, when shadowed sociologically, it is both simple and complex to see how Chicago, already known for its aggressive past, shifted forward—establishing a new reputation as the "gang murder capital of the Midwest." When observed with a close lens, it becomes easy to see how the true suffering that plagued the city far surpassed the reported murders.

Gang warfare defined this new, violent Chicago. And as the plague of violence becomes endemic, there is one rookie detective who takes on the challenge of not only ridding the city of this latest wave of gang brutality but, more importantly, understanding it as well. Along with members of the gang intelligence unit, especially his jaded partner—DoubleA—Myles Sivad wages a relentless battle to piece together the crimes, the reasons, and predators crushing the spirits of those who keep losing their children to this spreading violence.

These officers who, at times, were targeted by the gangs were men who walked a fine line in their fight for justice—warriors who sometimes lost their lives in this urban jungle.

CHAPTER 1

It was a grisly spectacle of blood, brain tissue, and death. I couldn't help gasping for fresh air. The stench of death was overpowering, yet we had to conduct an investigation—being especially careful not to overlook any key evidence. When we entered a boarded-up side entrance, we overheard a voice yell out, "The Bulls are coming." Suddenly, several suspected Blackstone Rangers made a beeline out of a rear window and down the fire escape. The year is 1974 and there is a gang war going on. The Blackstone Rangers—often referred to as "Stones"—is a street gang that has intimidated and destabilized the Woodlawn community through the use of violence and murder.

The scene was the abandoned South-Moor Hotel located on Stony Island Avenue, between Marquette Road and 67th Street on the Southside of Chicago. This was a horrid crime scene. We received information that a body could be found in a closet on the fourth floor. The anonymous tip was accurate. The victim was a male Black—approximately fifteen years old. His body was partially rolled up in a rug and stuffed in a janitor's closet. He was wearing a pair of blue denim pants, a white shirt, and a red sweater. A gray jacket and red cap were found lying next to the corpse. He had a gunshot wound from a large-caliber weapon—probably a 45—behind his right ear. His brains were literally blown out. Further examination of the crime scene, just outside of the janitor's closet, revealed blood and brain tissue scattered all over the walls and draperies. Both hands and feet were bound, and he was gagged. The body had begun to decompose and the stench was successfully compromising my will to continue. Even though the killer—or killers—had made every effort not to leave any evidence at the crime scene, they couldn't resist leaving their noted signature on the victim.

The victim had one white Chuck Taylor Converse All Star gym shoe on his left foot. The other shoe was missing. This appeared to be a signature that some gangs used to represent their code of conduct and the reason for murder. Apparently, this young man had failed to honor his association, his affiliation with his new family—or maybe he was simply caught stealing from the gang.

In Chicago there were several gangs that emerged during the late1960's and early 1970's. However, the Blackstone Rangers and the Devil Disciples were the dominate groups—and they were creating havoc in the Black community.

The South-Moor Hotel had been deserted for several years, and the Stones had taken it over. They conducted their meetings and gang operations in a building that was once the pride of the southside. While carefully searching through the area, I became distracted by the architectural remnants of the once luxurious and pricey hotel. I began to envision the elegant and extravagant furnishings that were the foundation of the buildings prominent past. The ballrooms and guestrooms were spacious and exquisitely configured. Just ten years ago, the South-Moor was hosting every upscale, bourgeois affair—including Greek fraternity and sorority gatherings. I once heard rumors that some organizers often denied admittance to individuals who failed to pass the "brown paper bag standard" set by a long-standing intra-race conflict established during the slavery era.

The "brown paper bag standard" was a form of intra-race conflict created within the Black community. The main position was the fallacy that light-skinned Negroes, who were the offspring of their White masters' established bloodlines, were superior to the rest of the members of the race. Stories were told of brown paper bags being placed on the door of an event at the South-Moor. Simply, anyone wanting to enter had to be the complexion of the brown paper bag or lighter.

While conducting my on-scene investigation, I instructed one of the uniformed assisting units to prevent any contamination of the crime scene. I requested the dispatcher to notify the coroner. Once the request was made over the police radio, officers from all over the area arrived on the scene to satisfy their curiosity and to offer assistance. This is a common practice. A hard working police officer always exhibits this trait. When something uncommon or extraordinary is heard over the police radio, no matter what he is doing, if a good cop has the opportunity he will visit the location.

The crime scene was defunct. I could not find any substantial evidence that would give us a lead. The hotel was cluttered; you could see there had been a lot of traffic. Trash, empty beer and wine bottles, drug paraphernalia, and cigarette butts were scattered throughout the area. We took the jacket and cap for evidence and placed them in a bag to be inventoried.

It was early spring. The homicide rate in Chicago had already surpassed first quarter projections by 112 murders, with a total of 231 before the month of March concluded. It was a clear sign that 1974 would be a record year for murder in the Windy City. Detective Aristotle Ashford and I were assigned to this most recent case by Gang Intelligence. Although it was a homicide, we got the assignment because the gang murder rate in Areas 1 and 3 outnumbered the murders committed in all of the other four police Areas. These areas represented the southeast and southwest sides of the city. The Stones had control of the southeast side, from the Dan Ryan Expressway to the lake, while the Devils Disciples managed the southwest side, from the Dan Ryan to Ashland Avenue.

Detective Ashford was a veteran detective. He had worked homicide, robbery, and vice before being assigned to Gang Intelligence. He knew the southside and the gang members. Ashford hated the gangs and just about any other Black male under the age of thirty-five. He said they were "traitors to the race," and they all needed to be eradicated before it was too late. His personal dislike for young Black males was daunting. It made me feel unsettled, because I was a representative of that same age group. "DoubleA," as he was known on the streets, always seemed unemotional and detached from the rest of us. He viewed life through a pair of deep-set eyes that came with a temperament bent by life experiences only he knew.

When looking directly at him, one of the first things you notice about DoubleA is that he has incredibly wide shoulders and unnaturally large hands. You kind of pick up on this right away because, by nature, DoubleA is a slim statured man. Standing 5'10" and carrying about 160lbs of sinewy muscle, he reminds you of a true middleweight boxer—especially when you note the wide-legged fight stance he always positions himself in. Always groomed, his neat and compact Afro is dark and short, graying just a little on the sides. And his fast paced walk—always stepping with long, determined strides—exudes the confidence of a fierce jungle cat. Whenever DoubleA arrives, everyone knows that a man of action is on the scene. More than anything, his imposing stature has to do with his voice. When DoubleA speaks he projects a low yet commanding range, kind of like a steak and potatoes meal would sound if it could talk. His pitch is consistently baritone, and when he addresses a room, he immediately captures your attention. Though not the biggest man on the job, he is an undeniable presence.

In the short time I had worked with him, I knew he had strong emotions about the present-day Black youth. In my mind, I began to develop my own suspicions about his dissonance.

The commanding officer of the Gang Intelligence Unit, Lt. Mike Nugent, a pug-nosed veteran of Irish descent, assigned us to work together. I believed that Mike knew that a rookie detective needed guidance and DoubleA was a veteran and a perfect match for my experience.

The streets were beginning to overflow with dead bodies. Mike was taking a lot of heat from downtown about the increase in gang violence, so he wanted an arrest made for every suspected gang murder committed in the city.

After scouring the crime scene and finding little evidence, we followed the squadrol down to the Cook County Morgue, located at Polk and Wood Street, to see what the coroner had to say about the time of death. The cause of death was obvious. Our only task was to find the responsible party and motive. We needed the time of death to begin our follow-up investigation and, more importantly, we needed to identify the victim. The coroner estimated that the victim had been dead at least four days. Now we had to wait on fingerprints and hope that his mother had reported him missing or would do so in the next twenty-four hours. This would give us a break on identification. We were accustomed to mothers reporting their children missing anywhere between three to four days later, especially if "Junebug" was a bad boy.

We examined the victim's clothing and inventoried everything. There was no evidence or laundry markings found that might have helped identify him, so we headed back to the area of the crime scene to canvass the surrounding neighborhood and see if a few snitches might be willing to help us out. Gang violence—especially shootings—was becoming very vogue. Unfortunately, real simple ass-whoopings to settle differences had just as quickly become old-fashioned.

DoubleA directed me to drive to Akins' Pool Room located on 63rd Street, just east of Cottage Grove. When we got there he went in alone. I watched him pick up the phone and make a call. He talked for a brief period and then hurried out, motioning to me that he was going to walk over to the EL station. DoubleA never traded any secrets. He was a sharp detective and he knew a lot of people on the southside, yet he always seemed reluctant to share his sources with me.

A short time later DoubleA came down from the EL and went into a Walgreen's drug store located just under the platform. I sat there and waited with the engine running. He came out and walked back up the stairs to the el platform. Ten minutes later, he came down and jumped in the squad car and instructed me to drive.

"Where we headed?" I asked calmly, purposely trying not to imply that I needed to know what kind of information he had obtained or whom he had gotten it from.

"Drive over to 64th and Woodlawn. I got somebody over there waiting on us."

Sometimes DoubleA didn't mind talking, but his hatred for gang violence often set him off and he wouldn't say much. I could tell he was upset and determined to find the killer or killers of the Black teenager found at the South-Moor.

We drove to the rear of the Haynes Hotel, located at 64th and Woodlawn. There we met a whore named Peachazz. She was a bleached blonde, about 5'4, 110 pounds. Guessing, I'd say she was around 28 years old. You could tell that before the needle got to her, Peachazz was a fine woman. Everybody in the neighborhood knew her. She was a whore, but she had a good heart and she knew the street and its horrors. Peachazz knew that prostitution was becoming a fading business in the area. She always said that the "gang niggas" were screwing up her trade. I could tell that the years of balancing her life between prostitution and heroin destroyed what was once an attractive young woman. Her hazel-colored eyes were the last reminders of what was, obviously, once a vivacious spirit.

As we drove up, Peachazz raced across the alley and jumped in the back seat.

"What took y'all niggas so long?" she complained. "I can't let anybody peep me talking to y'all. What's up?"

I drove east toward the Outer Drive. DoubleA instructed me to drive over to the lakefront, near La Rabida Children's Hospital. Once there, I found a snug little place to park and shut off the engine. DoubleA reached in his pocket and gave Peachazz a note. She took it, read it, and passed it back to DoubleA. I couldn't help feeling left out, so I gestured for him to hand it to me. DoubleA paused briefly, then handed the note to me. All it said was "Black Sonny." Black Sonny was an enforcer for the Blackstone Rangers. Peachazz looked alarmed. She seemed to clam up. I thought we were going to lose her help.

"Word on the street is Black Sonny executed a kid in the old South-Moor Hotel a few days ago," he said. "Some people believe it was because the kid didn't want to be involved in a gang. When he was ordered to perform an initiation ritual, he refused. I want you to find out if anybody knew of the murder or saw Black Sonny with the victim."

Peachazz sat there in the back seat of the squad car and didn't say a word. She had a look of panic on her face when she finally spoke. "DoubleA, I'm a whore. I don't want to mess with that nigga! He kills people for nothing. I'm afraid to even look him in the face. Man, I don't think I can help you with him."

"Do the best you can, baby-girl. You know what not to say. Just get me some information." DoubleA knew she had a lot of street wisdom and how to get information without arousing suspicion.

DoubleA was hoping that Peachazz would use her knowledge of the street and bring him some useful evidence. He always said the street had its own voice and street people knew the word. He was hoping that somebody saw something that would be enough to make a case.

Black Sonny was a vicious killer. His real name was Ivory Gilcrist, and he was "prison trained." He was arrested for murder at age 15 and sent to St Charles reformatory school until he reached 21. Shortly after his release, he was arrested for armed robbery and attempted murder. Black Sonny had received his education from several institutions of higher learning for recidivists. It would be hard to convict him without an eyewitness. Getting to him would be a complicated task. We knew he worked for the Stones and that he had rank. His name had been in the headlines before. We also knew somebody ordered our vic's murder—and that somebody sat within the top hierarchy of the Blackstone Rangers. We had a murder case with no known witnesses. We needed an eyewitness who could put Gilcrist at the murder scene, and we needed the murder weapon.

The overall picture was gloomy. We had Black kids dying at a record rate, and the suspects were not from another planet. Gang violence was plaguing the southside community. Every Black woman who had a man-child had a worry that provoked fear and apprehension in her everyday conscious state of living.

We dropped Peachazz off on 63rd and King Drive and headed south toward the 003rd District to call in and check our messages.

CHAPTER 2

As we entered the station, we could hear a commotion at the front desk. Two women were arguing with the desk sergeant. They were obviously upset. I couldn't help overhearing one of them complaining about not getting any police service. She also said if they were white the desk sergeant wouldn't treat them like that. The two women were handsomely dressed. From where I was standing, they looked like they were a mother and daughter. The older woman kept referring to passages in the Bible and how Jesus was keeping her from falling apart. When I walked by them the daughter grabbed me by the arm. She was literally begging me for help.

"What's the problem here ma'am?" I asked.

"My little brother hasn't been home in four days. We heard that gang members took him away."

I couldn't control the caustic feel that was released in my body when she said "four days" and "gang members."

I approached the desk sergeant and identified myself. "Sarge, I'm Detective Myles Sivad from Gang Intelligence. I'd like some place to interview these two women."

"Sure, son. Go upstairs and find a room."

DoubleA was on the phone calling both Gang Intelligence and Area 1 homicide division. I motioned to him that I was going upstairs and for him to get up there as soon as he could.

The older woman identified herself as Mrs. Bessie Williams. I was right. The younger woman was her daughter, Francine. They lived at 6626 S. Greenwood, the heart of Blackstone territory. The missing boy was Franklin Williams, age fifteen. Mrs. Williams was a middle-aged woman who had a nurturing face. You could tell by her mannerisms that she was sound in her spirit, yet extremely worried about the disappearance of her son.

"Franklin is a good boy. I've never had any problems with him," she assured me. "He goes to school everyday. He's a good student. I've fought hard to keep him out of gangs. He left home four days ago and has not returned," she concluded with a sob.

I couldn't control my tension because I knew it would be a miracle if the body found in the janitor's closet was not the boy they were reporting missing. I felt uneasy and found it difficult to ask questions without appearing nervous. Just as I was beginning to fold, DoubleA appeared in the doorway. I jumped up and stepped out to talk with him.

"DoubleA, the body found in the janitor's closet is more than likely the boy the two women in this room are reporting missing."

"Are you sure?"

"I'd be surprised if it's not."

DoubleA immediately re-entered the room and asked, "What kind of clothing did your son have on when you saw him last?"

"I'm not quite sure," Mrs. Williams replied. "I think he was wearing a white shirt and a red, or maybe maroon, sweater."

Her description was a match for two of the garments we inventoried at the morgue. We had a tentative identification. We knew that. But the difficult task was how to explain it to the family. Luckily, DoubleA was a pro and he knew how to handle a situation like this. As if by magic, he began to show a softer, warmer side—one I had never seen in the four months we'd been working together. I always took him to be cold-blooded and detached. Displaying feelings and emotions was not a known part of his character.

"Mrs. Williams," he said gently, "I want y'all to take a ride with us. I'd like to finish talking with you. I believe we can find some answers."

He never told them where we were going. They never asked. We drove towards the Cook County Morgue. When we arrived, DoubleA stopped the car and asked both women to get out. Taking control of the situation, he grabbed Mrs. Williams' hand: "Ma'am, I've some disheartening news about your son. We believe he's been murdered and his body is here in the morgue."

After realizing what Detective Ashford had said, Mrs. Williams swung away, screaming and flailing her arms, shouting, "Jesus no, Lord no, Lord no, not my baby!"

Francine immediately collapsed in my arms. I stood there struggling to keep her balanced as I watched Mrs. Williams stammer and stomp in a rage of sorrow and grief. The scene was heartbreaking. These women came apart. All I could do was stand there and wait until their emotions and pain subsided, so they could identify the body.

The morgue was located in the west wing of the Cook County Hospital. Any person who has had the experience of visiting a morgue can tell you the experience last a lifetime. The odor you encounter is distinctive; it bombards your sense of smell with a stench that you'll remember forever. The smell settles in your clothes and attacks your nostrils, causing unsettling sensations that teeter on being overwhelming. The room has dimly lit florescent lighting that, often, solicits fear and foreboding from an unsuspecting visitor. Naturally, homicide investigators and family members are the usual visitors. When family members have to view a body to make identification, it's usually a disheartening sight. They are brought into the examination room and the body is pulled from a refrigerator onto a sliding gurney. Next, the victim is viewed and identified. Afterwards, an autopsy is performed. This is followed up by a cause of death determination by the coroner. Finally, it is made a matter of record at a coroner's inquest.

As we entered an identification room, DoubleA attempted to shield Mrs. Williams from any further discomfort. Having to see her son would be devastating. The pain of seeing a loved one deceased is quite overwhelming; all of your emotions explode. There is no comfort until the reality of death becomes final. DoubleA suggested, "Miz Williams, Francine can make the identification. You can wait in the family waiting room."

"Oh, no! No!" she cried. "I want to see. I pray it ain't my baby, but I got to see. Please Lord, don't let it be my baby."

An assistant directed us to the section where the body could be identified. I began to feel apprehension and discomfort as the coroner's assistant pulled the sheet back. There was a sudden quiet, and then an emotional shrieking wail pierced the room as Mrs. Williams fell to the floor. "Oh, Lord, no! Jesus…Jesus, why has this happened to my child? Jesus have mercy!"

Francine buried her head in my shoulder and began to moan and weep as she tugged at my lapel. "Oh, God, why did this have to happen?" She wailed.

When the two women managed to regain their composure, we were able to get some information on who the victim's friends were and where he spent most of his time.

CHAPTER 3

It was Saturday morning. We had left the Area headquarters and headed southbound on Cottage Grove en route to Mary Ann's to have breakfast. Mary Ann's was a small restaurant located under the el station between Indiana and Prairie Avenue on 61st Street. The place had little decoration and the tables were small and uncovered. However, the food had its own reputation on the southside. Just as we turned off King Drive at 61st Street, we heard a simulcast that said, "Shots fired. Man shot at 65th and Maryland." We hit our siren and drove toward the scene. We were the second unit to arrive. A beat car was already on the scene attending to the victim. There was not much he could do. The victim, a young Black male, had been shot several times. It didn't look good for him. Cars from all over the area started arriving, and a fire department ambulance could be heard in the background.

I took one look at the victim and I knew he wasn't going to make it. I could see the fear in his eyes as he faded into shock. As I kneeled beside him, I could feel a surge of despair racing through my body. Suddenly, my mind wandered and I was thinking *who was this child and why was he dying right here in front of me?* I envisioned his mother wailing and screaming as she rushed to him. I saw DoubleA talking to me, but I couldn't hear what he was saying. He jerked on my arm and brought me out of it.

The victim was around seventeen years old. His death was assigned to two detectives from Area 1. We told them to send us a copy of the case report if they determined that the case was a gang-related murder.

We drove around for a few hours conducting field interrogations and attempting to locate any witnesses. Now, instead of breakfast, we settled on lunch at

Mary Ann's. As we entered the restaurant and searched for a seat, several people seated in the dining area waved or spoke to us.

"I spy the two that will," was heard from the corner of the room. "You boys look mighty hungry today. Take that table near the window." The waiter, a tall, lanky guy named Buddy, was always glad to see DoubleA. He seemed to jump for joy every time we stopped in. "I guess crime takes a break to allow you gentlemen time to replenish your source of energy, huh?" he continued teasing us. "Well, we got most every kind of energy replacement you boys need to keep crime off us working people."

Buddy seated us and, in his most professional manner, gave us Mary Ann's hand-written menu. He then poured us two glasses of ice water. Buddy was about 6'8". He had long arms and a very small head. He reminded me of the farmer on the Kellogg's Cornflakes box. His personality was very pleasant; he always presented a smile, accompanied by warm greetings and laughter. Most of the customers at Mary Ann's were regulars—many of them street people, gamblers, hustlers, blue-collar laborers, and politicians who needed good home-cooking to keep them going.

We dined on collard greens, onions and tomatoes, corn muffins, mashed sweet potatoes, and fried chicken. It was almost 2:30 p.m. when we finished lunch. We hadn't accomplished much. Our murder case was still hot, and we needed to find a witness before Black Sonny got wind of our tip.

Our next investigative decision was to visit Cornell Booker, the boy who Francine Williams named as a close friend of her little brother. He lived just a few blocks from the victim. We arrived at his house and rang the bell. A tenant on the first floor—a young, pudgy female—answered the door, asking, "May I help you?"

"We're detectives from Gang Intelligence, ma'am. We're looking for a young man by the name of Cornell Booker. We were told that he lives at this address."

"Sorry officers, but Cornell and his mother moved several days ago."

I hesitated for a moment. "Well, do you have any information on where they moved? Cornell Booker is an important witness in our investigation. We really need to locate him as soon as possible."

"Sorry. They didn't leave a forwarding address."

Our case was at an impasse. There were two other names given to us by Francine Williams, but she didn't know where they lived and she only knew them by their nicknames, Lil Will and Snake. As we directed our attention toward finding these two subjects, our investigation stirred up a new concern: even though the victim's mother was adamant about her son not being mixed up with gangs, the names Lil Will and Snake appeared to be street monikers—names you get through gang affiliation.

Not knowing exactly where to find these two, we were thinking we should hit the streets and see whom we could find that would give up our suspect, Black Sonny. In the short time I had been working with DoubleA, I'd learned that, in a murder case, when all looks doomed, a person arrested for something altogether unrelated—something as simple as "flipping" (not paying) the EL train—could provide you with coveted information just to beat the rap.

In our short moment of gridlock, DoubleA voiced his instinct. "Listen, Myles, I got a hunch. We should contact the old hustler, Papa. You remember him, right? The old-timer and ex-pimp. He still has a lot of connections in the Woodlawn and he might be able to help us."

I remembered Papa from a visit we made shortly after me and DoubleA became partners. Papa didn't live in the 'hood anymore. He pulled up and left when the Stones started running it. He said "them niggers ruined the entire Woodlawn community with their carnage and property devastation. A Black man who has any desire to live and prosper has to give way to them niggers or be willing die." He wasn't afraid to die, he said, but he needed a reason to make such a sacrifice and "ain't nothing in Woodlawn been reason." So Papa moved further south to 87th Place, just east of King Drive—a real fine neighborhood where Black people had stature and money.

DoubleA didn't stop to call Papa and tell him we were coming. He just drove up to Papa's doorstep, got out and rang his doorbell. A tall, silver-gray-headed man, roughly sixty-five or so, opened the door.

"Well, I'll be damned! If it ain't the Black Crow and the Sparrow," he greeted us. "The ghetto sleuths coming to the old master begging for salvation. DoubleA and Myles, come on in! Damn if I wasn't thinking about you two yesterday. How's the police business?"

DoubleA laughed and gave the old silver fox a big hug, saying, "We can't complain, Papa. Death in the neighborhood is our peril. It's getting worse everyday. We just left a boy shot dead on 65th and Maryland."

Papa didn't flinch; he walked over to his favorite chair and took a seat. "Yeah, I know what you mean. These punks have ruined a great community. What can I do for ya, men?"

Papa was a hustler from back in the day. He never claimed to be a pillar of the community. Loan sharking, gambling and numbers were his forte—and he made his money without killing or destroying the community. His kind of criminal behavior was acceptable to the community and he was well-known and well-respected.

"Well, Master, we're working on a murder investigation and it smells like a gang execution," DoubleA said. "We found a kid slain in the old South-Moor Hotel, shot in the back of the head at close range. We need some information on some possible suspects."

After Papa listened to all the facts, he got up and went into a bedroom and came back with a photo of a group of young men taken in a poolroom. There were seven people in the photo. Papa identified three of them as being the ranking members of the Blackstone Rangers: Jake Fontaine, Gene "Bull" Hardison, and Edney Bayels.

He explained, "These three niggers are the root of the Stones. They set policy, target competition, and direct enforcement. Bull Hardison is probably the power broker; everybody seems to follow his orders. Jake Fontaine is damn near illiterate, but he seems to have some charismatic powers. Edney Bayels is the enforcer, and he's closely aligned with Fontaine. They are responsible for the murders, the drugs, and the violence. There's only one thing I can say they did that was worth praising: they ran the goddamn Dagos out of Woodlawn.

"Before the gang came to power, the Dagos 'gangstered' all of the profits out of the community. They squeezed us without compassion for the big policy money, loan sharking, and other vices including big card and dice-game money. The policy money was big-time on the southside and we even had a nice little wire room they operated on 64th and Blackstone. They had two niggers performing the muscle and two Dagos raking the cash. The Stones rolled on them one night demanding a cut of the action.

"Them Italian boys laughed at them and told them to go get fucked. They didn't see the magnitude of the threat. Well, the Stones came at 'em hard. They killed the two grease balls and one of the shines. They got the message then. Ever since, the Stones have been in control."

I thought that was an interesting story, but I still couldn't put together the connection of what DoubleA was trying to find out.

"Well, anyway Papa, are you still in contact with any workers from the days when you were king?" DoubleA asked, changing the subject back to our mission.

His "workers" were guys who used to collect debts when Papa had his little gambling and loan sharking operations going on in the 'hood.

Papa seemed a little reluctant to give up that kind of information. He hesitated for a few seconds before he replied, "Well, one of my best boys is still living down there. He's been kinda staying out of the way, but he still knows how to get up on a nigger who's trying to cover his trail. I'll reach out for him and you call me in a few days; he might be able to help you boys a little."

We left Papa's house and headed north to the Gang Intelligence Unit located at police headquarters on 1121 S. State Street. I turned to DoubleA: "I noticed you never mentioned to Papa who we were looking for."

"Yeah. If we did that we would be putting too much information out too soon. We need to talk to the guy Papa turns us onto and then work him for some information."

We stopped in the parking lot just outside of the field house in Washington Park. DoubleA knew that I worked the westside and I didn't know the main players on the southside—or their rankings. He began filling me in about gangs and gang history. "The information we got from Papa was incomplete," he said. "Papa retired a long time ago and some of the information he gave us is old. For instance, the three guys he showed us in that picture were not the original Stones. DoubleA filled in the gaps:

"The Stones had been perpetuating havoc on the southside since the early 1960s. The gang originated as the Blackstone Raiders in the early '60s and then moved on to the Rangers in the mid-'60s. Three main guys—Chazz "Watussi" Rhodels, Brian "Bop" Bells, and the one guy in the picture, Gene "Bull" Hardison, controlled the gang. Jake Fontaine didn't rise to power until Bull went to prison.

"During this time the Stones were a coalition of Black street gangs on the southside. Jake Fontaine, in his effort to seize power, attempted to organize all of the gangs under one leader, himself. His efforts met resistance, which caused gang warfare and a series of murders and framing of gang leaders from opposing groups. Bop was the true leader of the gang before Jake took over. When Bull went to prison, Watussi Rhodels stepped to the side after Bells was indicted for murder, and then Jake moved up and seized power.

"Gang strife continued with the small coalition groups being taken over by little Jake and his crew. Jake was just a punk with big ideas, but he had charisma, which attracted people to him. Eventually, he shed his meek and punkish personality and became leader of the Black P. Stone Nation. He was successful in bringing all the satellite gangs, splintered groups of Black Stone Rangers who controlled gang turf throughout the projects and other locations on the southside, under one nation. Jake had power and he used it. He didn't show any mercy. If you didn't obey his rule, you paid the price. After Fontaine's stint in prison, he returned to the gang more mature and violent."

I asked DoubleA, "What did he do to go to prison?"

"In the late '60s Jake got caught up in an anti-poverty scheme—a $927,000 federally-funded program that created jobs for inner city youths. Jake and his main twenty-one gang leaders influenced hundreds of youths, getting them jobs and receiving kickbacks.

"Jake got convicted on federal fraud and conspiracy charges and was sent to prison. This was his first real hard knock, and the first time the "G, the federal government, came at him. At this point, the White folks realized that Jake was envisioning too many big ideas and he was becoming dangerous.

"While in prison, Jake picked up a new religious belief or what he called a religion: El Rukuan. This religion created a more developed and evolved Jake Fontaine. He had grown up a great deal. But prison did more to Jake than take him away from his gang. He hardened. I think he led himself to believe that he was done an injustice by being put away. Jake came out of prison on a mission to take everything from everybody. He became predatory." Black kids started dying in record numbers and gang violence was at the root of this new wave of violence in the Black community.

All of a sudden I could see why DoubleA was so hostile toward gangs. He'd witnessed the root of their fury and took it to heart. His twelve-year exposure to the annihilation of the fruit of his race disturbed him. He hated those responsible for snuffing out the hopes and dreams of so many young Black boys. It was enough to make him seek revenge, regardless of his sworn oath to protect life and property.

I had some knowledge of what was happening in this city, but I was having an arduous time keeping my focus. What had been occurring in the Woodlawn community the past eight years was also occurring in the Englewood community, just west of Woodlawn and across the Dan Ryan Expressway.

The Devil's Disciples, later named the Gangster Disciples, waged similar gang violence in the Woodlawn area. Both groups were in a struggle to recruit new members in Woodlawn, but the Stones were so ruthless in their attack that the Disciples were forced back across the expressway. During the late '60s, Woodlawn Avenue was the dividing line between gangs—with the Stones governing every neighborhood from Woodlawn east to the lake, and the Disciples controlling neighborhoods west of Woodlawn Avenue. With these men now archenemies—Jake Fontaine, leader of the Stones, and Nicholas DeSenzo and David Barkscale of the Devil's Disciples—gang warfare waged on the southside.

Interestingly enough, gang violence in the Black community was not new to Chicago. The city experienced gang violence in the late '50s and early '60s with the rise in gang conflicts between the Egyptian Cobras and the Conservative

Vice-Lords. These groups waged gang hostilities on the westside. However, their methods of aggression were centered around turf. When pressed, they used sticks, knives, and zip-guns in combat. The violence between them resulted in deaths, but not at this current rate. In comparison, the Stones and Disciples were responsible for a metamorphosis—spreading genocide amongst the young Black males in the windy city.

CHAPTER 4

Our murder investigation had stumbled to a straggle. We hadn't uncovered any new evidence and none of our leads panned out. We had not heard from Papa, and it didn't look like Peachazz was going to deliver any useful information. Two weeks had passed and we had no new evidence to work on.

We were reporting for duty one morning at headquarters when a voice over the PA system announced, "Detective Myles Sivad, you have a phone call at the front desk." I picked up the phone and heard the voice of Francine Williams, our victim's sister.

"Detective Sivad," she said, "I thought I should let you know that a few days after the funeral we went into my brother's room to sort through his things. I found $600 in cash in his pants pocket. We're not poor, but we can't figure out how Franklin got that kind of cash.

"Francine," I took a deep breath and did my best to phrase my words gently, "me and Detective Ashford would like to look through Franklin's room ourselves. If we can find additional evidence, it could help us solve his murder."

"I'll be home all day," she said. I sighed in relief.

When we arrived, Francine met us at the front door and escorted us into her brother's room. The room was small but everything was organized. Franklin had photos of his mother and sister on his dresser. I looked under his mattress and found a Polaroid photo of Franklin and three of his friends. I studied the photo and I could see that Franklin was affiliated. Two of the boys sported the far-famed red beret. The other one wore a red cap angled to the left, "representing"—showing their gang affiliation.

The photo was worn and crumbly, but you could see Franklin throwing up the "sign," and they all had their arms folded. Inscribed on the back were the words "Stone Love" and the names Lil Will, Snake, and what appeared to be a graffiti sketch of the word Reebok. It was clear to me our victim was not the good little boy his mama thought he was. I slipped the photo into my pocket for future reference. We continued our search of his room for any other significant evidence. I found several phone numbers and some smoking pipes.

"Ms. Williams, did Franklin use drugs or alcohol?" I asked.

"I believe so," Francine answered. "I suspected he was smoking reefers for some time. Mother had no idea what marijuana looked like but she told me his room always had a strange smell and I often found seeds in the carpet."

I also found an opened letter under his mattress mailed from the Cook County Jail. I didn't want to open it there, so I slipped that into my pocket. I told Francine she should hold onto the $600 and let us know if anybody contacted her asking for the money. I thanked her for calling. Before leaving I told her if she found anything else—anything that seemed unusual—not to hesitate and give us a heads-up phone call.

It was getting close to noon, so we thought we would spend the rest of our tour of duty looking through gang files and photos at headquarters. As soon as we walked into the squad room, Lt. Nugent stormed out of his office, kicking and screaming. He was in a tirade: "Those fucking politicians! They sit on their ass and complain about crime, but when you ask for more personnel they tell you to make do!"

With mounting complaints about gang violence and slow investigations, Lt. Nugent was clearly under pressure. He ordered us into his office for a briefing. "I just got off the phone with the Chief of Detectives and he informed me that Area 1 was leading the city in Part 1 offenses and the homicide index was causing citizens to complain," he explained. "Now, men, I'm not accusing you of not working hard, but I think we need to get some arrests for these murders."

After we detailed our investigation, Lt. Nugent told us to call a detective in Area 4, the westside's Detective Area, and talk to a dick named Jack Porter who was handling a homicide we might be interested in.

"I'll start looking in the gang files for the nicknames of Franklin Williams' two friends. You can contact the dick in Area 4," I said.

"Cool," DoubleA responded. "I hope that guy's got something good."

The Gang Intelligence Unit's gang file was an assortment of all the known gang members in the city. They were sorted by name, nickname, and section of city. Because the gangs were turf-conscious, you seldom found a Stone living in

GD, Gangster Disciple, territory. Although this theory was not always reliable, we found it to be the most useful when searching for identities and addresses of suspected gang members.

I ran the nicknames through our files and compared them to the Polaroid. Lil' Will was identified as George Buck, age seventeen. According to this, he lives at 6444 S. Greenwood. Not surprising, he's had six arrests since turning seventeen. Snake's birth name was Felix Hamilton, also age seventeen. His last known address was 6646 S. Drexel. He had two arrests for unlawful use of a weapon. I copied the information in my notebook and went to meet DoubleA. The two hits on the nicknames made me feel lucky, so I threw in our victim's name just to see if he had any history. Nothing came up. He had no arrest history, but that didn't mean that he was clean.

DoubleA was still on the phone with Detective Porter. As he was jotting down some notes, he summoned me to his side. He made a gesture for me to pick up the other phone and listen to what Detective Porter was saying. I picked up as Porter was describing a crime scene from three days ago.

He said, "I received a tip that a body was in the trunk of an old car in Douglas Park on the westside. When I got to the scene, I found the body of a Black male around eighteen years old. He had been tied up with duct tape, gagged, and shot in the head just behind the right ear. His body had probably been in the trunk at least two days. There was no blood evidence, so we can surmise he wasn't killed in the trunk or in the park. Oh, yeah, another thing I found to be peculiar was the victim had on only one shoe. It was on his left foot. We haven't made a positive identification, but the victim sported a tattoo on his right shoulder that read 'Lil Will.'"

This was vital information. It looked like young Franklin Williams and his pack had bit off a big piece and somebody ordered a contract on the crew. We had to find Felix Hamilton before he got whacked. Whatever these kids did, it was a serious violation of gang ethics and the penalty was death. We thanked Porter for sharing his information and requested he mail us a copy of his report through the department's intra-mail system. He promised to keep us abreast of his investigation. We would do likewise because it looked like this murder may have been committed on the southside.

We typed up our report, submitted it to the lieutenant, and then headed for Felix Hamilton's address. Felix had two arrests for carrying a gun. Experience dictated that we view Felix as a shooter. Moreso, he had to be alarmed about Franklin Williams' death and his other associate, George Buck, being missing.

We parked a few doors south of his address and walked up to his front door. Before we could ring the doorbell, an elderly man answered.

"Sir," I began, "my name is Detective Sivad. This is my partner, Detective Ashford. We are assigned to the Gang Intelligence unit of the Chicago Police Department."

The old soldier didn't let us get a badge into play before he answered. "I know who ya are. I saw ya get out of dat ther undercova car."

DoubleA made an effort to explain our presence, but again the old-timer beat us to it. He said, "The boy ain't been here in three days. We don't know where he is, but I'll tell you what, wherever he is, trouble is up on em! He ain't worth a shit. His daddy whazz'en shit. I knew that before Felix was born, and I knew he whazz'en gonna be shit. I didn't want my daughter to marry Felix's daddy, but she insisted. Now she done run off with another no-good som'bitch and left Felix's black ass here with us. Wherever he is, trouble is with em. Now what can I do for y'all?"

"Well, sir, we'd like to talk to Felix." Double A answered. "We think his life is in danger."

"Dangha! Dangha! The boy came into this world under the sign of Dangha! All his life he ain't been nothin' but bother. He's been in jail too many times for a boy his age. His daddy left him when he was eight years old. His mama couldn't do nothin' wit him, and I sure as hell couldn't. He left here three-fo' days ago with one of his no-good friends, a cut-up nigga who looked like somebody tried to write a message in the side of his face. I'll tell you two offisus somethin': I believe Felix done shot two or three people befo'. His time is up; it's time for him to pay dat debt. It won't be long befo' you find him 'restituted.'"

"Well sir, we'd appreciate it a great deal if you could call us if and when you hear from him. We'd like to talk to him about the death of two of his friends," I said.

The old man nodded his head. We never did get his name, but we thanked him for his input and left him a number to contact us if Felix showed up.

CHAPTER 5

Three days missing. That's about how long George Buck had been dead. We had to consider that Felix might have been with George when the Stones caught up with him and that both of them got knocked together. Yet, on the other hand, maybe not. Why would they whack George and Felix together and take George to the westside and not Felix? Felix was probably still alive and terrified. We had to find him.

When we pulled away from Felix's address, I had an idea. "DoubleA, drive over to Hyde Park High School. I got an idea."

"What's that?"

"I took a photo from Franklin Williams' bedroom, along with a letter from an inmate at Cook County Jail. The photo has four teens wearing gang paraphernalia and "representing". Now we know three of the youths, but number four is still a mystery. I think if we make a few stops in and around the school, maybe we could get lucky and find somebody who knows the identity of our mystery person."

We went right into the school building and asked to see the homeroom teacher of Franklin Williams. We were directed to a Mrs. Margrita Taylor. We located her in the teacher's lounge. Mrs. Taylor was a very light-skinned woman about 54 years old. She was about 5'1, 110 pounds. Her hair was cut very short. You could tell she was a heart stopper in her day.

"Are you Mrs. Taylor, ma'am?" I asked kindly.

"Yes, I am. May I help you?"

"Yes, ma'am. My name is Detective Sivad and this is my partner, Detective Ashford." I showed her the picture and asked, "Can you identify the boy on the end?"

"Yes. That's Cornell Booker. He attended school here for the past two years, but I understand he moved away and I have no idea where he moved. He was an excellent student, but he hung around with thugs. I had hoped he would break away from that environment, but he never did."

"We've been trying to locate him, but have been unable to find him. They didn't leave a forwarding address," I said.

"I wish I could help you officers. Booker was an outstanding artist. If he enrolled in another public school, he won't be hard to find. Contact the Chicago Board of Education and ask for the student enrollment section. They keep a daily record of all student transfers and discharges. If Booker enrolled in another school, you can find out where."

We had a fresh lead and it looked like we were heading in the right direction. The thought of showing the young woman the picture at Booker's old address didn't occur to me then, but I thought the information from Mrs. Taylor gave us a better lead to follow up.

While en route to the Chicago Board of Education, I reached in my pocket and took out the letter I had taken from Franklin Williams' bedroom. It was addressed to Franklin Williams, postmarked March 21, 1974. The letter was from an inmate named Ronald Jennings. The letter was basically written in code, but Jennings did mention two of Franklin's crewmembers and the word "violation" was underlined. I could decipher from several other sentences that Jennings was warning Franklin that he'd be dealt with if he continued to disobey orders.

Our investigation was opening up and we had moved from a creeping stall to a roll. Clues were panning out and we were starting to put things together. Sometimes during an investigation you could end your tour of duty at rock bottom of an investigation and the next day everything falls into place. An investigation culminates with an arrest and proper charges for sentencing. This murder investigation was taking on a life of its own, and it looked like a number of people would end up dead before we found out what precipitated the violence.

The lead on Cornell Booker did not pan out with the Chicago Board of Education. They didn't have any transfer information on him.

CHAPTER 6

We had been on the trail for two days, following up leads and looking for Cornell Booker and Felix Hamilton. We were driving down East 63rd Street around 6:30 p.m. DoubleA abruptly stopped the squad car, jumped out, and raced across the street. I was somewhat startled as I saw DoubleA approach a lone man walking westbound on 63rd from Stony Island. As soon as DoubleA got up on the subject, he slammed him with a powerful overhand right to the jaw. The man tumbled to the ground. DoubleA leaned over him and began to strike him repeatedly about the face. I jumped out of the car and ran across the street screaming at DoubleA, "What the fuck are you doing, man! Are you crazy?"

DoubleA stood up and began to stomp the man in the face while shouting, "You black motherfucker...what did I tell you? What did I tell you? If I ever saw your black ass again, I would stomp you in the ground. Didn't I? Didn't I?"

I grabbed DoubleA by the arm in an attempt to stop him from killing the guy.

DoubleA glared at me with a fierce and intense sordidness, a look that I had never seen in him. "This is the motherfucker who told the Stones we were in the alley. This bitch was responsible for the death of Alfona!" he yelled.

I had no idea what he was talking about.

I helped the man to his feet as he whined back at DoubleA, "I know you hate me DoubleA, but I had to tell them or my ass would be dead. They would have known that I saw you guys and didn't tell them." The man then fled down 63rd Street holding his hand over his mouth to stop blood from getting on his clothing.

We both walked back to the squad car and got in without looking at each other or saying a word. When he started the car I said, "Take me down to headquarters. I need to be excused."

DoubleA drove me to the front door and stopped. I got out of the vehicle and he sped off.

When I exited the elevator Lt. Nugent saw me and motioned for me to come into his office. "Where's DoubleA?"

"He just dropped me off, Lieutenant. I need to be excused."

Mike could see I was upset. "What happened?"

I tried to be a veteran and tough it out. "Nothing happened." But Mike was on to me. "Don't give me that shit, son. I can tell when things aren't right, so what happened between you two?"

"I don't know, sir. DoubleA assaulted a man for no reason. I've never seen him act like that. Maybe I need to find me a new partner."

"Okay, Myles, who was the man and what did DoubleA say to him?"

"I don't know who he was, sir. When I tried to stop DoubleA from beating the man he said something about him being the person responsible for the death of some guy named Alfona."

Mike immediately knew what had happened. "Sit down, Detective Sivad," he ordered. "How long have you known Ashford?"

"Sir, I met DoubleA when we were assigned to this unit in November of last year. I was promoted to detective in June 1973 and assigned Area 3 homicide. When the department announced that it was looking for detectives in the Gang Intelligence Unit, I volunteered. I met DoubleA on my first day here. Of course you know all this, because you assigned us to work together," I said snippily.

Before I could continue, the lieutenant interrupted me. "Listen here, son, DoubleA was actually one of the first detectives assigned to this unit in the fall of 1967, when the unit was first organized. He worked here for five years and then went to the Area 2 Detective Division before being reassigned back here in '73. He worked with a team of some of the best detectives this department has ever seen. During that period, the Gang Intelligence Unit was strictly an intelligence-gathering unit and did very little enforcement. Meanwhile, gang violence was rapidly increasing. Both the Gangster Disciples and the Blackstone Rangers taxed the skills of the Detective Division. The department began to realize that if we were to become effective we needed to specialize in our knowledge of their organizations, street activities, and development.

"I don't know if you were on the job during that time but, during the late summer of 1970, three Gang Intelligence detectives were sitting in a squad car in the alley behind the South-Moor, conducting a surveillance of the hotel, when a sniper fired a shot through the trunk of the squad car. Detective James Alfona was struck in the lower back. The bullet penetrated the trunk and the rear seat and entered Alfona's right side. The bullet split in half and penetrated his liver. Detective Alfona died after he struggled to survive. The loss of blood and the damage to his liver were just too much. There were arrests made and a trial conducted. Needless to say, the results of the trial left everybody with a serious hatred for the Stones. We learned during the trial that one of our key witnesses was actually the one who informed the Stones that the detectives were in the alley. That witness was the man DoubleA assaulted; his name is Rodney Fletcher. He had been a stool pigeon for DoubleA for several years.

"When DoubleA found out it was his stool pigeon who double-crossed us, he swore that if he ever saw him again he'd get even. You see, Myles, DoubleA and all of the men assigned to Gang Intelligence during that time were extremely close. They were some of the best detectives we had in the department. They worked hard on their assignments. All of the information we have on the gangs now is a result of those guys going out and turning information.

"Jimmy Alfona was a hell of a policeman. Everybody loved him. It didn't make any difference who he worked with, 'Everybody was blue,' he said, and he lived by that creed. When he got killed, I thought there would be some murders in retaliation because we all took his death hard, but there were never any allegations accusing us of any gang murders.

"Go home, kid. Get some rest, report for duty in the morning. I'm sure DoubleA will be over his mood."

I thanked the lieutenant and left headquarters. When I got into my car, I sat there for a while trying to put everything the lieutenant told me into perspective. I felt bad for DoubleA. I really hadn't shown up as a stand-up partner. When all was said and done, I had punked out over rules and training. I told myself I was lucky to draw a partner like DoubleA. I owed him an apology.

I started up my car and drove to 61st and Calumet. I needed to relax, and I hoped that I would see DoubleA there. Bennie's 357 Club was the "The Big Drink Saloon." Coppers from all over the city came by Bennie's to talk shop, examine their worth, and quench their thirst. Bennie's has a reputation for pouring the best drinks in town. You don't get any chasers here. If you needed cola or orange juice, you have to bring it with you. Many careers were adjusted at Bennie's.

Bennie Brady, the owner of the bar, played professional baseball in the Negro Leagues during the late '20s and '30s, and it was rumored he was one of the best.

He often bragged about how the Negro Leagues survived during the depression when major league baseball was about to go under.

I walked in and ordered my favorite drink, Jack Daniels on the rocks. I knew that after one drink I would be at ease. I took a seat alone in the corner, just to watch all of the people interacting and having a good time. I could see everyone was relaxed, not caring about what was happening outside the front door.

I gazed over in the corner across from me and saw a familiar face—Sgt. John Harde, a former instructor from the police academy. I waved hello, and he beckoned for me to join him. "Myles Sivad. Detective Myles Sivad," he said. "Well boy, tell me who do you know? You've been on the job for how long? Four years, maybe, and you're a detective already? Looks like you got a stinger who can do things."

"Naw. Not really Sarge. I really wanted to be a detective. When they gave the exam in '73, I did pretty well. I don't have no clout and ain't nobody been giving me no blessings."

"Myles, I admit you're a bright kid. What are you doing in this saloon? This joint is for old-timers who love the big drink."

"Sarge, I need to be around some old-timers so I can learn to accept the challenges of the day and understand how to be cool. My partner always talks about this place and I thought I might find him here tonight."

"Who you working with, Myles?"

"Detective Aristotle Ashford."

"DoubleA?"

"Yeah. We've been working together since November of last year."

"You working with a pro, kid. DoubleA is the best. He ain't got much personality, but he's a good cop and he don't take no kinda shit. We started out together in the old fifth precinct. DoubleA had just gotten out of the army. You know he served in Korea, during the War? He received a Purple Heart for a wound he received during combat. DoubleA was born in the south. I'm not sure, but it was either Mississippi or Alabama."

"Yeah, he told me he was born in Mississippi, but he didn't elaborate. I think he doesn't like talking about where he was born or what he did prior to joining the police department."

"You know, Myles, your partner keeps everything close to the vest. He's not the open and friendly type. I met DoubleA in the police academy in 1957. He was a quiet and very private person. He never talked much about himself except for one night, just prior to completing our police training, we stopped here for a drink. DoubleA was feeling unusually personal and he started talking about himself and life in the south before he came to Chicago. I remember feeling his pain when he described an incident in the sixth grade.

"He told me he had just enrolled in public school and his teacher attempted to introduce him to the class. She brought him in front of the room and told everyone she wanted them to meet a new student and she introduced him as Aristotle Ashford from, yeah, Bellzonni, Mississippi. He said when the teacher pronounced his name, he quickly corrected her and told her his name was 'Arist-tolee Ashford.' His classmates broke the silence with thunderous laughter because of the way he pronounced his name. He knew that for all of those years he had been pronouncing his name incorrectly, and here he stood in front of people he had never seen and they were laughing at him. The humiliation he felt made him want to disappear. It also made him hate his classmates.

"That night he confessed to me that he was never able to get over the shame and embarrassment he endured after coming to Chicago and being treated like some country-ass Negro from down south. But I tell you what, son. You will never meet a finer human being or a better partner to work with in this profession."

"You're right, Sarge. Partners don't come no better than DoubleA," I agreed, "but I think he still has a glaring dislike for young Black males. I don't think it's just the dislike for the gang violence, I think it's deeper than that. This generation of Black youth is guilty of something in his view, and I just can't identify it. What I'm struggling with is this; I'm a member of the generation he hates and, although he has never given me reason to be concerned, I find it difficult for him to exclude me from that group."

"Well, Myles, I don't think you've gotten to know DoubleA completely. He's not the kind of person who would disclose his opinions unreservedly. He's a very proud Black man and he has the greatest respect for the contributions Black men have made to America—even though our historians have failed to adequately include them in their chronicles. Perhaps when you get a chance to really talk to him about his experiences in life, maybe he will give you the answer to those questions. Anyway, Myles, you seem like you're on the right track. I bet the next time I see you, you'll probably be a lieutenant."

"I wish, Sarge. This job has not been the greatest experience. It took me three years to make it. I took the test four times. Each time I went to take the physical, I was told that I had a heart murmur. I finally made connections with an alderman who instructed me to go back down to Hubbard Street where I had taken my last physical and tell them 'Mr. Griffin sent me.' I paid the little Irish city worker fifty dollars. In turn, he changed the results on my physical exam record."

"Four times, hmmm? That wasn't so bad. Most guys who came on before you had to go through a lot more changes than that, and it cost them much more than fifty dollars!" he said, grinning. "You want another drink, Myles?"

"Sure. Jack Daniels on the rocks."

"Have you ever heard of W.E.B. DuBois, Myles?"

"Yeah, I think so. He opposed Booker T. Washington's accommodationist views on the plight of the Negro during the turn of the 19th century."

"Okay, well you should remember the term 'talented tenth.'"

"Yeah, I think he was talking about the Black elite of college-educated Negroes who would be responsible for the uplifting of the race."

"Damn, Myles! You know something about Black history, uh?"

"Not from my high school studies. In four years of high school—two in Catholic and two in public—the most I learned about Black history was 'the Negro was a slave.'" As we both laughed about the limits of public school education, I wondered how many people knew that I was a college graduate. I wondered how my fellow brothers of the badge would react if they learned that I'd actually deferred my acceptance to graduate school—or that, one day, I was planning to go back for my Masters.

"Well, anyway, the police department had its own one-out-of-ten strategy. You see, during the '50s and '60s, when a large number of Black men attempted to join the department, only one out of every ten or more applicants was accepted. That was by design, and, through racist policies, many Black applicants were turned away for false medical reasons, such as heart murmurs and 'flat feet.' If you didn't have somebody in there removing obstacles, you got turned away. It was difficult for us to be hired and promoted. A lawsuit filed by the African American Patrolman's League is still pending in federal court."

"Yeah, Sarge, I know all about that, but I didn't know about the department's hiring procedures during that time."

"Myles, I think I'm going to punch out of here. I've been here for three hours and you know anybody who stays here too long is a perfect DUI."

"Thanks for the drinks, Sarge. It was good talking with you."

I looked at my watch. It was nearly 10 p.m. and I wanted to get by the South Town YMCA to see Sam Jordan, the weight-lifting instructor, to get my schedule for his upcoming class, so I left when the Sarge did. I got home just before eleven; it was a long day and the Jack Daniels was ruling. I needed to get some sleep.

CHAPTER 7

The roll call briefing the next morning was discouraging. Lt. Nugent read off the number of murders that had taken place in the city over the past two weeks, and gang murders lead the list. Both southside Areas had six apiece, and seven of the total twelve were gang-related. There were two arrests made, but five homicide cases still remained open and unsolved.

I sat in the front row, so I didn't notice if DoubleA had come in. Lt. Nugent was addressing the roll call making sure that everybody knew the count. As he briefed us on three possible suspects, I heard DoubleA's voice from the back of the room. "Remember, guys, be sure that you debrief all arrestees and any possible suspects for any information. When the pressure is on, a proficient detective can get plenty of good information from an unrelated suspect."

The lieutenant then called out the assignments. "Stay safe, boys, and give 'em hell," he concluded.

I gathered my gear and headed to find our squad car. I met DoubleA in the parking lot. I felt a little anxious but I had to speak. "Say, man, I apologize for my behavior yesterday. I'm embarrassed and ashamed that I didn't stand up with you. I did some soul-searching last night. I want you to know I have confidence in you. No matter what else happens, I'll be there with you."

A big smile appeared on his face; this was the first time I had seen him look so pleased. DoubleA shook his head back and thanked me. "I guess that fucking Rodney Fletcher sparked a monster in me for a moment," he said by way of explanation.

We had just started to drive south when the dispatcher called our beat number, 6812B-Boy, over the radio and told us to report back to headquarters. We pulled into the parking lot and met with Detectives Clark and Folks. They gave us a phone message from our friend, Papa. He wanted us to contact him right away. DoubleA went inside headquarters and told me to wait for him in front of the building. I pulled around to the front as DoubleA was hurrying out of the door. He jumped in the car and told me to go to 411 East 63rd Street and park in the rear.

I wanted to ask him what he had, but I knew before we got there he would explain everything to me. When we reached 22nd Street, just prior to approaching the Dan Ryan Expressway, DoubleA opened up. "Papa made contact with his worker. He wants us to meet the worker at the 411 Club."

Discretion is often the better part of valor. I wanted to ask whom we were looking for, and how would we know him when we saw him—but I dared not. DoubleA had his own way of doing things and explaining what he was doing or thinking was not open for public discussion.

We pulled into the rear of the 411 Club. It was a small neighborhood bar just east of King Drive on 63rd Street. The place was empty except for a few regulars who were engaged in a conversation with the barmaid. We took a seat. The barmaid shouted over to us, "If you boys are drinking this early in the morning, you have to order from the bar."

"No, thank you, ma'am. We're waiting on somebody," I replied.

About ten minutes later, a tall Black man entered the bar and scoped us as he took a seat beside us. He sat there for a moment and then quietly stated, "Papa sent me."

DoubleA offered to buy him a drink, but he politely declined.

"My name is Wilson. Papa spoke very highly of you guys and he told me to help you as much as possible. What I've learned through the grapevine is this," he said, getting right to the point. "On the day the young boy was killed at the South-Moor, three known gang members were seen entering the hotel with a young teen. Nobody from the street knew what happened to him inside, but a junkman by the name of Sampson, who scavenges around the neighborhood, was inside the hotel when they went in."

"How do you know he was inside the hotel during the murder?" I asked.

"Word on the street is the junkman always travels with a old shopping cart. The cart was seen in the rear of the hotel, next to a back entrance. If the cart was there, so was Sampson. It was said that Sampson heard the conversation and witnessed the murder. Shortly after the gang members left, Sampson was seen fleeing the scene and he left the cart in the rear."

DoubleA quickly stepped in, asking "What does this Sampson guy look like and where can we find him?"

"Sampson lives on the street. He collects junk from the alleys and sells it over on State Street. He's about 6'4", 230 pounds, medium complexion, raggedy, and smelly. Nobody knows how old he is because he's always grubby, unshaven, and unclean. We don't even know where he really lives—or if Sampson is his real name. Basically, people have just seen him around the neighborhood pushing a cart collecting refuse and iron."

I thanked Wilson for his efforts and gave him our number at headquarters. "Give us a call if you find out any additional information."

I was excited; this information gave us the best lead yet. If we could find Sampson, bring him in and conduct an interview, take a statement, maybe we could get an arrest warrant for our boy, Black Sonny. Finding Sampson was an utmost urgency. We drove over to the Woodlawn area and started canvassing. Every person we stopped never heard of Sampson, the junkman. We went over to the salvage yard on State Street and spoke to the owner. We knew most of the scavengers in the area took their wares to him. He was an old Polish guy named Prunziski. He ran the junkyard on State Street, east of the railroad yard at 61st. He said, "Yeah, I got plenty junkmen who fit that description. To me they all look the same. If you want to find him, I'm open from 6 a.m. to 6 p.m., six days a week."

He was a smart-ass son-of-a bitch, but I gathered his rudeness was a front to keep us from uncovering his side activities. My suspicion led me to believe he was fencing stolen goods.

It was evident that we'd have to put in some additional hours if we wanted to find our junkman. We set up a plan for a stakeout to see if our guy would show up. The thought of sitting on a junkyard was depressing, but if we wanted to find our man it was the only practical thing to do.

We set up our surveillance at 6 a.m. the next morning. I brought coffee and donuts and we began our boring task of watching a mixture of bums, hustlers, and thieves scurry in and out of the salvage yard. DoubleA seemed to be accustomed to this kind of work. He sat there relaxed and energetic, making comments about the people we saw. Being there with him on this type of operation gave me a great opportunity to listen to his experiences and learn something about being a detective.

During that time I was able to learn a great deal about the man I was assigned to work with. "You seem to be accustomed to handling this kind of duty, DoubleA," I said. "How many times have you had to pull an assignment like this?"

"Shit, this is detective work, Myles. If you want to be a good detective you must develop an appreciation for patience. Good police work requires good observation skills and patience. Stick with me, my boy, and you'll learn how to be a good sleuth."

DoubleA didn't have any children, but he was quite fond of his nephew, Alex—his sister's only child. He mentioned the child's name only once, but it was with such fervor and excitement you could tell he loved the boy. I found myself becoming quite comfortable with asking him questions; some he answered candidly and with others his responses seemed enigmatic. I wanted to know how he felt about being a Black detective and what his views were on the plight of Black people in the United States.

I also wanted to know why he felt so hostile toward young Black males. "DoubleA, I want to ask you something but, to be honest with you, I'm afraid you might take it the wrong way."

"What is it, Myles? Take a shot. We got a long shift."

"To cut to the chase, I'm a little unsettled by your attitude toward young Black males. You seem to have a hatred for this group. I find it confusing because I'm a part of that generation, and I often wonder where do you stand when it comes to me. I don't think you hold me to this level of distrust, but sometimes the right answer is not always clear to me."

"Listen here, son, you're a good person, and you're going to be a good detective. I admire your resilience, aptitude, and integrity. For a man your age, that makes you an anomaly. You have a genuine respect for authority and you have shown me that you recognize the struggle of the Black man here in America. Most young men from your age group don't have a clue about what its been like to be a Black man under attack from a society that you are supposed to be a part of—a society that almost totally rejects you. Our struggle here is untold. If we are to make any new inroads into the American mainstream, we must all remember the struggle and make some type of contribution that will help uplift the race. It's not that I hate this generation. Rather, I hate their failure to recognize that they must contribute to the struggle. This carnage and massacre of the youth is a threat to our survival. Show me a race of people who have been taught to kill each other, who use self-hatred as ammunition, and I'll show you a race of people who became extinct. We need to stop all this destruction and realize the need to think and act collectively in a land where we've been denied."

I discovered DoubleA had a lot of conservative views. He did not believe in policies like affirmative action and welfare. He felt that social dependencies deprived our race of the strength needed to be enterprising. It was his belief that the growth of gang membership and gang violence was really an outcome of government social services that target the Black family for retrogression.

"Myles," he said, "the current established policies of our government today penalize the Black family. For example, if an unemployed father lives in the home, he must move because the welfare policy requires the home to be abandoned by the breadwinner in order to receive public aid. Black men who can not adequately provide for their families are too humiliated to sneak in and out of the home so that the "check" will not stop coming. After several decades of Black fathers not being at home, the women become unable to control the yearnings and rebellion of their virile children. This discord allows the gang family to establish a firm and decisive identity with the fatherless male child."

DoubleA thought programs like affirmative action lowered the bar so that Blacks could receive positions they did not deserve. It was his view that no matter how high the bar was, a brother could get over it if he disciplined himself and studied hard for advancement. DoubleA did not see the bar being lowered for White candidates who did not demonstrate any better skills than the Blacks; yet through political clout, nepotism, and prejudice, Whites have been given the opportunities for hire, assignment, and promotion.

That first day of our stakeout was an education. I learned a great deal of important information from and about Aristotle Ashford. However, on our next tour of duty, DoubleA reversed the trend. He wouldn't allow himself to be the orator.

As soon as I directed a question toward him, he shut me off. "Wait just a minute, my friend. I think it's my turn to do some interrogation here. You ain't going to get away with questioning me all day. Tell me something about yourself, young fellow. I think you can start by telling me who's your 'Chinaman.' It's obvious that you got somebody pushing the envelope for you. You've only been on the job for a little more than four years and you're already a detective. Where did you work when you finished the academy?"

"Well," I answered, "when I graduated from the police academy, I was assigned to the 008th District, Chicago Lawn, but that didn't last six months. My most vivid memory from that assignment occurred just a few days after I had completed my probation. I was working a one-man car on midnights. I responded to a fire somewhere on South McVickers Street. When I arrived on the scene a woman ran up to the car and told me her baby was still in the house. Hell, I didn't know what to do. I radioed the dispatcher and told them a child was still in the house. It was about 3 a.m. and I didn't hear any fire sirens approaching, so I raced into the burning house.

"I wasn't a fireman and I didn't know what I was doing. I raced up to the bedroom. Smoke was bellowing from all sides. I couldn't locate the child and I found myself trapped in the midst of the fire. My eyes were burning and the smoke was so thick I couldn't breath. I could see myself dying as I fell to the floor. Suddenly, I saw a wall crashing down on me, and then I saw a light. I just knew the light was from the tunnel between life and death. Instead, it was a fireman with an ax and he was chopping away. When he saw me on the floor he reached down and grabbed me by the arm and pulled me toward the window. Another fireman came through right behind him and they took me to safety.

"They found the woman's baby in the next room. I later learned the child survived. I laid up in the hospital for three days, suffering from smoke inhalation and minor burns. In those three days all I could remember was the voice of my grandfather. As a child he always reminded me that God looks after babies and fools.

"I never got a 'good job' or a 'thank you' for my brave yet foolish attempt, but I learned a lesson: wait for the fire department if you can, and never run into a burning building without determining how you are going to get out. It was a foolish rookie mistake. Four months later, I transferred.

"I wanted action, so I transferred to the 007th District, Englewood, in May 1971. Englewood was fast and I learned a lot quickly. Coupled with the fast action of robberies and shootings around the clock, I discovered that some of the officers assigned to the district were quite intriguing. I recall my first day in the 'Wood'; I was scheduled to work a beat car. After roll call, I found my partner sitting in our car in the parking lot. He was a veteran officer and I was really excited about coming to work with him in a high crime police district. I approached the car and attempted to get in when he grabbed the door handle and said, 'Just a moment, my man. Do you take money?' I was startled and I didn't know what to say. I finally said no. His next response was, 'Where do you want me to pick you up at and at what time.' I realized then that that this guy was a thief. He had already planned his day, with a partner or without one. Then, in 1973," I continued, "I went to the westside to the Special Operations Group West. That was an education. My first day driving around the westside on 5th Avenue, Wilcox, Kostner, Madison, Fillmore, and through K-Town is still a vivid memory. This was all new territory to me. I was working with a guy named Billy Lumpkin. We both were from Englewood and we found that first day on the westside to be an expedition. Driving around the neighborhoods and watching a part of Chicago that was unfamiliar seemed strange. The west-side brothers were unpretentious;

they hustled like brothers on the southside, yet they seemed to have a deeper respect for authority.

"People looked and acted different. What we both found to be so unusual on the first day was the number of men we saw standing around on the streets on crutches or with some type of cast on one of their legs. We couldn't figure it out until we asked a guy on the street why so many brothers were on crutches. The guy looked at us and began to laugh. He found it amusing that we had no idea why so many males sported orthopedic hardware. After gathering his composure, he replied, 'You dudes must be new around here.' Then he said, 'The reason why you see so many brothers with crutches is because they either broke their ankle or leg running from the police with those got-damn platform shoes on!' We both began to laugh hysterically, but it was the biting truth. You could see platform shoes strolled all over the westside—in the streets, on the sidewalks and curbs."

DoubleA laughed at that revelation and mentioned he once heard Dick Gregory, the comedian, accuse the police of inventing the platform shoe.

I found that amusing and continued to keep the dialogue going. "Back then, I noticed another peculiarity on the westside," I said. "The habitual abuse of the legally prescribed drugs, Talwind and Pyribenzamine—known on the street as T's and Blues. These drugs were obtained from pharmacies with a prescription from greedy doctors who were milking the state government's Green Card subsidy program. Addicts would purchase the two drugs in a pill form, crush them together, place them in a bottle cap and mix a liquid substance with them. Then they would use a hypodermic syringe to extract the mixed substance and shoot it into a vein. This combination of drugs created a feeling similar to heroin; however, many users suffered from infections that caused their hands and arms to swell. I often saw guys standing around looking like they had boxing gloves on because their hands were so swollen and infected."

"You know, Myles," DoubleA commented, "that investigation has not started, but believe me, son, in the future you'll see a lot of doctors looking for a new profession after their trial is over."

We spent three twelve-hour shifts searching for our junkman. On the final day of our surveillance, we concluded that the salvage yard was taking in more than junk. We noted on several occasions the same individuals came by at the same time each day. They would back their cars up close to a trailer and open the trunk. We could see men placing items into the trunk of the vehicles, but we were unable to determine what they were placing there. We took note of the times the vehicles showed up, and we wrote down a description of the vehicles. We would pass that information on to the tactical officers in the 003rd District.

As the day was ending, our conversations met on the same path. We both began to doubt the information on the junkman, Sampson, and we decided we would contact Papa and have him set up another meeting with his worker, Wilson. It just didn't seem like this guy Sampson existed.

Toward the end of the tour, DoubleA began to tell me about the death of Detective James Alfona. He described the incident from the very beginning: "During the late summer of 1970, three Gang Intelligence detectives were cruising behind the South-Moor Hotel conducting surveillance when a shot was fired from the fire escape. The bullet hit Alfona in the lower back. When the other officers realized that Jimmy was hit, they scrambled to find safety, believing that more sniper fire was incoming.

"You see, kid, that bullet was intended for us, members of the Unit's B team. We had a reputation for kicking the Stones' ass. It didn't make no difference what we stopped them for. If we caught them in a group, we stomped them. On the night of the shooting, Alfona was not working with his regular partners. He was the third man on a team that was usually assigned to the Disciples on the west end, in Englewood. They were covering for us because we were downtown. They made the mistake of traveling through the alley behind the hotel. They didn't know that this was one of our routines. The Stones knew our habits. Each night members of the B team would cruise behind the hotel looking for activity. The Stones knew this, so on the night of the shooting, they blocked off the alley with some old couches so that the squad car couldn't get through. When the squad car stopped, they opened up on it. It was a trap."

He continued, "The detectives put the news of the shooting out over the police radio and all hell broke loose. Officers from as far as the westside responded to the scene. It was like a wild episode right out of the movies. What took place on the city's southside for the remainder of the night could have been described as a police riot. It was estimated that over one thousand rounds were fired into the hotel's windows, doors, and concrete walls. We set out through the Woodlawn community searching for every Blackstone Ranger we could find. Any person wearing the gangs noted red tam was taken into police custody. Once we had them in custody, we literally kicked the shit out of them and took them to jail. We were devastated.

"What was so disconcerting about the whole night is that the morning papers printed a story that said the police never fired a single shot during the entire incident. The two detectives in the car with Alfona had to be relieved of their weapons and placed on restricted duty. Roll call the next morning started out like a planning session for a murder conspiracy. All of the department's brass had to address us to warn the detectives that any type of retaliation would be viewed as a conspiracy and all parties to such a response would be charged accordingly.

"I never heard any mention of retaliatory actions, but many detectives have been accused, even to this day, of snatching Blackstone Rangers from their dedicated turf, taking them into enemy territory, and forcing them out of the squad cars. They then would let the rival gang members know that there were Stones in the area before leaving the block.

"After this, Myles, the hatred for the Blackstone Rangers was at its highest point. The White detectives despised them for killing one of them. The Black detectives shouldered a double disdain because they killed one of the finest human beings with whom you could be associated with, and because they were responsible for the destruction of Black youth during a period when America was engaged in simultaneous struggles of civil rights, Black revolution, and civil unrest."

Our stakeout didn't yield any fruit, but it gave me an opportunity to recognize the shroud of a man who I was growing to admire and respect more and more each day. DoubleA never mentioned his service in the military or his life growing up in Mississippi, and I dared not ask. I recognized that he was a very private person and those subjects were personal. To ask him any questions about those aspects of his life would make him think I was invading his privacy.

We saw almost one hundred people go in and out for the three days of our stakeout. None of them was our guy. I thought that this guy must be a ghost or, more likely, that we had been spun.

"I never did get any good vibes from that name," DoubleA snapped. "The name Sampson doesn't have any flavor. I stayed up half the night calling around to people I thought would have some information on the junkman, but nobody knew of him. I did find out that a strange-looking street person had been seen coming around the area since last summer, but he's disappeared."

The sudden arrival and apparent disappearance of Sampson made DoubleA more suspicious. We gave up on the stakeout, but we contacted the 003rd District and requested that they be on the lookout for a junkman fitting Sampson's description. We also reported the suspicious activity we observed at the junkyard.

On our way to headquarters that evening, we were given a message over the radio to see a Mr. J.C. Gilmore at 6646 S. Drexel. The name was not familiar, but the address was. It was Felix Hamilton's grandfather's house. We pulled up to the address and the old-timer met us on the steps. He looked upset.

"Got-damnit, that som'bitch Felix got me. He done come in here and stole my gitback."

Mr. Gilmore told us that Felix had snuck into the house through a window during the night and took some fresh clothes and one of Mr. Gilmore's prize shotguns. Felix forced his way into a storage room in the basement, taking a LC Smith 410 shotgun and two boxes of double-odd buck ammunition. Gilmore said, "I wish to God I had ah been able to catch him. Y'all wouldn't be worrying where he's at now! I'da sent his black ass straight to hell. You would've been able to see what was in front of him if you was looking at his back. He's armed and dangerous now, and the boy is experienced in killing. Y'all better catch up wit' em before some undeserving Negro has ta die for being in his way."

We took down the old-timer's gun registration information and again thanked him for notifying us of his grandson's actions. It appeared that Felix was desperate and that he knew that his life was in danger. The theft of the shotgun gave him some protection.

"That 410 is about twelve to sixteen inches shorter by now," DoubleA said. "He can conceal it on his person while he scurries about the neighborhood hoping to avoid the contract of death that has felled his two cohorts."

Our investigation was approaching three weeks and we had encountered hot and cold leads that kept us busy. We contacted Papa as soon as we reached headquarters. We told him to reach out for his worker, Wilson, and have him meet us at a south-side restaurant on 79th Street, near Rhodes, around ten the next morning. We considered moving our place of contact to an area away from the section of the city where we were known by many of the people who lived and worked there. This was a distance away from the zone where the Blackstone Rangers' gang activity was concentrated.

CHAPTER 8

The next morning we arrived at Izola's Restaurant, a quaint south-side dining room filled with resplendent paintings of Black accomplishment. Pictures of jazz musicians, politicians, and folk heroes covered the wall in the main dining room. You could listen to a collection of blues, jazz, and contemporary artists while you dined on a down-home hardy breakfast, lunch, or dinner. We entered the restaurant and took a seat in the main dining room near the rear exit door. We ordered coffee and fresh donuts. We felt comfortable and relished our anonymity and the fact that we did not have to be concerned with being identified as police officers. The donuts and coffee were a clear giveaway, but we didn't concern ourselves with being suspicious. We just wanted to appear to be two guys having a coffee break.

Wilson entered the restaurant after we had finished our first cup of coffee. He located us sitting in the rear. He nodded and came over to take a seat. Before we could express our concern about the mysterious Sampson, he blurted out, "The boy done vanished, huh? I got word that ain't nobody seen him since the murder."

"Yeah," I responded. "We can't find a trace of him."

"Are you two detectives the only cops looking for Sampson?" Wilson asked.

"Why do you ask? I'm sure if some other team was working on this case we would be aware of it by now," I responded. I assured him that we would investigate and make sure there was no other investigative body working the same case. It was improbable, but not impossible.

"Well, this guy Sampson definitely saw the murder," Wilson said, "and he was seen leaving the scene shortly after the three Stones fled. Right now I think only you guys, my information source, Sampson, and I know this. But it could be possible that the Stones know this. Sampson may be on the run. I talked with my source about Sampson. I asked him every question I could think of which would give me a better assessment of him, but he still remains elusive. There is something very mysterious about Sampson. I just haven't figure it out yet."

"Okay, Holmes," DoubleA snapped, "when you figure it out, and if it happens before Christmas, please give us a call."

Wilson didn't like DoubleA's surliness, but, before leaving the restaurant, he insisted that he would solve the mystery of Sampson before we got taken off of the case.

DoubleA and I sat over another coffee and began to go over our investigation. We had checked police files under death investigations and other mysterious causes of death such as drowning, accidental deaths, and asphyxiation, and had found no reports that aroused our suspicion. The mysterious disappearance of Sampson, as we would later learn, was as puzzling as his appearance in an area where none of the junk collectors and scavengers who had lived in the neighborhood for some time really knew him or his rightful birthname.

Our extended canvassing of the area had revealed that Sampson initially began coming around the area in late August 1973. Sources stated that one day he just appeared with a cart, traveling through the alleys foraging for whatever he could find. He never mingled with the scavengers in the area, and it's not clear if he gave the name of Sampson or whether it was hung on him by competitors because of his size and build.

After breakfast we headed toward headquarters to complete our delinquent reports and to talk with Lt. Nugent about our investigation. Mike told us there was a message for us from Bessie Williams and that the coroner's autopsy and inquest reports were on our desk.

"I'll take a look at the reports and you can call Mrs. Williams," I suggested.

The pathologist report was submitted by a Dr. An, and it stated that the victim had expired as a result of a gunshot wound to the brain. The coroner's inquest ruled the cause of death a homicide. I had begun to type my supplementary report, when DoubleA bent over the typewriter and told me to call Mrs. Williams. He said she really wanted to talk to me. He had a scheming look on his face that he tried to camouflage and I didn't know why. I couldn't understand why Mrs. Williams didn't tell DoubleA whatever it was she wanted to say. He finally said it was a dinner invitation.

I called the Williams residence and she answered the phone.

"Hello Mrs. Williams. This is detective Sivad. My partner told me you wanted me to call you."

She hesitated for a moment then she answered, "I'm preparing a good meal for dinner this evening and I would be honored if you and Detective Ashford would be our guests." Although she never mentioned DoubleA's initial response, she seemed perplexed by me calling her after she had already talked to DoubleA.

"I'd be delighted Mrs. Williams; that is so thoughtful of you to invite us. What's a good time to come?"

"Any time after seven. I know you two boys won't pass up a good home-cooked meal."

It was Friday evening and DoubleA and I decided to finish up early. We had the weekend off and I really looked forward to having some time to relax.

I arrived at the Williams' residence at seven. Mrs. Williams greeted me at the door asking, "Where's Detective Ashford? I invited both of you to come."

I wasn't a bit surprised she asked, but I made an excuse for him and told her that he had made plans prior to the invitation. She seemed a little disappointed but said she was thankful that I came.

Mrs. Williams was a good woman; she had worked hard raising a family. She told me her husband died in an accident while doing construction work. He fell seventeen floors from a scaffold. She had been a widow for twelve years, left alone to raise a fourteen-year-old daughter and a three-year-old son.

Francine was busy getting dressed, so Mrs. Williams tried to entertain me until she finished. "Well, Detective Sivad, how come you ain't married? A fine-looking young man like you ought to have some protection."

I was a bit taken aback by her question, and I wondered how she would know whether I was married or not.

"I know this isn't none of my business, either," she added, "but do you have any children? I can tell you've been raised properly cause you're well mannered and you have a radiant spirit. What church do you belong to?"

I couldn't give her an answer.

"Aren't you saved, child? Don't you believe in the Lord? My heart tells me you're a good man, but you need to get in the church, boy. You must find salvation in your life through Jesus Christ."

"Yes, ma'am, I do believe in the Lord and I have been to church on a number of occasions. I just haven't been lately."

"Oh, mother, please," Francine voiced from the bedroom. "Give Detective Sivad a break. Let him know that we wanted him to have dinner with us to express our gratitude for his kindness and the comfort he offered during our time of grief. We don't want him to think we're trying to save his soul."

Francine suddenly came out of the bedroom. I was star-struck. She was gorgeous. Her hair was long and shimmering and it hung down to her shoulders. It gave off a glowing shine, so full of luster and bounce. When she took her hand and slightly moved her hair from the right side of her face, I noticed how a soft glaze of makeup highlighted a deep, honeycomb complexion. I stood there frozen, asking myself why I hadn't noticed her beauty the first time I saw her. As my eyes swept over her figure, I noted that her hips were high and her butt was round—but not too wide. When she dropped her arms to her side, I noticed the heavy curvature of her breast. All these features just accentuated her most gorgeous traits—those high cheekbones and almond shaped eyes. With a smile on her face, Mrs. Williams noticed my surprise and teasingly told me to wake up and come have a seat at the dining room table.

As I entered the dining room, I noticed that the table was set for four people. There were candles that emitted a fragrance of plum; they gave off a scent that aroused my already stimulated libido. There were fresh flowers centered on the table. The dinner consisted of braised lamb chops, baked potatoes, and broccoli. A bottle of vintage Chardonnay wine sat on the table and a tossed green salad complemented the meal. It wasn't the down-home meal I expected. I suspected that Francine chose the menu and not Mrs. Williams.

It was an evening chosen to show gratitude and appreciation for our efforts. Mrs. Williams gave me a card and told me to read it before we began dinner. I opened the thank-you card which read: "Dear Detectives Ashford and Sivad: I know in your profession you have witnessed the pain and suffering of many people, and I know you could never afford to allow yourself to carry their burdens. The loss of my son was another tragedy that my daughter and I have to endure in our lives. We could not have sustained our grief without your extension of sympathy and goodwill. The kindness and understanding you exhibited will always be remembered. We thank you so much for helping us get through such a difficult time."

It was signed Bessie and Francine Williams.

I said, "Ladies, I'm deeply moved by your recognition, but I must assure you that everything we have done is all a part of being a good detective. And I promise you, we are doing all we can to solve Franklin's murder."

After dinner Mrs. Williams thanked me for coming and reminded me to be sure that I convey their sentiments to my partner. She then retired to her bedroom. Francine and I moved to the living room where she showed me pictures of her family and friends. I found myself wanting to see Francine again, as soon as possible.

We spent the rest of the evening entertaining each other's questions. I found her to be extremely intelligent and affectionate. She was very versed on contemporary social and political issues. When she talked, she looked you directly in the eyes. She brushed her hand across mine while delivering her thoughts. I was falling for her and I wanted to stay and talk with her all night, but it was getting late. "Francine, I want to thank you for the invitation. I really enjoyed the evening. You're fun to be with and, if it's okay, I'd like to see you again."

She seemed delighted and welcomed the suggestion. I wanted to kiss her as we stood in the front doorway, but I didn't have the courage to make a faint attempt. I left, but I knew that I would be rushing to get back. I thought that I had found someone who could possibly contain my interest.

Chapter 9

I mused about Francine all the way home. I was so stunned by her attractiveness. I couldn't understand why I had never noticed her beauty until tonight. I concluded that I had been working too hard and was getting too involved in my duties. I've never considered myself to be a player, but when you miss such beauty because you are too wrapped up in work, you need to take a rest.

I arrived home around 10:45 p.m. It was still rather early and I didn't have anything planned for the remainder of the evening. I put a couple of sounds on the box and poured me a nice stiff Jack Daniels on the rocks. The sound of "My Favorite Things" accompanied by the seasoned horn of John Coltrane with McCoy Tyler on piano and Elvin Jones on drums eased my tension. I leaned back on the sofa and reflected on the evening with Francine Williams. She was a real prize. The ice cubes didn't float too long with the Jack before the "Train" completed his last track. I was traveling within the universe, still dressed with my badge and gun in their working positions.

The sound of the phone woke me up. I reached for it blindly without opening my eyes. It was DoubleA. "Hey dude, you up yet?"

My head was still spinning from the heavy shots of Jack Daniels. "Naw, man. What time is it?"

"It's almost ten-thirty, kid. What did you find last night? How was the dinner party?"

"Aw, DoubleA, I feel like shit! What's happening?"

"Nothing, really. I just wondered what are you going to do with a day off. I thought you might be interested in going to a party tonight."

"Party? Sure, man. What time?"

"I'll pick you up around nine."

"Cool, brother. I'll be ready."

Damn, DoubleA wants me to go to a party with him. That's great. I thought he was beginning to accept me as his partner. That made me feel good. I wondered what kind of a party we would be attending. I figured I should lay me out some threads. I wanted to look impressive. DoubleA was always talking about my style. It reminded me of how Dexter Gordon ragged Miles Davis about his Brooks Brothers' shirts and Ivy League style of dressing. I felt he was probably jealous because he couldn't catch up to my style, but I wouldn't ever say that because I couldn't stand his comeback. He's full-fledged. Anything you say about DoubleA will definitely solicit an attack on your family, your mama, and your ass.

I looked over at my music system and realized that I hadn't shut the power off last night. As I reached over the table to punch the button, I saw a piece of paper on the table with something I had scribbled last night. I could see that I had written the name Francine a number of times and her number was written beside it. Shit! I hope I didn't get drunk and call her last night. I only had two drinks, but they were like Bennie's 357 shots. I wanted to find an excuse to call her right then, but I decided against it. If I did call her last night, she probably wouldn't want to be bothered with my silly ass now. "Damn! Got-Damn!"

I got dressed and drove over to the South Town YMCA. I had obtained a membership in February and had only been there twice since joining. The Y offered a membership in the Triangle Club, which provided some of the best health maintenance activities you could find. Steam, sauna, whirlpool, swimming, exercise, and weightlifting were all combined with lounging, TV, and a professional masseuse. Just walking through the dressing room felt good. I like working out. I like what it does to my body. I guess I've always been considered athletic because of my physical build—plus the fact that everybody knows I've always been diehard about football. At 6-feet, 193 pounds—according to today's scale—I'm a pretty good size; and, I must admit, I'm proud of my build. In college, people always said I looked like a baby faced Jim Brown. Nowadays, everybody says I look like the "Juice" but, frankly, I don't see the resemblance. Actually, I've always kind of seen a more rugged version of Herbie Hancock staring back in the mirror—even though I'm not sure if I like the direction of this new, synthesized *Headhunters* album.

I took a dip in the pool and swam a mile and then topped off my morning with a stint in the steam room. I sat down on the couch and attempted to watch a little television but soon found myself dreaming.

When I woke up, it was 4:50 p.m. I raced to get dressed and headed over to Volois, a steam-tabled lunch counter on East 53rd street in the Hyde Park community. It offered wholesome meals at a bargain price. I dined on fresh broccoli, pork chops, and steamed rice along with a slice of lemon meringue pie. It was almost six o'clock when I finished. I needed to head home and get a little nap before DoubleA arrived.

DoubleA knocked on my door at nine; he was always on time. I opened the door and invited him in for a drink before we left for the party. This was the first time he had been to my apartment.

"Myles, I like the setup. You got good taste, man. How long you been living here?"

"Oh, shit, I just recently moved in. I'd been looking for an apartment in Hyde Park for months. While searching the area, I noticed this apartment was vacant. I stopped by to inquire about it, but the landlady told me there were no vacancies. I figured she didn't want to show the apartment to a strange-looking man, so she lied. I wasn't offended because I realized that I had to be realistic about how some females think when they see an unfamiliar Black man. So I came back in full CPD uniform and inquired about the same vacant front apartment again. The same landlady asked me who the apartment was for, and I told her it was for me. She looked ashamed because she knew I was the same man she had lied to, but I didn't want to scream discrimination. I really didn't give a shit. I wanted the apartment. I did what I had to do to demonstrate sound employment and good character. What was most attractive to the landlady, probably, was the idea of police security on the premises. She showed me the apartment and gave me an application. I filled it out. Three days later she called me and told me the apartment was mine."

I didn't have a lot of fancy furniture, but a few original oil paintings by Clifford Lee, along with the interior decorations, complemented the picture window in the front. The picture window gave the flat a full view of the street.

I asked DoubleA what was his pleasure, and he responded, "Tangueray, if you have any." Fortunately, I had a bottle stashed in the kitchen. I poured myself another Jack Daniels and we took seats in the living room. I already had the box going. I was listening to Dexter Gordon's "A Night in Paris."

DoubleA was a jazzman from the '40s. If it was jazz, he knew the musician and the title of the tune 99.9 times out of 100 compositions selected. "Yo, Holmes. You a jazz man? Well I'll be damned," he said. "I had you pegged as a doo-whopper." "I'm that too, but I come from a jazz family. My father played the saxophone and my brother played the clarinet. Jazz has always been a main staple in my family."

We finished our drinks and headed south toward the party. DoubleA stopped at Al Par's Liquors on East 71st street and picked up a bottle of Tangueray and a bottle of Jack Daniels for our host. The party was held in the plush Pill Hill community, located on the southeast side, at a beautiful ranch-style home owned by retired Captain, Benjamin Bluecrest. Captain Bluecrest had served the department for twenty-eight years and was one of the most outspoken critics of the department's treatment of Black citizens.

Parking was tight in the neighborhood, so we had to park on the next block. I knocked on the door and an attractive young woman opened it. As soon as she recognized DoubleA, she stepped out to hug him. "Detective Ashford, you are looking too good here. I don't think them momma's downstairs will be able to keep their hands off of you. Why do you make it so hard for a woman to choose?" she teased.

DoubleA smiled and returned the cuff. "You can't talk. How many times have you asked me what to do when one of them country boys was pressing too hard? By the way, Natalie, this is my partner, Detective Myles Sivad."

"Hello, Myles. It's a pleasure to meet you," she replied.

Natalie was Captain Bluecrest's oldest daughter. She was very attractive, tall, slim and sexy. She took our jackets and the drinks and directed us to the basement where most of the people were.

The music was jazz, of course, and the basement was just as I had expected—expertly finished with teak paneling and tiled floors. There was a large pool table in the middle of the room and a large wet bar that extended from one wall to the next. The walls were covered with historical pictures of Black men in action. There were also pictures of police officers killed in the line of duty and firefighters at fire scenes. Black Congressman Hiram Revels from Mississippi, elected shortly after reconstruction, was centered on a wall adjacent to the pool table. The sight of these heroes drew me in. I was overcome with a deep sense of racial pride as I moved from one picture to the next, identifying the heroes who where pictured in the gallery.

I noticed that encased on the bar were three pictures of Black police officers: James L. Shelton, 1872, Chicago's first Black police officer; Cornelius Wilson, the first Black police officer killed in the line of duty, May 19, 1912; and William Childs, the first Black promoted to the rank of sergeant in the city of Chicago. A brass plate centered beneath the pictures read "Have a drink for these guys!" It was an honorable tribute.

Smoke filled the room and the chatter from all the people present created an echo of voice and sound fused together with the savory sound of jazz in the background. The bartender was none other than Sgt. John Harde, my mate from Bennie's 357 Club. He greeted us and reached for the Jack Daniels while asking DoubleA what was his choice of poison. DoubleA ordered a double Tangueray on the rocks with a twist of lime. We gathered our drinks and moved through the crowd. While making our way, DoubleA turned to me and said, "Listen, kid, don't talk too much. You will learn a great deal about the people here and the Department if you just look and listen. I'm going over in the corner to talk with some old friends. You can mesh with the people and get your notepad ready."

I stood in the crowd sampling my Jack and listening to the stylistic voice of Nancy Wilson singing "Guess Who I Saw Today." This crowd was a mellow group, and there were conversations going on in every segment of the room. I could see officers from all ranks, along with noted politicians and familiar city workers. When I eased back toward the bar for a refill, I stumbled on a conversation between Captain Bluecrest and several other ranking officers. He was discussing gang violence in the city and he didn't show any forgiveness when he blamed past and present police officers for their failure to address this crisis.

Captain Bluecrest was a very articulate man. His voice carried across the room as he began to reveal his personal convictions: "Gentleman, the current increase in gang violence has not been given the faintest attention by the city or the police department. We as police officers have failed to evaluate the growing gang violence. It's my belief that if more resources had been directed toward programs which provided alternatives to gangs, the gangs would not have flourished and many young people would not have lost their lives."

We all stood around in a quiet hush, as the captain continued to provide facts to support his beliefs. "Black gang violence began to proliferate in the '50s. By 1966 we were headed for record numbers in shootings and homicides," he said. "From 1966 through today, the Department's strategy to combat gang violence has been through arrest and prosecution. It never considered putting police officers out there to educate the younger kids against gangs and gang violence. Between 1965 and 1970 the homicide rate in Chicago increased 169 percent. Anybody here want to guess how many of these murders were of Black boys between the ages of fifteen and twenty-four? The Department didn't give a shit about how many Black kids lost their lives. 'We'll get the winners and prosecute them' was the Department's foolish reply".

"Black police officers didn't do any better. We saw the gangs as our perpetual enemies and never once did we view them as dispossessed little boys who languished for a piece of the pie, fatherless and scorned in a society that bred contempt for the poor and the less fortunate. We accepted training that taught us that these kids were criminals and had to be treated as such. The playgrounds, YMCAs, and boy's clubs that saved us when we were that age could not provide the social leadership to these groups because the situation had gotten too violent. If a child wanted to participate in a program offered by one of these organizations, he couldn't—unless he was associated with the gang that controlled that turf.

"We alienated ourselves from the community, believing that this was the only way we could do our jobs effectively. We allowed the uniform to present us with a dichotomy that defined us as being different because we were police officers, and the difference which separated us was based on a misleading rationalization of the problem."

I stood there and listened to the Captain, wanting to pitch in and say something—but I thought better of it. I was getting a lesson that was invaluable. Most importantly, the professor was a retired, experienced official who knew the "poke was coming before the punch landed."

He continued. "For almost a decade, Black boys had to option educational choices in favor of survival. When their association conflicted with their home turf and school, their only choice if they wanted to remain whole was to give up school."

I found myself squeezing closer to the bar as the Captain continued. "The White police officer didn't give a shit about our Black youth problem or us. All they wanted to do was lock a nigger up!"

After listening to Captain Bluecrest's last statement, I drifted back to one of my own personal experiences. I recalled when I was in the police academy. During that period in June 1970, the Department and city of Chicago were doing some collateral damage repair to the Department's image. Police training of recruits was increased from fourteen weeks to thirty-one. We were required to take junior college courses in the behavioral science field. Graduate students from the University of Chicago were hired by the City Colleges to teach young police recruits cultural diversity. A young Jewish guy named Fred Lazin taught my class. He was very instructive, knowledgeable, and sensitive to the problem facing the Department. Mr. Lazin worked hard to change some attitudes, only to realize that he had failed.

When he gave our class a final exam, he offered extra credit to any recruit who provided an answer to the question: "What do you think of Dr. King's speech, 'I Have a Dream?'"

When Mr. Lazin returned to the police academy on Monday morning after the exam, he looked very distraught. He told us that one of our classmate's response to the question was, "Dr. King was a Nigger!" Mr. Lazin could not hide his pain and anger when he said it was officers like our classmate who would be responsible for another White officer getting shot in a Black community. What pained me so was that the son-of-a-bitch signed his name to the paper. This showed his utter disregard for Black people—that he didn't give a shit who knew where he stood.

By this time the Captain had finished his monologue. There were more than twenty people gathered around the bar. I made eye contact with Sgt. Harde and requested another drink. As the Sarge poured me another round he said, "What do you think of the Captain's lecture?"

"I approve. It was a valuable lesson and I'll be taking that information with me for future reference."

I could tell Sergeant Harde had great respect for the Captain as he continued to talk to me. "Captain Bluecrest could have stayed around another ten years," he said, "but he became fed up with the racism and politics of Chicago, so he retired. He's running a good security business and he does some training for other security agencies. He still demonstrates a certain excitement and concern for the plight of those young punks out here and doesn't hesitate to remind us all of our responsibility to change their plight."

I took my drink and found a seat in the corner next to a little guy who was taking a photography break. I introduced myself to him.

"Glad to meet you," he responded. "My name is Jimmy Withers. I'm a friend of the Bluecrest family."

"That's a nice camera you have there. Are you a photographer?" I inquired.

"Yes, sir. I'm a freelance writer and a photographer. The host invited me to come and take pictures of his guests."

Withers was a small-statured man. He was highly respected by his peers and very proficient with that camera. He continued to take pictures of the guests while we chatted about the party.

"What unit do you work in, if you don't mind me asking?"

"I'm assigned to Gang Intelligence."

He looked surprised. "I thought all of those guys were old-timers. I've never met any young guys assigned to that unit."

"I'm new. I just started working in the unit last year."

He seemed to know a lot about the Department and my curiosity wouldn't let him get away without asking him who he knew in the unit and how. "So tell me

Jimmy," I inquired, "who else do you know here that works for the Department?"

"Back in the '60s, I worked for the Woodlawn Organization," he responded, "and I met quite a few detectives assigned to the unit. I was quite familiar with all of the men assigned to the B team."

I had no knowledge as to whom he was talking about as he mentioned names like Foster, Ford, Branch, Peck, Clisham, O'Rourke, Foy, Clark, Folks, Patton, and Jackson. I told him that I was working with Detective Ashford and that he was here at the party.

JW smiled and said, "Mr. DoubleA is a fine person and we shared some similar views about the gang strife in the city."

"Oh, yeah. What kind of views, if you don't mind me asking."

"Well, during the rise of gang conflict in the Woodlawn community, the Woodlawn Organization and the University of Chicago were engaged in a struggle to keep the gangs from proliferating further north and east of their current theater of violence. Property values diminished as people became afraid to invest in the area, and property owners struggled to attract new tenants. Gang intimidation of some property owners forced them to walk away from sound investments or face the wrath and violence of assault. The property owners became desperate as they faced a crisis in which they had to balance their personal safety against the reality of demanding payment of rent. Many property owners just walked away and left the property to be claimed for unpaid taxes. The slumlords that owned dilapidated buildings left the property unsecured; many of them were set on fire for insurance claims. The community was being devastated."

My glass was empty and I asked JW if he wanted a refill, but he happily declined. I headed toward the bar again as the Jack was working its wizardry on my expansively mellow perception. I thought about what JW had said, and I remembered what our old friend Papa told us about "people having to give way to the gangs or die."

When I arrived at the bar, I saw DoubleA talking to the Captain's daughter. She looked a bit taller and more voluptuous since the first time I had seen her. I knew the Jack was in control, so I didn't make an issue of it. I walked up to them and said, "Natalie, are you enjoying the party?"

She smiled and said, "My name is Nadine. I'm Natalie's sister." I felt a little embarrassed. Luckily I had a nice buzz, which allowed me to pretend like I hadn't said anything.

"So you're the handsome guy my sister was talking about," she said.

I felt a bit uncomfortable, and the blushing smile I had on my face was clear evidence of my personal distress. I regrouped and asked her name, again.

She replied, "Natalie."

I was stumped. I knew then the Jack was "taking the lead." I had had my last drink for the night.

"I'm sorry for not being able to tell the difference," I stammered. "I guess on a better day I might not have made that mistake."

She recognized my confusion. "Oh, that's okay. People do it all the time."

DoubleA recognized my dilemma and whispered to me that the sister had been asking about me. My good detective partner, in his infinite provision of wisdom, asked me, "Are you okay? You seem to be befuddled here, my boy. These girls are top-shelf. They ain't no ho's, brother. You gotta have game if you thinking about camping here, dude."

"I'm not shopping," I replied. "I'm here with you, and I ain't in no shape to be trying to put down no game. I'll just fade here in the corner and be cool."

I found my seat next to JW and rested my head back against the wall. I took in the chatter around the room and mellowed with the sound of Gene Ammond's "Canadian Sunset." I had been sitting for what seemed like quite a while when one of the Bluecrest girls touched me on the sleeve. I looked in her direction, but I dared not say anything. It was Nadine. She said, "Would you like to have a drink?"

"No, thank you, but I'll join you while you have one." I got out of my seat and walked her toward the bar.

"I saw you when you came in and wanted to say hello," she said.

I was cool, but not for obvious reasons. "What're you drinking?" I asked.

"A gin martini. What about you?"

"I'll have a ginger ale."

"So you're Detective Ashford's new partner? He told me about you some time ago. He said you were a very nice person, and he thought I would like to meet you."

I didn't settle with that. I wanted to know why DoubleA told her about me and not her sister, but I had no idea how I could get that concern across without sounding brainless. Instead I said, "You and your sister look so much alike, it's easy for someone to get you confused."

"It happens. But if you really want to make a quick distinction, you'll notice that Natalie is always smiling," she said.

I was still under the spell of the Jack Daniels. I didn't want to start rambling and let everybody know that "Jack ruled," so I let her do most of the talking.

She noticed my silence. "You don't talk much, do you, Myles?" she said with a pleasant tone.

I felt compelled to defend my game. "I'm not shy," I answered, "it just seems that way for a spell until I get comfortable with someone. Do you talk with DoubleA often, because I'm wondering how did you and DoubleA get on the subject of Myles Sivad?"

"Don't fret, Myles. My dad and DoubleA are very good friends. Their friendship started some time ago when DoubleA was working with my dad. Daddy kind of took DoubleA under his wing, sort of like a mentor. He always said that when things got rough, he wanted DoubleA beside him. They talked about you several weeks ago when daddy asked him how was work. He said he was working with a pretty smart kid and that you were not accustomed to his style but were a fast learner. I made a remark about how I liked smart men, and he said he would take me up on it. I guess he brought you to this old folks' party to meet me."

"Old folks!" I exclaimed. "I wouldn't say that. Many of these people have been where I want to be and beyond. The music is great and I'm enjoying myself."

It was getting late. DoubleA motioned for me to come over to him. I told Nadine to walk over with me. Double A was talking to Captain Bluecrest. When I approached, DoubleA introduced me saying, "This is the kid I've been talking to you about. Myles Sivad, this is retired Captain Benjamin Blucecrest."

I extended my hand and the Captain extended his.

"Please excuse my left hand, son. I use the left hand only because it's nearest to the heart and it symbolizes my respect for you."

I thanked him for the recognition and for the wonderful party he hosted.

DoubleA had given me the sign that it was time to go. I searched the crowd for Nadine. I approached her to say goodnight.

"Nadine, it was a pleasure meeting you and I hope to see you again."

"The feeling is mutual, Myles. Take care of yourself."

DoubleA and I gathered our coats and headed for the front door. Nadine met us as we approached the door and slipped a note in my hand as I walked past her. I put it in my pocket and thanked her for her hospitality.

As we walked to the car, DoubleA remarked, "Nadine is a nice girl. You owe me one."

He dropped me off at home and I went straight to bed. I was feeling fairly high and tired. I didn't waste any time getting to sleep.

CHAPTER 10

I was in the first stage of sleep when I heard a faint sound of a telephone ringing in the background. I kept telling myself that someone's phone was ringing. I just wished they would hurry up and answer it so I could continue sleeping. The sound kept getting louder and louder as if it was moving closer and closer to my ear. I finally realized that it was my phone.

I reached toward the phone as I glanced at the clock next to it. It was 4:30 a.m.

Before I could say hello, DoubleA spoke in his usual tone, "Myles, we got a murder on 66th and Dorchester, next to the IC tracks. It looks like the victim took a shotgun blast to the head."

I hesitated before I responded, attempting to analyze what he had said and still hoping I was dreaming. "I thought we were off this weekend," I said, expecting he would say, "Oh, that's right." But he didn't.

He came right back with, "Welcome to Gang Intelligence. I'll be outside in fifteen minutes."

When he arrived, DoubleA barely stopped to let me get in the car before he sped off. "We got this assignment because there is evidence that it's linked to our original investigation. Looks like this is the work of our boy, Snake. Preliminary information indicates that the victim took a shotgun blast to the face with some heavy shelling."

"I wonder who the vic is? Who said that this murder might be linked to the Williams boy's case," I asked?

DoubleA's response was slow. In his own way, he was attempting to remind me that I had passed the detective's exam. "So why is it so hard to think that the cases are related? We got a renegade who lost two of his close friends, his ass in on the lam, so why wouldn't he strike first if he knows that his life is under contract? Our boy stole his grandfather's 410, didn't he? What else do you need to know, detective?"

"Okay, boss. I'm still sleepy and my cerebral cortex is still swimming with Jack. I know what you're saying, but who else knows this much about our investigation that they can receive information about a shotgun murder in this area and link it to our original investigation?"

"Well 'Joe Friday'—If you can connect the dots—remember that the detectives in Area 1 map all the murders occurring on the south and east sides. They compare each incident to the existing reports and then the data is analyzed. When an incident is reported to them they just look at the map, make the analysis, and notify the specialized units involved. Guess whose names are listed close to this file?"

When we reached the crime scene there were detectives, police officers, and supervisors on the site. The area was taped off and classified as a crime scene. Our victim was sitting in a late model Cadillac, the engine still running. No effort had been taken to examine the crime scene or remove the body. I crossed the tape and began my investigation.

There was not much left of the victim's face. He took a frontal blast, which indicated that he probably turned to face the shooter just prior to the blast. Crime lab technicians were photographing the scene as people began to gather and try to get a closer look at the slaying. DoubleA had begun the long task of canvassing the area, hoping to discover a key witness who saw the incident.

I opened the car door from the opposite side to prevent contamination of any evidence that would help the investigation. I looked in the glove box and discovered the vehicle registration, which came back to a female, born in 1952. Her name was Rosetta Collins and she lived at 4858 S. Vincennes in Chicago. I also found several rolled joints. I took a peek under the driver's seat believing that the victim was ranked—which led me to believe that he was likely armed. I was right. Stuffed between the hump where the seat meets the floor, I discovered a fully loaded Browning 9mm automatic. I was careful not to taint the evidence as I reached for my handkerchief to remove the weapon and disable it.

The homicide detectives, Cole and Banahan from Area 1, had completed their preliminary on the scene and requested that the body be moved to the Cook County Morgue. When the body was rolled out of the front seat, underneath was a stash of an unknown substance contained in individual packages. There was no money found, but we believed there should have been some. The evidence was given to the beat officer who had been assigned the paper work. A search of the victim's body did not reveal identifying information. After additional photos and fingerprints were taken at the post-mortem, that would have to be done at the morgue.

Our investigation was complete. The dicks from Area 1 would wrap up the investigation and complete a supplementary report and send it to us as soon as identification had been made. Our objective right then was to find Felix Hamilton. It was a sure bet that he was the shooter and that this murder was in retaliation for the death of Franklin Williams and George Buck.

We headed back to 6646 S. Drexel to talk with Felix's grandfather, J.C. Gilmore, to see if he could provide us with any kind of information that would lead us to Felix's location. It was Sunday morning, approaching 10 a.m., when we arrived at the house and rang the doorbell.

As we waited patiently for someone to come to the front door, a voice from behind us called out, "What can I do for you offisus this mo'nin?"

We turned and faced the old-timer, offering greetings and recognition of his sly and guarded approach.

"Mr. Gilmore, how you doing this morning?" I asked courteously, hoping not to get him started on one of his sermons.

"It all depends on what y'all bringing. I still ain't got over that little greasy som'bitch stealing my prized gitback. I don't reckon y'all come to tell me he done got restituted and y'all done found my 410."

"No, sir, Mr. Gilmore. We ain't been that lucky. We just come to talk with you to see if you can provide us with some information that might lead us to Felix's location."

"Well, I tell you, I don't know too much about Felix's friends. He didn't have too many, you know. Just awhile back I do remember him mentioning a street called Cecil Court or something similar. One of his girlfriends was s'pose to be living there."

I'd never heard of it, but DoubleA had an idea. "Cyril Court? Would that be the name of the street, Mr. Gilmore?"

"Yeah! I believes so," Mr. Gilmore said excitedly, but he could not give us any other pertinent information. He didn't know the girl's name or apartment number. We thanked him for his patience and headed toward Cyril Court, a street just south of 71st off of Jeffery Blvd.

When we arrived at the location, 1962 East 71st Place, we were floored. The building was a ten-to-twelve-story complex with about a hundred apartments. It was the only apartment building on that short block. It was huge. It extended all the way around the corner to Jeffery. We would have to set up another stakeout and hope that Felix came through. The way the building was positioned made our observation angles difficult. We couldn't just sit on the same block and conduct surveillance, because the block was too short and the other end was a through street. There was limited parking and a bad view. We decided that we would set up on the through street, anticipating that Felix would stay off the main streets during his travels and hit Cyril Court from Euclid, one block west of Jeffery Blvd.

While we sat on the stakeout we discussed the investigation, reviewing all of the suspects who we needed to locate to wrap up the case. DoubleA wondered about Peachazz. We hadn't heard from her in weeks, and she usually kept in good contact with him. She would leave messages at locations she knew DoubleA visited often, such as his barbershop or his favorite watering hole. Even I didn't know where he liked to drink. He always reminded me I was a detective and should act like one and figure shit out on my own without asking him.

After a short while, DoubleA got out of the squad car. "Look here, Myles," he said, "I'm going to look inside the apartment building to see what it looks like from the inside and make a mental note of its layout."

I sat back behind the wheel and reviewed our notes while occasionally looking up to see people and cars going by. My eyes started to get heavy and I began to drift between a conscious and dreaming state. Suddenly I heard a loud thud at rear of the car. I reached for my 9mm as I turned to look out the rear window. I saw DoubleA standing behind the squad car. I jumped out and moved quickly to the rear.

"What's going on?" I asked.

DoubleA responded, "I had to fuck 'em up! I saw this nigga getting off the elevator and recognized him. When I approached him and asked him his name, he took a swing at me and attempted to run. I faded away from his punch and caught him with my slapper right over his left eye. When he went down, he realized that his eye was flooding with blood. He was dazed; he just didn't know it. Then I cuffed his ass and drug him out."

It was our boy, Felix Hamilton. I searched him before putting him in the car and found three 12-gauge, double-odd-buckshot gun shells in his right front pocket. We drove off toward Area 1 homicide with our suspect. Old Felix had been on the run, and he was hiding out in the large apartment building. We figured that the murder weapon was still in the building, so we had to locate it before he was allowed to make any phone calls. If Mr. Gilmore was right about him knowing a girl in the building, we had time to find her before she got word that Felix was in custody.

When we arrived at Area 1, we took him up to the Detective Division and called for the two dicks, Banahan and Cole, who had the initial homicide investigation. It was our arrest, but we figured we would let them work the interrogation since they were homicide detectives and experienced in breaking down a suspect.

It was nearly 5 p.m. and they were still on duty, but they had not yet returned from the morgue. The desk officer said they had called about two hours ago and reported that the victim had been fingerprinted; they were waiting for the results to be sent to them at the Area 4 Detective Division over the facsimile. We called them and told them we had Felix and would wait for them to come to Area 1.

Detectives Banahan and Cole arrived at approximately 6:45 p.m. with the name and background information on our murder victim. His name was Arthur Shelby, age thirty-three, and his last known address was 6229 S. Ellis. Arthur was in our gang files as "Artie the Brute." His arrest history listed him for one murder as a juvenile, two murder conspiracies, and four aggravated batteries with a firearm. He had also been arrested three times for carrying a loaded handgun. He was a ranking member of the Blackstone Rangers, known to be ruthless.

Detective Banahan came into the interrogation room and signaled for me to come out into the hallway. "Look here, Sivad," he said, "our murder victim is a no good son-of-a-bitch. I didn't recognize him on the scene, but I arrested him for murder two years ago. He beat the case. A key witness refused to testify against him because he and the gang had threatened the witness' family. He was a back-shooter feared by all who knew him, just like our main murder suspect, Black Sonny. I guess death came as a surprise to him. He got bushwhacked by an eighteen-year-old who decided that if he was going to die, he might as well take somebody with him. He picked a well-deserving candidate."

Detectives Daniel Banahan and Sidney Cole would conduct the interrogation. They invited us to witness it through the two-way mirror in the next room. Sound would be transmitted so we could follow the process step by step.

I suggested, "DoubleA, why don't you observe the grilling while I contact Mr. Gilmore. We need to find out the name of Felix's girlfriend so we can get the shotgun before she finds out that Felix is in custody."

I made contact with Mr. Gilmore over the phone.

"Mr. Gilmore, this is Detective Sivad. We have Felix in custody. Looks like he's going to be charged with murder. What I need from you is the name of Felix's girlfriend, the one that lives on Cyril Court."

He never questioned my information. "Well son, that was quick. I hope y'all boys found my 410. It's a fine hunter's treasure and I sho' would like to get it back."

"No, sir, we don't have it yet. I believe it's in Felix's girlfriend's apartment, but we don't' know her name or what apartment she lives in."

"Hold on for a second," he instructed. When he came back to the phone he said, "Alls I can tell you is they calls her Penny."

That wasn't much information considering the size of the building, but it was time to find out what kind of detective I was without DoubleA providing the supervision. I decided I had to get over to that building and find Penny to get that weapon. I knew that I couldn't go there looking like Dick Tracy and just ask her for the gun. I needed to improvise, develop a scheme that would get over. I decided I'd go home and put on some street clothes and snoop around.

I dressed in denim jeans, a bulky beige sweater, and a knit cap and drove over to the apartment building. I scanned the names listed on the bell and found "P. Green." This seemed to be the best bet. I went to her apartment and knocked on the door. Several seconds passed and then I knocked again. A scratchy voice answered from behind the door, "Who is it?"

I didn't know what to say, and without any preparation my response surprised me. "Hey, Penny, I need to talk to you right now. It's important."

She replied, "Talk? Talk about what? Who the fuck are you?"

"I'm down with Felix. The police had us in the lockup at 51st Street. He told me that the police would be looking for you to find the shotgun he hid over here. He wants me to get it and get rid of it before they find out what apartment you live in."

Penny opened the door and took a hard look at me. She asked, "What's your name?"

"Paul Stone. We're in the same family." Whatever that was supposed to mean.

She paused for a moment then said, "Wait a minute."

I waited for a brief moment until Penny returned to the door with a green garden bag and gave it to me. I opened the bag and looked inside. Bingo. It was the 410.

I said, "When the police come, just tell them you don't have a clue as to what they are talking about and let them look for themselves."

I hurried out of the building and raced back to the station. When I arrived, the detectives and DoubleA were gathered around a desk in the open office area. I walked up to them and put the garden bag on the table. Detective Cole opened the bag and sighed, "Well, I'll be got-damn if it's not the murder weapon."

He took a piece of paper from the desk and used it to reach into the bag and remove the cannon. It was a 410 shotgun, cut down to about eighteen inches. After Detective Cole laid the weapon on the table for examination, I glanced over at DoubleA to see his reaction. He was beaming like an instructor who just realized his teaching was having some impact. I nodded my approval of his response.

"Have you contacted Lt. Nugent and told him we have Felix Hamilton in custody?" I asked.

"Not yet," he replied, "but you can do the honors. And while you're at it, have someone check our desk for messages."

The detectives then went back to the discussion they were having before I surprised them with the weapon. I went to the administrative desk and dialed our office on the Pax phone line. Lt. Nugent was not in the office. The officer who answered the phone said he would have him contact us when he returned.

"Are there any messages for Sivad or Ashford?" I asked.

"There's a message from a woman named Hilda Cox from the Cook County Hospital."

When I returned to the interrogation area all three detectives were in the room with our arrestee. I tapped on the door and motioned for DoubleA to come out.

"We got message from a Hilda Cox from the Cook County Hospital. Who's Hilda Cox? Is she somebody we know?"

DoubleA quelled my suspense: "Hilda Cox is Peachazz. She's probably a patient there. The life of a whore is filled with many emergencies—social, environmental, and medical. We'll get up with her when we get a chance."

We went back into the interrogation room and broke the shotgun down. To our amazement, one spent shotgun shell was still in the weapon. We had our case; now it was time to convince Snake that the charades were all over. It was time to get Felix to cop a plea.

When we put the 410 on the table in the interrogation room, Felix's eyes bulged for a second and he put his head down. DoubleA lit right into him. "My man," he said, "you looking at murder one. Conviction by trial guarantees you ten to thirty. Make it easy on yourself. We know what you were up against—the fear of being killed after what your boys suffered. With the right mouthpiece you could plead self-defense. It would probably help your case."

Felix placed his hands over his face and took a deep breath. Then he said, "They tried to kill me. They tried to kill me first. I was with George Buck when they caught up with us. We saw Artie and Black Sonny when we turned the corner at 67th and Dorchester, in front of the funeral home. They saw us, too, so we split up. I could hear shots being fired but I never looked back. Later, I found out that they had caught George and took him away. I knew they were going to kill him and me too."

DoubleA interrupted, "Tell us why your crew was targeted for murder. If you guys are all in the same family, what happened that triggered y'all to be contracted for murder?"

Felix looked up at us and began his story: "Me, Franklin, and George were spotters. The Stones have a house on 65th and Ellis where they keep all of their drugs, guns, and money. All day members come in and out of that house—bringing in and taking out products and weapons."

"What's the address of this house?" I asked.

"I don't know the exact address, but it's the gray stone building in the middle of the block. They keep a lot of cash, too. Our job was to keep the block under surveillance and to make sure that if the police was around to alert them. If a strange vehicle moved the block too slow, we had to signal. All of the main-ranking players knew us and liked the way we handled our business.

"One day Frankie told us we could make a sting, and nobody would ever know it was us. He suggested that one of us sneak into the house and rip off the gang for its stash. Frankie was a daring nigga. He wasn't afraid to take chances. He was real smart and slick. I was skeptical of his plan but he said that if we were all in, he would go in and get the money while we kept watch. The house was often empty during the mid-afternoon, when all of the ranks were out on the street."

DoubleA seemed to be suspicious of all the information Felix was providing. "You telling us that all of this was Franklin's idea and you just went along, even though you knew that if you got caught the penalty would be death."

"That's the truth! I know we shouldn't have took such the chance. We fucked up!"

Detective Banahan couldn't resist the temptation as he stood over Felix displaying his two pearl-handled Colt .45's, one on his right hip and the other in a upside-down shoulder holster: he taunted, "You damn right you fucked up. So what happened next?"

"We made our move and hit for almost two grand and some drugs—T's and Blues. Those drugs were new on the street and all the junkies were wild over them because they were cheap. When the Stones questioned us, we told them we were out there all day and nobody strange was seen on the block. It made them think it was an inside job. What fucked us up was that fool-ass George Buck, who was in the poolroom spending too much money on weed. Because of him, they flushed us. Somebody told them we stole from them and that we were in the hood 'high-spending.'"

"Who told?" I asked.

"I don't know. That jag-off George Buck was a fool. He could never do what he was supposed to. I should have followed my first thoughts and stayed out of that scheme."

"So what happened after you guys got exposed?" DoubleA asked calmly.

"Franklin got caught first. Word on the street moved like a fire in a matchbox. I found out Black Sonny and Artie had Franklin in the trunk of a car riding around looking for George and me. I went low and stayed off the street, but I would contact George to see if he was okay. The day they caught George we were coming down from the train tracks around 2 a.m. trying to get to a friend's house to lay low for a day or so. Several days later, I heard that they had killed George the same way they had killed Franklin. I had nowhere to hide. I knew that when they caught up with me I would be 'One Shoed.'" Felix was cold-hearted; you could tell he had a rough life. I could see he had learned to survive—that he did whatever was necessary.

"What about your friend, Cornell Booker? What was his role in the ruse?" I inquired.

"Cornell was just a guy who grew up with us. He wasn't aggressive and he didn't go in for that gang shit. Cornell was an artist. He liked drawing his name on shit like abandoned buildings and el trains. He never got down with the gang violence. He was our friend and we never bothered him with the work. His mother was a Jehovah Witness; she stayed on him all the time. He just wasn't cut out for what we did."

Detective Banahan, after listening to Felix, stepped in: "What about the murder of Artie the Brute. You can save us some time so we don't have to wait for ballistics to charge you with the murder. If you confess, you would be doing yourself a favor..."

Felix didn't let Banahan finish. "I ain't confessing to shit! Y'all got me and y'all got what you think is a murder weapon. Y'all didn't catch me with no fucking weapon and ain't nobody done said they saw me kill anybody. I ain't confessing to a got damn thing!"

We decided we had to wait for the crime lab to examine the evidence before we could proceed. We could hold Felix for suspicion of murder and keep working on him until he broke down.

DoubleA called us all back to the open office area and conferred with Detectives Banahan and Cole to tie in what Felix had said concerning Black Sonny being with Artie the Brute when they caught up with him and George Buck. We had unsubstantiated information that Black Sonny was involved in the murder of Franklin Williams, but we had no eyewitness. Felix's testimony could put him in the loop, but it would be useless in court without corroborating evidence tied to a motive. Detective Banahan told us all the officers had been given instructions at roll call to be on the lookout for a junkman named Sampson, but so far he had not turned up. We ended our conversation with the decision that both teams would continue pounding the streets looking for additional evidence that would solve this case.

A voice came over the P.A. system requesting that Detective Myles Sivad or Aristotle Ashford pick up the Pax line. I went to the front desk and answered. It was Lt. Nugent checking on us.

"Yeah, Lieutenant," I informed him, "we got our boy Felix Hamilton in the interrogation room"

"Good work, Sivad. You guys also got a gal from Cook County Hospital calling here."

"We got that message. We'll get to her as soon as we finish up."

I took the shotgun, marked it, and completed an inventory form for it. We would drop it off at the crime lab at police headquarters. I told Detectives Banahan and Cole to keep working on Felix. Once the crime lab examined the weapon and found his fingerprints, it would be all over for Felix. I took the weapon and headed for our office at headquarters.

Chapter 11

En route to our office, DoubleA decided we would make a quick stop at the Cook County Hospital and see if Peachazz was still a patient. We checked in at the desk, identified ourselves, and requested a pass to see Hilda Cox. The clerk gave us a pass for Ward 432. We went up to the fourth floor and asked for assistance in locating her bed.

Peachazz was sitting up when we walked in. When she saw DoubleA she tried to fix her hair and wipe her face. "Sho' took y'all niggas long enough to come see about me," she complained. "I've been calling y'all for three days. I thought I was your girl, Mr. Detective. Seem like when you need me you always around."

DoubleA smiled in his usual, impersonal way and said, "Baby girl, you know I'll always be around for you. What the hell happened to you?"

"Some freak got hold to me. I should've followed my first thought. I had made me some money and didn't need to be greedy. I should've told him that I was through for the night. He persuaded me to get in his car; he just wanted a blow-job. I rode off with him and when we got to a spot, he started calling me all kinda nasty bitches and telling me that all whores need to die. He pulled out a knife and began stabbing me in the hands and arms. I took a good one in the side. I was able to get away from him, but then I collapsed a few blocks from the scene. The next thing I remember, I was waking up in this bed. They said I had lost a lot of blood and was gonna need surgery."

"Damn, girl, aren't you lucky. What'd this trick look like?" DoubleA asked.

"I don't even know. I do remember he was driving a nice car with a raccoon's tail hanging from the mirror."

"You're lucky this time, Peachazz. You better get out of the game before you meet your last trick. By the way, did you get the information we requested the last time I saw you?"

"Nobody I talked to saw Black Sonny take the boy into the hotel. But Gladys said the junkman ain't no junkman."

Both DoubleA and I responded simultaneously, "What! What do you mean? Who's Gladys?"

"Gladys, my friend, said she had heard you were looking for the junkman and never found him. She said she saw Sampson leave one day with two White men. They were parked on Marquette Road near the cemetery, and Sampson left his cart and jumped in the back seat and they drove off. She said it looked like Sampson knew the men and they looked like cops."

We both stood speechless. If Sampson was working undercover and not for the Chicago Police Department, then who was he working for? Three ellipses stood out imperiously in my mind: F B I—the Federal Bureau of Investigation. When I began to recall all of the things DoubleA had told me about Jake Fontaine and his hard knock for stealing government funds, it was clear that the "G" still had an interest in what Jake was up to and whom he was involved with.

DoubleA made up with Peachazz and gave her some money. She said, "I'll be home in a few days. You can call me then."

We were both discouraged. Our feelings were contemptuous. If Sampson was an FBI agent or a mole, then the "G" had an eyewitness and they weren't telling us. We headed to our office to talk with Lt. Nugent. He had to be brought into this conflict. If the information could be corroborated, there would be fireworks at headquarters and the federal building.

We reached our office around 11:30 p.m. Only the desk officer was in. The lieutenant had gone home around 9 p.m. He'd left word for us to see him after roll call in the morning. We decided we had done enough for the day. I checked our desk for messages. There were two—one for me from Francine and an old one for DoubleA from Peachazz. I told DoubleA I would see him in the morning and headed home. I arrived home a little after midnight; it was too late to make a phone call, so I took a hot shower and went to bed.

I arrived for work early Monday morning only to find DoubleA sitting in the lieutenant's office having a cup of coffee.

When he saw me, DoubleA shouted, "Holmes, you learning fast. Any good detective arrives for duty early when he has a case that's hot. Come on in here. I was just briefing the boss about our findings."

Lt. Nugent looked disturbed. "Our relationship with the Feds is already bad enough," he complained. "We've made several efforts to improve relations by working on some joint investigations, but it seems like something stinks in Denmark. Judging from what you heard, it looks like those bastards are still treating us with distrust. I'll have to let the Deputy Superintendent know; we may be getting involved in another controversy. If they knew, they should've told us about the murder. We could've charged Black Sonny and kept their agent undercover until the trial. They continue to think that they are the supreme law enforcement agency and there is no equal. Bullshit! This is going to be messy. You guys continue with your investigation. When the fireworks start, be ready to come down to the Deputy Superintendent's office."

We left the lieutenant's office and went into the roll call briefing. Sgt. Angelo was conducting roll call and giving us the statistics for the month of March. It was April 11 and the department's monthly stats were out. "There were 68 homicides in Chicago for the month of March," he announced. "Gang-related, 21; Gang-related arrests made, 16; Blackstone Ranger victims, 7; Devils Disciples, 11; Vice Lords, 4; and 7 unknown but associated."

The teams working the Devils Disciples were having a horrific time with increases in shootings in the Englewood (007th) District. There was an internal struggle within the Disciples. Their leader, David Barkscale, had been murdered, and it looked like there was an internal scuffle for control. They began to call themselves the Gangster Disciples, and a new leader, Barry Clover, was rising to the throne and murder incorporated was his colleague.

When roll call was over, I went to the phone to call Francine and was told she was not working today. I called her at home and she answered the phone. She was surprised to hear from me on a Monday morning.

"Myles, how are you? I'm so glad you called," she said. "I called you at home yesterday—all day yesterday; then I called your office. They told me you were out in the field, and they didn't know when you would be back in the office. I left you a message. I thought that you'd forgotten me."

"No, I could never do that, Francine. I'm glad that I caught you at home this morning. I just took a chance on calling you."

"I usually work on Mondays, but I stayed home from work today because mother has not been feeling well. I thought I might have to take her to the doctor."

"I hope she's feeling better. I've been busy, but I'll call you when I get off duty."

"Thanks so much for calling. I'll be here waiting on your call later today."

I met DoubleA in the hallway. He told me we had just gotten a call from Wilson. He wanted to meet us by the 63rd Street beach house. We took the elevator down to the first floor and went directly to our vehicle. In the parking lot, we met with Detectives Baker and Brownfield who told us of a meeting between ranking members of the Blackstone Rangers and the Vice Lords. Word on the street was they were trying to negotiate a peace settlement without violence. The Vice Lords were accusing the Stones of trying to move in on them on the westside. Jake Fontaine and several ranking members were seen at the meeting. We thanked the detectives for the information and asked them to keep us informed. Then we headed for our meeting with Wilson.

As we rolled up, we spotted Wilson sitting in a 1971 dark blue Lincoln Continental. He blew his horn to get our attention; before getting out of his vehicle and taking a seat in the back of the squad car. He didn't waste any time providing us with the information he had uncovered.

"I talked with a junk guy named Cecil. He's been salvaging junk in the Woodlawn area for twenty years. He knows the terrain, the people, and the problems. He told me that he tried to talk with your boy, Sampson, and he concluded that what Sampson was looking for was not junk.

"What made him believe that Sampson was on a different mission?" I asked.

"He said he could tell when a person is out here trying to survive because he has to. Your hands are always grimy, you don't have clean fingernails, your eyes are watery, and your nose is running. The life of a man trying to squeeze a living from the garbage of a neighborhood is a hard life. The wet and the cold tax your survival skills. You can't pick through garbage and rubbish for a living and not show signs of degeneration. You can see it in the eyes and skin. That kind of life wears a man down. A man living that way is always hungry and cold, but he's determined to survive. Sampson wasn't cut that way. His eyes were clear and his skin was soft and smooth. He wasn't full of sniffles and lice. My guy said he always suspected Sampson was looking for something other than junk."

We now had two people telling us similar stories about Sampson. We were sure the stories were valid, and, when the time came, the battle would come to the surface and both sides would have to duke it out. The intensity of the confrontation created a chemistry of apprehension and despair in me. I tried to imagine whom the key adversaries would be when the elements of the conflict were presented. The Cook County State's Attorney would undoubtedly represent the interest of the Chicago Police Department. Our Deputy Superintendent, Mike Spiotro from Investigative Services, would spearhead our charge. The "G" would probably defend their position from the U.S. Attorney's Office, hoping that the confidentiality of their investigation would outweigh their failure to take action or report the murder. Either direction they chose, in my opinion, would not support their failure to take some action rather than to do nothing at all.

Wilson had an unparalleled knowledge of the streets. His career as a collector of "Juice Loans" for Papa during the '50s and '60s provided him with a wealth of contacts who knew something about everything that occurred in the 'hood. His pervasive knowledge of street life made him a welcome contact. What I liked most about Wilson was his charge. When asked to find something out he was relentless. He didn't quit until he got the information he was searching for.

"Look here, Wilson, I appreciate your efforts. If you ever need us for anything, don't hesitate to give us a call," I said.

"Thanks, Detective Sivad. I'll hold you to that promise."

It was approaching noon as we headed back to Area 1. We needed to see how Detectives Banahan and Cole's interrogation was coming along. When we arrived, we discovered that Detective Banahan was down at the County Morgue retrieving the coroner's report. Detective Cole had just brought our suspect upstairs and placed him in the interrogation room for another round of whodunit questioning.

Felix looked worn down. The night in that little cell had not been pleasant, so he had plenty of time to start thinking about how many nights he would spend sleeping in a cell. Being locked up starts to wear on you. You begin to recognize that maybe you can negotiate the amount of time you have to spend in custody.

When we began our little inquisition, Felix started where he left off: "I ain't confessing to shit."

Detective Cole immediately jumped in, declaring, "I'm not going to spend my day questioning this asshole. If he wants to stick with the same got-damn story, he could do that without me sitting here begging him to come clean. I'm taking his punk ass back downstairs to the lockup. When the State's Attorney arrives, he'll be charged".

Both DoubleA and I agreed. We could hold Felix for seventy-two hours without charging him. But after that you had to be painstakingly creative in presenting a reason for continued custody.

Detective Cole put Felix back in cuffs and said to him, "If you feel like talking, have the lockup keeper give me a call."

DoubleA paused for a moment then walked over to Felix and whispered something in his ear.

Felix turned and faced DoubleA and said, "I'll think about it."

"Yeah, you do that, son. Everyday you waste before trial is not considered time served."

CHAPTER 12

We left the Area and drove toward the eastside. It was a pleasant day; the sun was shining and it was around sixty-eight degrees. The streets were crowded. This was the first nice day of spring. We were headed south on Cottage Grove when we heard a simulcast announcing shots fired at the police coming from the rear of a building at 6211 S. Drexel. I hit the siren and raced toward the scene. Cars were coming from all directions as the dispatcher, caught up in emotion, worked intensely to give out vital information.

"Units on the zone, we have shots fired at unit 327 at 6211 S. Drexel. Be alert," he warned.

Seconds later, the dispatcher transmitted a second broadcast that deflates the spirit of every police officer. "Officer shot! Officer shot! We are now getting reports that an officer is down in the rear of 6211 South Drexel!"

My body erupted with an array of bubbling fluids that threatened to cloud my concentration. I felt hyped-up yet empty. I was nervous. I felt I couldn't respond to the present situation effectively. When we reached the mouth of the alley, I could see the fallen officer lying on the ground beside his squad car. There was a garage on the west side of the alley, but the building was on the east side. It was between two vacant lots that did not provide any cover for responding units. We sprang from our vehicle and took cover in the rear. On the south side of the building we could see another vacant lot and a garage. The building next to the second lot provided adequate cover to units responding from the north. Several other officers were taking fire just south of us as they approached the scene. I could not tell if the wounded officer was alive, but he wasn't moving.

DoubleA rose up from his crouched position and laid down a stream of fire at a suspect who was firing at us from the third floor; it appeared to be a man positioned behind a refrigerator that had been pushed close to the banisters. After a minute, I realized what DoubleA was doing, so I began to fire at the suspect, too. DoubleA made it to the rear of the injured officer's squad car and attempted to communicate with him. The downed officer never responded. The shooter was using an automatic weapon, probably an M14, M16 or an AK47; worst of all, he was accurate. He could tell that DoubleA was trying to rescue the wounded officer, so he kept up a continuous stream of fire so he could keep DoubleA pinned down.

The alley was full of police officers—all trying to establish a position and return fire. We were constrained by the width of the alley; this prevented a number of assisting units from laying down accurate support fire. The shooting suspect was screaming profanities at us as he continued to reload and fire. We had called for the department's heavy weapons vehicle and a sniper team, but they were miles away. The most important thing we had to do was get to the wounded officer and get him to the hospital. We could worry about taking the shooter out later.

Our communications with the uniformed officers was limited because most detectives don't carry portable radios. I couldn't talk to DoubleA and neither could supporting units. I could see that he needed some support firepower, enough to put the head of the shooter down until he could rescue the wounded officer. Several uniformed officers looked over as I yelled for them get ready to open fire in unison. When the shooter paused to reload his weapon, I signaled for DoubleA to make his move and that we would aid him. When DoubleA rose again from his crouched position, we began to lay down a barrage of fire that picked a rapid succession of splinters from the wooden porch.

DoubleA moved swiftly toward the fallen officer and dragged him to a garage that shielded them both from further gunfire. DoubleA signaled to us that the officer was alive, but that he needed help in bringing him out. I moved hurriedly with two uniformed officers to assist DoubleA. We managed to bring the officer out to an awaiting ambulance. He was shot in the chest. He had lost a lot of blood, but he was still semiconscious.

Once the officer was safely in the ambulance, we turned our attention to the shooter. It was obvious he was determined to shoot as many police officers as he could. The voices over the police radio were in a state of panic. Communications were frantic as units crowded the frequency with conversations that clashed and jumbled together. We needed radio supervision, someone to take control of the communications. Uniformed officers were crowding the radio zone with traffic and they were stepping all over each other. The dispatcher was so emotional that he couldn't take command of the radio zone. He was causing confusion and needed to be removed. Suddenly, a female voice took over. She was poised and experienced, and she didn't hesitate as she commandeered control.

"All units, all units on this frequency, standby. I have control of the communications on this zone. No one will be acknowledged unless I acknowledge you. "We cannot all talk at the same time!" she roared. "Now everybody stand back, take a deep breath, and let's get this shooter into custody!"

The radio went silent and we could all hear her next statement clearly: "All units, I have a caller who states that the suspect is a Vietnam veteran who has displayed mental illness. Be cautious in your approach."

A lieutenant—Tim Ellison from the 003rd District—arrived on the scene and took over supervision. I knew Lt. Ellison when he was a sergeant in Special Operations. He ordered all units at the north end of the alley to pull back. We met on the 62nd Street side of Drexel where he began to devise a plan. While we were developing our strategy, I looked around for my partner. I didn't see DoubleA anywhere. I started to get concerned because we had been devising a strategy for over fifteen minutes and still DoubleA had not shown up.

The lieutenant told us that he had sent several officers to the front of the building and that we needed to keep the shooter occupied while they made entry. The reports that would later come back would reveal that the stairwell was dimly lit and cluttered with furniture. This impeded passage and risked officer safety.

"All units, all units, the heavy weapons vehicle is about twenty minutes away."

The shooting was sporadic as we continued to exchange intermittent gunfire. Communications from the building disclosed that we had officers on the third floor, but they were unable to gain entry. Suddenly the shooter rose up from his position behind the refrigerator and placed a heavy burst of fire down at the wounded officer's squad car. We didn't understand why he was doing that; there was nobody near the vehicle. He stood there as if he was daring us to return the fire when, seemingly without a reason, he looked quickly to his left and wheeled his weapon in that direction. We heard three rapid shots. Suddenly, we realized that they were coming from the south. The shooter's weapon abruptly dropped from the third floor, and he followed it like a wounded sparrow that couldn't open its wings. The thud of his body striking the ground made me cringe. As I let out a deep breath, I knew that it was over.

We were all startled. And then, adjacent to the second vacant lot next door, we saw Detective Aristotle Ashford removing his black shooting glove and placing his weapon back in its holster. He was just standing there looking completely composed.

Police officers began to leave their shielded areas and approached the offender's body as he lay in the dirt about thirty-five feet below his sniper's nest. He had three gunshot wounds—one to the head, neck, and jaw. His eyes were set frozen as if to indicate that he was surprised. His weapon was a M16 automatic rifle with a 30-round clip. He wore a combat fatigue jacket with about eight to ten pockets. He still had four loaded clips in his pockets. He had on combat boots and a utility belt with a large bolo knife holstered in a case.

We moved quickly up the stairs to the third floor porch. The back door was unlocked and, along with several uniformed officers, I went inside. We still had our weapons drawn. We could hear a baby crying as we entered the dining room. The sound was coming from a room up front. We carefully approached and observed a toddler huddled under the body of a woman. The woman was lying between the couch and the wall. There was blood all over her and the toddler. I felt for her pulse, but there was none. The apartment was in terrible disarray, as if a fierce struggle had occurred. Furniture and clothing were scattered all over the room. Blood was everywhere. I took the child to the rear porch and instructed one of the uniformed units to take him downstairs to safety.

Lieutenant Ellison entered the apartment. "I want all personnel to clear this crime scene. I only want the report-writing unit and the dicks here."

He made sure that there was no further contamination of the crime scene. He found a telephone in the apartment and tried to make a call to headquarters, but he quickly realized the phone was out of order. The tenants who lived in the building had fled when the shooting started. They were trying to get back into the building, but the police downstairs refused to let them in. The remaining coppers who were allowed to stay stood around the kitchen and the rear porch, waiting for the mobile crime lab unit to arrive.

I didn't notice that DoubleA had entered the apartment until he called me to come to his side. "Are you alright?" I asked.

He nodded affirmative. "When I left the alley I came to the front of the building. A neighbor next door saw me and waved for me to come into his building. He led me up to the third floor apartment where I could see the shooter's position. I didn't want to step out there and have him notice me. There was no cover if I stepped outside. But when the shooter laid down his last barrage of fire, he had to reload. That's when I stepped outside—before he could finish. I shouted out to him to drop the weapon. He never intended on doing that. He tried to turn so I 'lit' him up. I couldn't risk trying to talk him down. When he refused to obey my order, I squeezed off three.

"I see he killed a woman here. I wonder what caused him to flip out. That picture in the living room of the young couple is a sad tribute. Another young man and woman dead, and another Black child who will have to grow up without ever remembering the warmth of his mother's bosom and the mettle of his father. This kind of violence we have to witness every day sometimes wears you down. Day in and day out somebody dies. You know, Myles, policing can be depressing, especially when you see your own people always being victims."

When Lt. Ellison entered the room he apologized for not recognizing me when he arrived on the scene. "Sorry Myles, I had too much adrenaline flowing when I approached the scene. When I got here it was pure pandemonium. Shots were being fired from both sides and the radio zone was in complete chaos. I couldn't get through because of all of the squad cars blocking the street.

"I've requested the zone operator to make a call for additional detectives to come to the scene. I want the entire block canvassed to ensure that there are no additional victims. All police officers that discharged their weapons must go in to Area 1 and stand by for debriefing and reports."

Lieutenant Ellison was a very efficient supervisor; he made sure that he covered every detail.

"Myles, you and your partner stand by. You have to be interviewed by the Assistant Deputy Superintendent and give him an account of your actions. Detective Ashford, you will be designated as the lead detective. You'll be required to give a written and verbal statement describing your actions." Finally, the lieutenant said in a lucid baritone, "Men, you all did an outstanding job. I want to make it clear to you that your superiors will be informed of what took place here today."

We prepared to leave the scene, just as additional detectives started arriving. As each team passed us, many of them stopped to acknowledge DoubleA and offer him a handshake or a nod of approval. DoubleA kept the same stoic facial expression, never once smiling or showing any sign that he was proud of his actions. He looked like he was unaware of his environment and somewhat removed from the present.

We returned to our squad car and headed toward Area 1 for the first round of questions. It was going to be a long day of report writing and questions being asked by department heads and the State's Attorney's office. There was nothing to fear; DoubleA's actions were certainly within department guidelines; however, if a police officer is shot or if he shoots someone, the reporting and filing procedures are time consuming. Every detail must be examined and noted.

Assistant Deputy Superintendent Richard Clark arrived at the Area shortly after we did. He looked glum. "Men, Officer Glen Hill has succumbed to his wounds."

A leaden silence covered the room, heads fell and hearts languished. Every person in the room stood there grieving. We were all devastated and, more than that, we were angry. Another police officer had lost his life while performing his duty.

Superintendent Clark continued, "I want you all to pray for Officer Hill's family, and remember that we are a family who has lost someone. Now is a time for all of us to come together as one and stand proud of the job we must do day in and day out. I know the pain that each of you feels will not go away for a long time. Right now we have to complete this investigation, no matter how unimportant it may seem. Now it's our duty to finish."

The investigation took almost seven hours. Each officer who fired his weapon had to submit a report and turn his weapon in for ballistics. Everybody except DoubleA was able to leave, take their weapons to the crime lab and get temporary replacements. DoubleA had to talk to the Assistant State's Attorney and the Assistant Deputy Superintendent one-on-one to give an account of his actions.

I told DoubleA I'd take his weapon to the crime lab for him and get a replacement.

"Don't worry Myles, I have my snub and another .45 at home," he said.

I returned to the Area after I obtained a replacement weapon to see how my partner was doing. He looked fatigued and irritable. When I came into the office, the ADS (Assistant Deputy Superintendent) told me they were almost finished and maybe it would be a good idea if we found some place to relax when they were done. I sat in the outer office area until DoubleA came out. He was quite reserved and didn't make much conversation. I knew he was tired and needed to get home, but I thought we could have a few drinks to take the edge off and come to grips with the events of the day.

"You want to stop at Bennies and have a drink? I'm buying," I offered.

"That's a good idea, Myles. I really need a drink to help me get past this day."

We left the Area and headed for the Big Drink Saloon, Bennie's 357. It was a Monday night and you would think the crowd would be light but, on the contrary, Bennie's was packed. Coppers from all over were out grieving and trying to drink away the pain of losing a comrade. As we entered, guys started moving toward us offering congratulations to DoubleA and making comments about how he took the police killer out.

When we made it to the bar Bennie had two big drinks waiting for us. "Compliments of the house," he said. "To two of the finest men I know."

The crowd around DoubleA was relentless. When one copper left, another would take his place, encouraging and complimenting DoubleA. I moved out of the way and found a seat with a couple of old-timers who were having a conversation about DoubleA.

"What's your name, boy?" one of them asked me.

"Myles Sivad," I replied.

"You a lucky kid to draw a partner like Aristotle Ashford," he said. After taking a sip of his drink, he introduced himself: "I'm retired Commander Bob Harness, former commander of the Old Wabash 005th District; this here gentleman is retired Sgt. Alton Curtis."

I was jolted. The Commander was out with the troops, offering support and comfort to many of the men he once led.

"DoubleA worked for me in the 005th, back when I was a lieutenant," Commander Harness continued. "You got one of the best men this department can offer, son. Bank on it. I met your partner when he came on the job. I was impressed. I'm still impressed with his service."

Shaking his head over his glass, the commander asked, "Did you know Ashford served in Korea and was wounded? He took some shrapnel to the back when a grenade exploded near him. His outfit was under attack by some North Koreans somewhere near the Chinese border. DoubleA was pinned down in a foxhole while most of his platoon got out. This man has exhibited courage in combat throughout his career, Sonny. Thank God you pulled the straw that partnered you up with that hero." The commander's voice was deep but scratchy. You could tell by the way he talked that he was a rugged man.

I knew everything that Commander Harness said was true, and I was proud to be working with DoubleA. I knew I still had a lot to learn from him. I began to realize working with him was not so much the luck of the draw, but his willingness to work with a rookie detective.

The fact that I was sitting at the table with Bob Harness, known legendarily as "The Crusher," was also a privilege.

"Commander, I heard so much about you while growing up. You're a legend. You know," I chuckled, "during my teen years I had the dishonor of being a guest in the Wabash lockup."

The commander seemed amused. "What happened?" he asked.

"One night, during my misguided teenage years, I had the misfortune of being 'tuned' by two Wabash beat officers. The incident escalated into a brawl that I lost, of course."

Commander Harnness looked at me with a sort of knowing smile. "Did this wrangle take place inside the station?"

"Yes sir," I replied.

He broke out with a big reverberating laugh. "Well I'll be got-damned! You're the son-of-a-bitch that took on my whole watch. How about that! I got a call that night from a lieutenant who jokingly told me that some young kid had whipped the shit out of my whole watch. I called the captain and told him to get the kid's name. Hell, I was ready to sign him up the next day. So you're that same kid? Well, son, I see that ass-whopping you took that night didn't discourage you from wanting to be a police officer, huh?"

"No, sir. It made me respect the Chicago Police."

I saw DoubleA moving toward my table so I waved him over. Commander Harness rose from his seat, gimpy-legged and cane-assisted, and gave DoubleA a fatherly hug.

"My boy, you're still a wonder. I guess you have to show these young farts how to be a policeman. God bless you!"

I looked at DoubleA and saw tears in his eyes. The sight of Commander Harness leveled him. It was like a son seeing a father after being away for a long time.

"Commander, what are you doing out tonight, Sir?" DoubleA asked.

"I'm out here because one of us went down today. I had to be next to you men. This policing of today is dangerous; these young niggas don't respect us anymore. We got to let the dogs out and recapture our glory, or folks gone have to leave this city!"

The sergeant who was sitting with the commander was quiet. He acknowledged our presence, but he seldom said a word.

"Is something wrong with him?" I whispered to the commander.

"Yeah, there is. The deceased officer is his nephew. He's taking it hard, because he encouraged Glen to join the force."

Sgt. Curtis was an empty soul now; he couldn't come to grips with the tragedy. I offered him my condolences and told him that we would be there to support him. He never said a word; as he sat there and sipped his drink, his eyes filled with tears.

It was getting late and we had to face roll call in the morning. We finished our drinks and thanked everybody for their concern and support.

"DoubleA, I'll take the squad and drop you off at home," I offered.

"Don't bother, Myles," he insisted. "I'll drop you off and pick you up in the morning."

I knew better than to argue with him. We made it to my residence at approximately 12:40 a.m. I couldn't wait to get to sleep.

CHAPTER 13

It seemed like I had just locked the door and laid down when the phone rang. It was DoubleA. As I rolled over to look at the clock, I saw that it was already 7:40 a.m.

"Yo, Myles, I'll be outside in fifteen minutes."

I jumped up, took a quick shower, and was outside in twenty minutes.

When we got off the elevator at headquarters, Lt. Nugent was standing there waiting. "I figured you guys would be arriving around this time. I want you men to take the day off. We are all kind of down around here and—well, after the experience you went through yesterday, the day off will do you both some good."

We were glad to be excused from duty. I knew that the department would be busy making arrangements for the funeral of Officer Glen Hill. His would be an honors funeral with all of the ceremony and escorts that the department could provide. Members of his unit of assignment would be selected for honor guards, while his close friends on the force would be selected as pallbearers. Lt. Nugent told us that the funeral had been set for Friday, April 14. The immediate family had not determined the time and place yet, but department preparations could be completed prior to the finalizing of the services.

I asked DoubleA to wait for me while I called Francine at work. It was 9:20 a.m.

I forgot she had given me her direct line when a woman's voice answered the phone, "South Shore Bank, customer service department. May I help you?"

"Yes, may I speak to Francine Williams?"

"Myles, is that you?"

"Yes. Hi, Francine."

"Myles, I'm glad you called. I was hoping to hear from you before I got off work."

"Listen, I'm excused from work today because of the police shooting. Yesterday was a bad day."

"I know. I saw the incident on the evening news, and I read about it in the morning papers. I hope you're okay."

"I'm alright, thanks. But the reason I'm calling—I want to see you tonight. Would you like to take in a movie?"

Her response was delightful. I couldn't believe the excitement in her voice. "Of course! I'd love to."

"Good. We can catch 'Uptown Saturday Night.' It's playing at the Roosevelt Theater in the Loop. I'll pick you up at six and we can have something to eat before the show."

She was enthralled.

Instead of heading home, I stopped at the South Town YMCA for a morning of exercise and relaxation. The club was full of members who often started their morning with a workout. The businessmen's club attracted some of the most successful Black executives and businessmen in the city. Men like Stu Collins from Seaway National Bank and Collins Foods, State Senator Richard Newhouse, Truman K. Gibson Jr., who replaced Judge William H. Hastie as Special Advisor to the Secretary of War during World War II, Cecil Troy of Grove Juice, George Jones of Joe Louis Milk, retired Police Sergeant Carl Nelson, Mark H. Allen, Secretary of the Amalgamated Meat Cutters Union, Local # 74, George Easton, Al Lee, Pegg Abernathy, Albadea Smith, and a host of other accomplished Black entrepreneurs, were frequent visitors to the club.

I hadn't planned on playing racquetball, but an old friend from the 007th District, Don Roberts, challenged me to a game. We played three games of fast-moving and hard-slamming black ball. Don's skills were superb. He gave me a good workout. I was exhausted but revitalized, as the anguish and trepidation of the previous day subsided. I was slowly letting go that experience and getting back to normal, forgetting for a moment the visit of death to the ranks of our fraternity. I showered and laid down on one of the club's couches for a short nap.

I awoke shortly after two and decided to get home and spend the rest of the afternoon in my apartment. I arrived home about three-thirty, flipped through my mail, and started to straighten up when the phone rang. It was DoubleA.

"Yo, Myles, I got the arrangements for Officer Hill's wake and funeral.

His wake is going to be at the Metropolitan Funeral Home on Thursday from three 'til nine. There's going to be a gathering there at seven o'clock of all sworn department members—a time to assemble and pay tribute to the life of our fallen hero and recognize St. Jude, the patron saint of all police officers. The funeral will be held at the First Church of Deliverance, 4315 S, Wabash avenue, Friday morning at 11:00".

"Cool, man. I'll put this information in my notebook and pass it around."

I had a couple of hours before my date, so I put a few sounds on to further my relaxation therapy and cool down. The impressionable horn of Sunny Stitt's "Cherokee," a tune my father loved, mellowed me out and soothed my anxious will. I never really stopped to realize the pace I had been going, and it was time for a few moments of self-evaluation.

Being a detective was demanding; your mind was always conducting some type of investigation. No matter what your thoughts were or your present condition, you solved all of your problems through investigation. I started thinking about Francine Williams—about how I had met her, and how I never really stopped to recognize how attractive she was. She was warm and beautiful, but I never noticed that until I saw her as an ordinary person and not the sister of a homicide victim. The pace I was working over the last few months was getting to me. I needed to take time out for myself.

My thoughts drifted from me to my partner. He certainly was one hell-of-a detective. It's funny. No matter how much I get to know him, he always seems to have another gear to shift into. I suddenly realized Aristotle Ashford had a lot in common with my father. They both kept their feelings close to their hearts. All I can say is that I have learned a great deal from the both of them.

It was after 5 p.m. now and I needed to get dressed. I picked up Francine at 6:15. She was dressed in jeans and a suede jacket. She looked radiant and her scent—Jasmine, I believe—was knee buckling. I just wanted to grab her, squeeze her, and give her a line. Maybe tell her I'd been looking for her my whole life. We headed downtown to the Roosevelt Theater on State Street, just south of Lake Street. The movie was scheduled to start at 7:10, so we were a little early. I took her around the corner to Tad's Steak House for coffee and a bite to eat. I had a bounce in my step. Just that quickly, I had forgotten all about the experiences of the past few days. I was alive, vibrant, and thrilled to be in the company of the most beautiful woman in the world.

The movie," Uptown Saturday Night," was hilarious. Sidney Poitier was one of my favorite actors. I wasn't a big moviegoer, but I always had great respect for the mold he was creating. He was a pioneer in the film industry. I remembered the "Mesay Day-O Man," Harry Belafonte, from the time when I was a child and visited my grandparents on the weekend. Every Saturday night we would watch the "Lucky Strikes Hit Parade" TV show. During that era you didn't see too many Black faces on TV, and, when you did, you were excited and proud because you had someone to identify with. Bill Cosby was also pretty popular at that time. He added the comic flavor to the all-star cast.

As we sat there in the dark theater watching the movie, I just couldn't stop gazing at Francine. I wanted to talk, but I dared not disturb the other moviegoers. When the movie was over, as we walked back to my car, she reached out and grabbed my hand. Her hand felt warm and supple, so I gripped it tight.

"You want to stop on the lakefront on our way home for a moment and talk?" I asked.

"I'd love to, Myles. I really don't want to go straight home."

We stopped at the lakefront on 31st Street, walked over to the water, and found a seat on the rocks. The sky was clear. Looking upward, you could distinctly make out the three-quarter shaped moon, which was slowly clearing from the shadows of the clouds. The appearance of the half crescent moon annoyed me because it was the symbol used by the Stones to mark their turf. Everywhere you looked on the southeast side you would see it—on garage doors, buildings, schools and playgrounds. There was no mistaking the threatening symbolism of the half-crescent moon accompanied by a pyramid and a five-pointed star. No matter what history these symbols actually denoted, in Chicago they meant Blackstone.

Francine began talking about her little brother, Franklin. "Myles, I was afraid that Franklin was involved with the gangs. Gang activity has plagued our community for some time. Franklin and his friends were close. They hung around together all the time. I never knew their real names, only the street names they called each other. They all met in the sixth grade at Alexander Dumas Elementary School. Franklin was a very bright kid and his friends seemed to follow him in whatever he wanted to do".

"My mother wouldn't allow herself to believe that Franklin was involved with gangs. No matter what evidence she saw or what people told her, she denied its truth. I suspected that he was doing something when I began to see him with older boys. He started coming home with things that I knew he didn't have money to buy. When I asked him where he got certain items, he would tell me he'd just borrowed them from some person he knew. Then they began to look like little thugs. He even started sneaking out after mother and I went to bed. I didn't have anybody to turn to and…I guess I wasn't doing a good job of keeping him away from the gangs. Since his death, I've had a hard time not blaming myself."

Francine had tears in her eyes and my heart sunk. I wanted to lift that burden off of her. I wanted to erase what had happened; I suddenly wished that I had been there for her to turn to when she needed someone to rescue her little brother. The tears in her eyes looked heavy.

I reached for her hand and I pulled her close to my body. I held her tight and squeezed her.

"You shouldn't blame yourself for what happened to Franklin. You did all you could to steer him away from harm. Nobody can blame you for what happened," I told her.

We stood there, on top of a rock with the moon shining bright in the sky, holding each other without saying a word. The traffic in my body was log-jammed. I felt happy and sad, weak and powerful, championed and frustrated, yet complete. Holding her in my arms gave me a feeling I had never experienced in my entire life.

Francine gently took her hand and placed it behind my neck. She looked straight into my eyes as she pulled my head towards her lips. We kissed, just as our bodies were tensing for an explosion. Her tears told me that she was as captivated by me as I was by her. At the height of our shared moment, she whispered, "I want to tell you something, but I'm afraid you may not understand."

"You just have to trust that I will."

Her voice was soft as she stepped away from our embrace. "Myles, the day I met you in the police station, before you stepped onto the second floor, I could feel you coming up the stairs. My spirit alerted me to look toward the stairwell. When you appeared, I knew that a prayer was being answered. I didn't think it was for me, but for my mother. Now I feel that the prayer was for me, too. I'm so glad that I met you."

We sat there on the rocks for a good while, hugged close to each other, not really saying a word.

Finally she started to open up again. "Myles, I feel so protected with you. You are such a strong man. I bet your phone never stops ringing."

"Not really, Francine. I'm not a player. I have friends, but I don't have a girlfriend. I guess I haven't found that special person."

Francine didn't seem to respond too well to that statement. I guess she thought better of it for the moment. Then we embraced again as our shadows reflected over the water. The kiss was definitive, full of emotion, sexual arousal, and genuineness. I didn't want to let her go, but it was getting late.

"Are you ready to go?" I asked halfheartedly.

"I guess so. We both have to work tomorrow."

"Yeah, I think it's time we headed home."

I double-parked in the street and walked Francine to her doorstep. She hugged me very tightly and gave me a sensuous kiss.

"Drive home safely and please call me tomorrow," she whispered.

All the way home, I felt aglow. The echo of her voice was still circling my senses. My heart felt warm and stimulated. I knew we hadn't known each other long enough to mention love, but who designs love? It comes to those who want it and are capable of recognizing its vigor. My feelings for her were becoming undeniable. The challenge was whether it would be long lasting.

I arrived home just after midnight, took a hot shower and hit the sack. My flex day off was spent well. I relaxed, entertained myself, and had a good evening. I had a great day.

Chapter 14

Roll call the next morning was solemn; the death of Officer Glen Hill still gripped the entire department. Lt. Nugent's summary of gang homicides was the topic, but most of us couldn't care less. He discussed the funeral arrangements and reminded all of us that we had to be in dress uniform for both the St. Jude's wake and the funeral.

After roll call, Lt. Nugent called DoubleA and me into his office and handed us a memo from the Superintendent. It summarized our murder investigation and identified his concern with the Federal Bureau's failure to share information about the murder. Superintendent James Rochard directed us to meet with his executive assistant at nine the next morning.

Lt. Nugent wasn't happy about the situation. He grumbled, "The brass is highly upset with the 'G's unwillingness to give us a tip on their information."

The way the department viewed their actions was simple: keep your secret investigation going, but let us know about the evidence you have. Since we had a key witness under raps all we had to do was arrest Black Sonny, charge him with the murder of Franklin Williams, and hold him in custody until a trial date was set. Once he was in custody, we had 120 days to prosecute. That should be more than enough time for the Feds to finish their secret investigation of the Stones. We didn't give a shit about their investigation; all we wanted was to get Black Sonny off the street.

The conflict between the Federal Bureau of Investigation and the Chicago Police Department was age-old. They never trusted us since the corrupt days of Al Capone, and we never trusted them because we knew the bullshit they sold the public about their investigative prowess.

We stopped by our desk to check our phone messages. There were three messages from Peachazz, one marked urgent. I gave them to DoubleA while I read the crime lab report on the sawed-off 410 shotgun. The analysis concluded that the 410 recovered from Felix's girlfriend was indeed the same weapon used to kill Artie the Brute. It had Felix's fingerprints on it. The one casing found in the weapon was determined to be the original shell used in the blast. We decided to make a stop at Area 1 and see if our friend Felix was ready to cooperate.

We met Detective Cole upstairs in the Area 1 and he briefed us on our suspect: "Felix is holding steady to his defense and is not being cooperative. He told Detective Banahan we would have to convict him on circumstantial evidence because we didn't have an eyewitness and he would take his chances on that. It appears that Felix has been talking to a jailhouse lawyer. He firmly believes that without an eyewitness he can beat the rap."

After listening to Cole's report, DoubleA said he was going to make a phone call and that he would meet me downstairs when he finished. When I got downstairs, he was still on the phone. He looked up, saw me and hung up. He motioned for me to follow and we exited the rear door of headquarters. We jumped in our squad car and hit the expressway.

DoubleA drove over to the Parkway Gardens, the housing complex that Peachazz's mother lived in. "Wait here. I'll be right back," he said.

I sat there until he returned.

He got in the car and turned toward me, "Peachazz was waiting for me to bring her a few dollars. She's been down on her luck since the assault and she needed some money," he explained.

I didn't say anything, but I think DoubleA sensed my curiosity. When he started up the squad car, he began to talk about their relationship.

"Before Peachazz started whoring, she was a very attractive woman," he said. "We met when she was just twenty-one at a cabaret party at St. Elizabeth's Hall. She was fine as she could be. We dated for a couple of years. Eventually, she got pregnant. She wanted to get married, but I didn't think she was ready for a life of marriage with me. She was young and too impressionable. She didn't know how to keep niggas off of her. Every time a dude made a pass, Peachazz didn't know how to back him up. When I told her I didn't want to get married, she got pissed with me.

"She hung around with a couple jealous-ass bitches that filled her head with a lot of bullshit. She couldn't see that they were envious of our relationship because most of the niggas they got up with weren't shit. Peachazz started drinking and hanging out with a bad crowd. Then she lost the baby. I never forgave myself for being so selfish, but she was young and I couldn't see myself married. I would have taken good care of her and the baby, but she just wanted me, no excuses.

"After she lost the baby, she started skin-popping heroin and got hooked. I must have put her in five different detox facilities, but each time she would go right back to the same crowd. I gave up on her. Next time I saw her; she was a drug addict-whore. Life's a bitch, ain't it, Myles? I thought I might as well tell you the story before some lying-ass copper gives it to you all fucked up. So now you don't have to sit there being confused, trying to figure out what's with Peachazz and me. I talk to her sometimes about the job. She knows a lot about our investigation—but don't worry. Peachazz is loyal, even though she shoots dope. She would never betray me.

"Now enough about me, my friend. Let me ask you something."

"Cool, man, shoot away."

"Well, I know you recall the other night at Bennie's, talking with Commander Bob Harness."

"Yeah. Yeah, I remember."

"I couldn't help overhearing you tell him about the time you had the "dishonor of being a guest" in the Wabash lockup. What year was that Myles?"

"I think it was 1965. Right. The summer of 1965. What about it?"

"Believe it or not, I was in the station that night and I recall the incident. When I heard you tell the commander that was you, I was amazed. Man you raised a lot of hell that night. Tell me, what made you act like that?"

"It's a long story, DoubleA. I was on the street when the police responded to a disturbance. Some of my friends were upset because one of our boys got stabbed. Two cops approached me and told me to get in the squad car. I hadn't done anything so I asked them why. The little cop slapped the shit out of me. Now listen, I have a very unpleasant history of being slapped. My grandmother and my mother were both 'face smackers.' Then in school, teachers and nuns had the same bad habit. I made my mind up one day that I wasn't going to allow it anymore. I guess I picked a bad time to take a stance. It could have been anybody. Why the fucking police?

"After the little cop slapped me, I tried to take his head off. They called for help, and I guess every car on the street responded. They stomped the shit out of me. When I got to the station, I lied and said I was sixteen. When my mother and sister arrived, my mother told 'em I was seventeen. That meant I had to go back into the lockup. I was already stewing over the ass-whopping I took on the street, so I cut loose with a right to the officer's head. I backed myself up in a corner and screamed at them to come and get me. The room was full of cops; I know

now they were having their early shift roll call. When the commotion started in the back of the squad room, the captain told the officers to break rank and get that situation under control. I was doing well for a moment, but the next thing I remember, I woke up in the bullpen feeling like I was having a nightmare. I didn't realize the trouble I was in until I had to go to court. Shit, I was facing a stint in the county jail. The charges were dropped against me because the two cops didn't come to court and my lawyer was a classmate of the judge but, man, my ass was out there."

"Sounds like you had a bad police experience, my boy. But tell me, how did you get past the background investigation with that arrest history?"

"Funny you would ask that question. As soon as the two background investigators discovered I had been arrested for '*fighting with the police,*' they disapproved my hiring and sent my file to the Civil Service Commission. I had to go there and justify my hiring.

"I went to the 3rd Ward Democratic Organization and asked for mercy. My mother worked for the Board of Election. She was a precinct captain and she knew the Alderman, but he wouldn't help me. He told my mother I was too violent. He never once thought the police were wrong. The incident is as clear as day in my mind. My mother was crying because that chicken-shit son-of a-bitch wouldn't bless me. I finally got help from a guy named Sam Patch. He sent a message to the Civil Service Commission through a friend of his, Quentin Goodwin, a Civil Service Commissioner. He convinced me to have my hearing rescheduled so that I could seek legal counsel. The rest is history. After the hearing I was accepted and hired about three months later."

"You know, Myles, and this is a fact, when Commander Harness heard about you and all the shit you stirred up in the station that night, he jokingly told the watch commander to send a man over to your house and sign you up for the police department. The rumor was you kicked everybody's ass on the watch. Harness never did let that shift forget that they let a kid kick their ass."

Before I could answer, we got a call over the police radio to meet two detectives on the westside, at 14th and Springfield. We had no idea who they were, but they specifically asked for us. This was a long way from the southside, so whatever these detectives wanted it had to be good.

We met Detective Bob Brownfield and Detective Ed Baker, two westside veterans who had a suspect in the back seat of their squad car. When we rolled up, Detective Brownfield got out of his squad and walked back toward us and began talking about the suspect in the back seat of his car.

"We've were sitting on a house looking for a murder suspect when we grabbed the guy sitting in the back seat of our squad," he said. "This guy was holding a big sack of heroin. We squeezed him a little, and he told us about a murder that had occurred on 66th and Dorchester several days ago. As soon as he started singing about the murder, we called Area 1 and found out that you guys were handling the case."

DoubleA informed him that it was our case. He didn't leave out that two dicks from Area 1 were actually conducting the investigation; he explained that we were conducting a gang intelligence investigation, one that ties directly into the murder. We took the witness and sat him in the back seat of our squad. I asked him his name and what he knew about the murder.

He replied, "Donovan Jackson. I'm a friend of Felix and Franklin. On the morning that Artie got offed, Felix came by my house right after he had wasted Artie and told me what happened. He stayed at my apartment until later that morning when I drove him to Penny's apartment on 71st Place." He described the murder weapon and wanted a play on the dope charge if he helped us with the investigation. "I know you guys can help this dope charge disappear if I help you with this case."

"You mean you'll testify as a witness for the state?" I asked.

"Yeah, if I can get the right help on these drug charges. I don't want to go back to prison."

"You'll have to go with us to the criminal courts building and talk to an Assistant State's Attorney to see if we can take you in front of a grand jury."

Jackson was a convicted felon on parole. Any kind of arrest activity would stir up his "promise to be good" and send him back to the joint to complete his sentence. The parolee pondered the offer and agreed to tell a grand jury about the conservation he had with Felix Hamilton the morning after Arthur Shelby was murdered. Detectives Baker and Brownfield turned Donovan Jackson and the sack of dope over to us. We took him directly to the criminal courts building.

We located a friendly Assistant State's Attorney who took the time to listen to the facts of our investigation and make a decision as to how the state would pursue the charges. Assistant State's Attorney Thomas Ryan agreed to calendar the case, but he wanted Donovan Jackson booked on the heroin possession. After the state got his testimony, Ryan said, they would work out a deal on the charges. We had to contact Baker and Brownfield and have them come in and do the paperwork so that there would be no question regarding the chain of evidence. This was necessary since they made the collar and recovered the heroin from the person of Donovan Jackson.

That arrest of Donovan Jackson by Detectives Baker and Brownfield was a stroke of luck. We knew we had leverage over Felix Hamilton. When he found out what we had, he would have to "do the dance" and figure what was the best route for him to take.

On our way back to the southside, DoubleA broke out with a sudden burst of laughter.

"Myles, I want to be the one to break the news to Felix. I got a nice presentation I want to make to his smart ass. He'll be singing a different tune when he finds out that one of his 'homeboys' rolled on him."

When we arrived at Area 1, we learned Felix had been charged and sent to the Cook County Jail. We had to turn around and head back to 26th Street. Prisoners on lockdown awaiting trial were housed at the Cook County Jail. We had to make a request to see Felix regarding his case.

When Felix entered the visiting room, he had a terrible attitude. "What the fuck do y'all keep coming to see me for? I ain't got shit to say!" He snarled.

DoubleA lit right into him. "Hold it, dude. Let me tell your nothing ass something! Why is it when a nigga commits a crime, he thinks that he gonna get away with it, and when the police asks him some questions the nigga cops an attitude? What you thinking, boy, you done committed the perfect crime? Here's the lick—we offered you a deal, fess up, and we'll make it light on you. Plead self-defense, your boys got killed and you knew you were next. You were overcome with the fear of being killed—a jury would buy that; self-defense, you could get acquitted. Or you could risk seven-to-ten for voluntary manslaughter. Or, you can keep claiming you didn't kill nobody and stonewall us!

"Well, peep this outcome: You go to trial on the evidence we present, bench trial or jury trial, you lose. Now that seven-to-ten becomes ten-to-life. Now guess what? We ain't going to flip a coin. Confess and ask for mercy. Oh yeah, by the way, we ran into one of your homeboys on the westside, a Donovan Jackson. Man that nigga was carrying some weight, and he traded the package for your black ass. You got twenty-four hours to cry out my name, dude!"

The look on Felix's face told the story. He just dropped his head into his hands and covered his face. We got up and left the interviewing room while Felix sat there looking stricken.

DoubleA had a look on his face, too—one that reflected triumph. He knew he had Felix where we wanted him and there would be no further need to disturb the prisoner. He would be calling out for us to make him an offer of mercy.

Our ride back to the southside was a happy one. We knew the murder investigation of Arthur Shelby would be cleared and closed by the end of the week.

Now we had to concentrate on getting Black Sonny off the street. Our alleged FBI agent, Sampson, was out there somewhere and somebody knew it. The "G" would hold on to his confidentiality until they were forced to give him up. Our task was to find someone who knew Sampson was in the hotel at the time of the murder.

The next morning we were sitting outside the Superintendent's office. We observed four people directed into his office by his receptionist. We recognized Mike Spiotro, the Deputy Superintendent of Investigative Services, and Frank Stibby, the Chief of Detectives. DoubleA and I were discussing our case when the door opened, and the Superintendent came out and told us to come in. He introduced us and we learned that the other men in the office were David Carey, the chief prosecutor from the Cook County State's Attorney's Office and George Thompson, the assistant to the U.S. Attorney.

The Superintendent laid out the conflict for all to examine: "Gentlemen, I don't think I have to explain why we are here. This incident is going to be bad news for the public. If we don't come to some kind of compromise, this issue is going to be embarrassing."

Assistant U.S. Attorney Thompson carefully took notes and made several attempts to explain the government's position. "Our stance must remain the same right now, until I can get some direction from the Bureau on how we can work this out."

Superintendent Rochard didn't want to hear that. "You guys are stalling," he complained. "We need the government to come forward with information that will put our suspect in custody. I'm demanding the government identify the mole and allow us to use his testimony to charge our suspect and take him off the street."

Thompson refused to disclose the "G's" investigation and stood firm on not identifying Sampson. "I'll have to discuss this matter further with my superiors," he insisted. "I'll meet with you after a decision has been made."

When the meeting was concluded, we were told to wait around until everybody left. Superintendent Rochard escorted everyone else out, then returned to his office and gave us some additional information. "I want you men to meet with a Chicago police officer who is assigned to the Intelligence Division but is detailed to the U.S. Attorney's Office. This man is one of the first Chicago police officers to receive training at the Federal Bureau of Investigation's training facility in Quantico, Virginia. He was asked by the Bureau to come back and teach a class for new federal agents. His name is Ramone Smoothe, a veteran who has been with the department since 1957." He gave us a contact number and told us Smoothe may be able to help us identify Sampson.

While on the way to our office, DoubleA told me he knew Smoothe from the police-training academy. "Me and detective Smoothe graduated from the police academy together. He's a decorated veteran from the Korean War. When he was discharged he had reached the rank of lieutenant. Once we completed training, Smoothe was assigned to a special detail. I didn't see him after that. I had heard Smoothe was working with the "G." Word is he has been providing them with information about the rising drug traffic in the city."

Back at our office, DoubleA went directly to the phone and dialed the number he had received from the Superintendent. I stood by awaiting a response. The call only lasted about a minute.

"I just talked with Smoothe," DoubleA filled me in. "He wants to meet us downtown in a restaurant called Miller's Pub. It's located on Wabash, just south of Monroe."

It was 11:30 a.m. when we left headquarters and headed to Miller's Pub. We found a parking spot and went inside. As we entered the restaurant side of the establishment, we saw a male subject sitting at a table in the northeast corner smoking a cigarette. DoubleA nodded to him. As we approached his table, DoubleA whispered in a low voice," Smoooooothe, my brother." The man stood up to greet us. He gave DoubleA a big hug and extended his hand to me. He introduced himself as Detective Ramone Smoothe.

Detective Smoothe was about 6'2" with a thin build. His complexion was olive, and he had long, mingled gray hair. He looked like he was still active in the gym, even though a long, non-filtered cigarette was burning in the ashtray. We sat down and looked over the menu. Smoothe had a pleasant-sounding voice, very clear and distinct, and you could tell he had studied the King's English. After he and DoubleA exchanged some reserved conversation about their training at the police academy, Smoothe asked us about the hindrance in our investigation. DoubleA gave him a clear account of our situation and asked if he could help us identify Sampson.

Smoothe had it all waiting for us before we could begin to give him a description of Sampson. "I have a mental file that I prepared when I learned the particulars of this investigation," he said. Then he confirmed our suspicions, adding, "Sampson is an FBI agent. His real name is William Oliver. I was allowed to review his file as a favor," he informed us.

We learned he had attended Lindblom High School and later enrolled in a program at the Woodstock Country Day School called 'A Better Chance' in

Woodstock, Vermont. From there he entered Dartmouth University in Hanover, New Hampshire. He was raised in Chicago—Englewood district—and was recruited out of college by the Bureau in 1973. They sent him to Omaha, Nebraska. He came back to Chicago when an investigation opened up on the Blackstone Rangers. "He volunteered for the assignment," Smoothe said.

Smoothe showed us a picture taken of Oliver during the Bureau's Chicago Christmas party last year. From the looks of it, his height and weight matched the description we received on the junkman. Smoothe didn't know much about the kind of investigation the "G" was doing on the Stones, but he did mention that the "G" was bent on disrupting their dynasty and dishing out some heavy jail time.

"I think the next step in your investigation should be to return to the table with the Superintendent and his staff and have them bring the Assistant U.S. Attorney back in the circle," Smoothe suggested. "Offer him a proposal on how to settle this dispute. Once an agent's identity has been exposed, the government doesn't have much of a choice. They'll have to agree to your terms and allow Oliver to testify in front of a judge about what he saw the day of the murder."

Everything was set; we ordered lunch and closed the subject. It was an interesting morning, and we were ready to move forward in our investigation. We thanked Detective Smoothe for his cooperation and wished him well.

When we reached our squad car, we discovered it had been ticketed for illegal parking in Chicago's downtown area. "Now ain't this a bitch," DoubleA snapped. "I guess it's real hard for these dumb-ass sons-of-bitches to see this is a squad car!"

"Don't get upset, man. You know these uniformed officers down here don't have too much crime-fighting to do. We can run over to the traffic court building and get the ticket non-suited (stricken from the file) before it hits the system."

En route to traffic court, DoubleA started telling me about Lt. Ramone Smoothe's Korean War experience. "Smoothe's platoon-size detachment annihilated more than two hundred enemy soldiers during an operation in a battle ten miles south of Chorwon. They prevented a flanking maneuver by the North Koreans," DoubleA said. "It was rumored that Smoothe killed thirty North Korean regulars when they tried to out-flank his platoon. He received the Bronze Star for his service." DoubleA was beaming with pride.

"During that same time period, I was in Yech'on, a town recaptured by another distinguished Black fighting man, Lt. Colonel Sam Price. Myles, I guess you can tell by now I keep up with events. I try as much as possible to pass on history to the next generation. When a Black man makes a good contribution to the race, we all need to know about it."

The traffic court building was located at 320 N. Clark Street. When we drove up, I took the ticket and went inside. I stepped on the escalator and looked up at the top of the stairs where I saw a Black, high-ranking police officer standing in full uniform. I recognized his face. A slight sweat began to moisten my neck and my heart began to pound irregularly. It was Assistant Deputy Superintendent George Simms standing as tall as John Henry. I froze as the escalator reached the top. I wanted to say something, but I couldn't find the courage.

George Simms was my hero. It was his shoulders that I stood on to become a detective. He stood up for Black police officers when others wouldn't. During the federal trial, in which the African American Patrolman's League sued the City of Chicago for discrimination, Deputy Simms sacrificed his career. It was his testimony about unfairness and racism in the hiring, assignment, and promotion of Black police officers that gave victory to Black policemen and forced the city to cogitate its next move in a federal class-action suit.

I thought I would never have another opportunity to say to Deputy Simms what I felt in my heart, so I found the courage to walk toward him and get his attention. My hands were all clammy and I had a lump in my throat, but I moved forward.

"Deputy Simms," I stumbled, "my name is Detective Myles Sivad. I just want to shake your hand and thank you for your commitment to justice. I read the transcripts from the trial. I don't know how we'll ever be able to thank you for the courage and fortitude you exhibited when you gave your testimony. It's men like you that I'll always respect. I hope that some day during my career I'll be able to stand up with the same amount of determination and guts to support my people."

Deputy Simms looked at me with a huge smile on his face. He seemed gratified when he responded, "Young man, thank you so much. If I never hear another soul mention what I did during that trial, I'll consider your recognition enough. You have assured me that my testimony was for the good of all young Black police officers here in this city. No matter what happens in my career, I wouldn't hesitate to walk the same path again if it meant it would help us overcome racism and bigotry in this department." He extended his hand and shook mine, adding, "Your temperament is a true example of what I stood up for."

I was overwhelmed with emotions and tears rushed to my eyes as he walked away. I felt like I'd just finished talking to General Eisenhower or Patton; my respect for Deputy Simms was that profound.

I took the ticket into Room 110 and informed the clerk that it was written on a squad car. She took the ticket and told me she would take care of it. When I got outside, DoubleA asked me what took me so long. I was still feeling overwhelmed when I answered, "Today is a day of generals." I knew he wouldn't understand, so I told him whom I'd met in the traffic court building and what I said.

"Myles, that was honorable. I wish I could've been there. You know, George Simms is a war veteran with combat experience, too. He was discharged from the military as a lieutenant, and then he distinguished himself during the 1968 riots on the westside. His testimony during that federal trial turned the department and politicians against him. His decision to give favorable testimony on behalf of the African American Patrolman League cost the city the use of $76 million in federal revenue-sharing monies. The mayor refused to comply with the court's decision, and the city was forced to borrow $55 million from local banks to stem the tide until other revenue sources were identified. Simms' decision hurt his career, but he doesn't seem to mind. George Simms is a man of principle, and he always knew that the department had a long history of discrimination. He had endured it throughout his career. He felt it was time that somebody stood up and forced the issue."

We left the downtown area, heading south to Area 1 to meet with Detectives Banahan and Cole. We wanted to give them an update on our suspect and have them pay Felix Hamilton a visit to see if he was ready to cooperate. We gave them a complete rundown of events. They agreed that we had enough evidence to make Felix flip over.

After roll call the next morning, we met with Lt. Nugent to review our investigation and discuss our dilemma with the Feds. Mike seemed concerned about the conflict, but he assured us that the department would back us all the way. "The Superintendent requested a report from Detective Smoothe after I talked to his commanding officer. The battle will be a struggle, but we have sufficient reason to force the Feds to cooperate," he told us.

Chapter 15

It was Thursday and the city was in mourning. All twenty-one police districts, headquarters, and all six of the cities police Areas had black-and-blue mourning bunting hanging over their main entrances, and all city buildings flew the American flag at half-mast. Martin Luther King Drive, the street where the funeral home was located, was shut down from 47th to 43rd streets. "No Parking" signs were posted, restricting parking in this area from 9 a.m. to 7 p.m.

The wake for Officer Glen Hill was scheduled from 3 p.m. to 9 p.m. The St. Jude's prayer assembly was scheduled to begin at 7 p.m. We were preparing to pay tribute to a hero. Nothing seemed more important than bestowing honor to our fallen comrade.

Still, we had work to do. I left headquarters and went to Branch 49, which was located on the second floor of the 007th District, to testify in an old misdemeanor case I had when I was assigned to the Englewood District. The case was a burglary that was reduced to a theft because the victim and the offender were related to each other and the State's Attorney didn't want to risk losing the case by trying to get a felony conviction. The arrestee took a plea, so I didn't have to testify, but the prosecution wanted me present in case there was a change in the agreement.

After the case was over, I stopped downstairs to talk with some of my old buddies who were still assigned to the "Wood." It had been a while since I had seen some of the guys who taught me "the principles of policing." We shared many adventures. It was here, in the Englewood District, that I learned to be a police officer. Everybody looked out for each other, and every call of "a man with a gun" brought four or five cars. A call of a suspicious person aroused the curiosity of every working policeman. There were characters of all kinds working in the Englewood District, including the hustlers who thought that anybody they stopped had to pay a tariff. The veteran officers looked out for the rookies, always offering to share their experience without hesitation. It was an experience that will always be with me, and I'll cherish the lessons forever. It has only been six months since my promotion to detective, so I still feel close to those guys. I always will. They are like family. I'm always glad to see any one of them during my travels.

When I reached the front desk I saw an old friend who had his back to me, but I recognized him anyway. I shouted out, "Peace if possible," and before he could turn to see who had said that, he responded, "But justice at any rate." It was my old friend Morris Carter, an old-timer whom I had spent many a shift with, listening to his stories and sharing his wisdom.

Morris was a wise creature who loved being the police. He would entertain me each night during our tour with stories about how the job used to be. He boasted of the time "when the streets were lined with gold and we didn't need a pay raise." "Just bring back the good old days," he'd say. He was educated and carried himself in a dignified manner; yet, he never rose above the rank of patrolman. He didn't let that disturb him because he knew how difficult it was for a Black man to be a police officer and how the system was designed to reward the White officers and the ones who had clout. Morris didn't give a shit about being promoted, but he let me know that he cared if I never got the opportunity.

At 6:30 p.m. we began gathering for the St. Jude's prayer assembly. Large crowds, both foot and vehicular, began to create congestion in front of the Metropolitan Funeral Home, located at 4435 S. Martin Luther King Drive. King Drive was previously named South Park Boulevard and prior to that Grand Boulevard. Its boundaries began at Cermak Road (22nd Street) and ended at 115th Street. This area was considered the heart of the southside, offering a scenic view of tree-lined parkways from 35th to 55th streets.

Police cars and civilian cars were parked in every foot of space. The parkway, which provided extra parking spaces, was filled on both sides of the street. I remembered how as a child I used to play football on the parkway and how the magnificence of the structure and the landscaping of the Poll Roll Beauty College mystified me. The College was housed in a beautiful mansion of three stories with a black wrought iron fence in the front. The rear yard reminded me of paradise. It was surrounded by a seven-foot brick wall, which sheltered berry trees and greenery. To me, at a young age, it symbolized peace and contentment.

I stood at the entrance of the funeral home and witnessed a sea of uniformed and plainclothes police officers lined up adjacent to the winding driveway to pay their last respects. It was our tradition to honor our dead by gathering at the wake in large numbers—to grieve our loss and let the world know that we accept death as a part of our profession. We gather together to demonstrate our honor and respect to the family of the fallen paladin.

All of our high-ranking officers gathered at the head and foot of Officer Hill's casket as the remaining rank and file lined up on each side of the room. The grieving family members sat in the middle aisle, as Father Nagel called us all to prayer.

The room fell silent as he spoke of the tragedy and reminded us that the danger of being a police officer was awaiting us all. "At anytime, when responding to a citizen's call for help, any one of you could lose your life. I hope that what I'm saying here, tonight, will give each of you the strength to continue addressing the ills of society. When you leave here tonight and the call for help is assigned to any officer in this room, I know you will give the dispatcher a '10-4' and respond to the call."

While Father Nagel continued his service, I began to drift into a semi-conscious state, thinking about what he said and how it related to police officers. I could see the blue-and-white squad car on patrol and the dispatcher giving the assigned officers a job:

"Beat 715, you have a call of a man with a bazooka at 55th and Halsted."

"10-4, squad."

And the beat cars on zone 7 would fill the air traffic with "712, I'm going;" "717, I'm headed that way;" "716, squad, hold me down, responding to that call."

I fell deeper into my thinking, analyzing the contents and our response without question. A call of a person with artillery far superior to any weapon a police officer might have is always a possibility, yet we accept the responsibility even when faced with insurmountable danger. We are sworn to protect life and property, and there is no hesitation in accepting the assignment, nor is there ever a hesitation to back up another officer. It's "duty calling." I returned to the present with a feeling of despair.

The funeral on Friday morning brought police officers from all over the state. The body was taken to the First Church of Deliverance, located at 4301 S. Wabash. All traffic on 43rd Street from the Dan Ryan Expressway to Cottage Grove was shut off. After the funeral services, the cars lined up for the procession to the cemetery. There were more than two hundred police and civilian cars in the procession, spanning over twenty blocks. When the procession arrived at the cemetery, the police mounted unit was lined up on each side of the entrance to the burial ground. The Chicago Fire Department had two hook-and-ladder companies create an arch for the procession to travel under.

The last prayers were recited at the gravesite, and then Officer Glen Hill was laid to rest. The ceremony was solemn. There were tears and sounds of mourning as we stood in full uniform, stolid in the mid-spring winds that blew across our faces sweeping away our tears and reminding us that in Chicago death was a fate all too familiar.

CHAPTER 16

I spent the entire weekend being very low key. Work just seemed to be less important than usual, as many of us still lamented the lost of a fraternal brother. Our unit seemed solemn. No one had much conversation. Crime was not important. DoubleA and I worked a half-day on Saturday and Sunday. It just seemed like no one gave a shit about duty.

Monday morning appeared, too soon. After roll call, we were back in the Superintendent's office with Lt. Nugent, the First Deputy Superintendent Mike Spiotro, and Chief of Detectives Frank Stibby. Superintendent Rochard briefed us on a phone call he had received from the "G," explaining their position and offering to cooperate. However, the time line for a showdown would have to be extended because our suspect, William Oliver, aka Sampson, was in Ghana on loan to the U.S.I.S.—the United States Information Service.

The U.S.I.S. did not sound familiar and we took it to be a euphemism for the CIA. The type of assignment Oliver was on was not explained to us, nor were we given a possible date for his return to the U.S. We couldn't argue any further. We had to wait for his return, if and when it would ever happen. The Superintendent told us that we should go out and arrest Ivory Gilcrist and try and break him down. Let him know that we have an eyewitness, and see if he would be willing to make a deal. The Superintendent's rationale sounded good for a TV series, but, in the real world, hardcore criminals like Black Sonny had to taste their fate before they would agree to roll over on themselves.

We left the fifth floor and walked up to our office. DoubleA was quiet until we reached the stairwell. As soon as we were alone, he broke out in a rage. "What the fuck is this? The makings for a television series! Here we have the got-damn

'G' telling us some bullshit. Our boy Sampson is on some secret mission for the U.S. Information Service, whatever the hell that is, and they don't know when his mission will be completed. This all sounds like some TV shit for the wannabes. This bullshit might go on forever!"

I agreed with him, but what else could we do? The Superintendent was telling us to go out and arrest Black Sonny, but we both knew that was not our best option. We needed to find out if Arthur Shelby was the person with Black Sonny when Franklin Williams was murdered or if somebody else was an accomplice. It was time to talk with the Detectives Cole and Banahan to see if they had taken the investigation any further from when we handed them a prime witness who could maybe close the case.

I called Area 1 on the Pax line and talked with Detective Banahan. "We need to meet with you and Cole and have a round-robin discussion about the case."

He agreed, "Good idea. How about the Woodlawn Hospital? We can have lunch there. The food's good, too. They serve a good menu that's within the budget."

Woodlawn Hospital was located just west of Jackson Park, on 61st at Ellis. It was a small hospital that looked like a high-rise apartment building with an old-fashion fire escape on its east wing. The dining room was located in the basement of the hospital. When we entered, it was obvious that Detective Banahan was hungry and very interested in the menu. The dining room was very small; however, we got there early and were able to get a table. The menu for the day was smothered chicken, smothered pork chops, liver and onions with rice, mashed potatoes and mixed greens.

Banaham was right; the food was down-home and delicious, and the price was an extra bonus. Police officers always looked for a good serving that did not cost much. When they could put the squeeze on, they looked for a police discount. As a matter of fact, most coppers expected a police discount. We were conditioned to believe that the discount was an entitlement that came with the job. It's almost funny how so many police officers screwed that up by abusing the public and getting greedy. After awhile, it became embarrassing when a copper would ask for a discount and the shop owner refused to give him one.

Our conversation began after lunch. We wanted to know if Banahan and Cole had gone any further into the murder investigation after we delivered Felix Hamilton.

To our surprise, Detective Cole gave us the history on Arthur Shelby and his connection to the Stones. "The Stones hired Shelby and Black Sonny to kill Franklin Williams and his crew for ripping them off for their money and drugs,"

Cole said. "Arthur Shelby, aka Artie the Brute, had made a deal with two brothers—Lloyd and Lester Holmes—who were friends of the Williams' crew, in an attempt to get them to locate Felix Hamilton. Our witness, Donovan Jackson, was also part of their crew, even though he is several years older. He got word to Felix that Artie was looking to take him out of the game and told him to come and lay low at his flat.

"When Felix learned of his planned demise, he became desperate and decided he would get Artie first. He knew Artie picked up his dope money on 66th and Dorchester and that he would be there late at night waiting for his mules to bring in the cash."

Detective Cole then reminded us that Artie did not have any cash on him when we found him. Cole believed that Felix probably rolled him after the hit.

"We also interviewed Penny Green," Cole said, "and we took a statement from her about the murder weapon that Felix brought over to her apartment."

DoubleA quickly countered when Cole mentioned that Penny cooperated, yelling "Damn! That bitch didn't give you any trouble when you questioned her?"

"Nope. She answered every question we asked, and she gave us the dates and times Felix came to her apartment."

DoubleA was satisfied with their progress and commended them: "You guys did good. I want to apologize for thinking that y'all took credit for the arrest and then sat on your asses without looking any further into the case."

We finished our lunch and thanked the two detectives for sharing their information with us. Detective Banahan informed us that since they were unable to tie Artie directly to the Williams murder, they were still looking for any witnesses who could supply them additional information.

It was approaching two-thirty as we got back into our squad car and received a message from the dispatcher. "Beat 6812B, your office called. They want you to see a Mr. J.C. Gilmore at 6646 S. Drexel."

"10-4, squad, we'll respond."

We weren't that far from Mr. Gilmore's address, so we decided to stop by and see him first thing. As usual, we parked in front of his house. Before we could get the car door open, Mr. Gilmore stepped out onto the front porch. He was wearing carpenter's overalls and a railroad cap. He stood at the top of the steps and waved hello as we exited our vehicle. "Don't reckon y'all brought my 410 with yous'? I talked with that no-good grandson of mine. I asked him 'bout my 410 and he told me y'all had it. I'd like to sign for it and get it back. You know, it's been in my family for a long time." He was smoking a hand-rolled cigarette.

I tried to respond professionally but stammered and tripped over what I wanted to say.

Before I could recover, DoubleA stepped in and began to tell Mr. Gilmore what happened to his prize shotgun. "Sorry, Mr. Gilmore. We really wish we could give you that piece back, but it was used in a homicide. Besides, Felix ruined it by cutting it down fourteen inches so he could conceal it. Honestly, its value has diminished. Besides, it's illegal to have a shotgun that size."

Mr. Gilmore dropped his head in disappointment and said in a sharp but somber voice, "That som'bitch. He lied to me 'bout my prize. I hope y'all keep his black-ass in the shithouse 'til I'm gone, cause if I ever lay eyes on his no-good ass I'm gonna commit a sin! And, gentlemens, I really 'preciate y'all coming when I called. Y'all's two very fine police offisus."

We left the old man standing on his front porch. He was waving goodbye as we headed toward our squad car. It was getting close to our tour ending, so we settled for what was accomplished that day and called it quits. DoubleA drove to headquarters where I got in my own car and headed south toward my apartment.

When I arrived home, my phone was ringing. I picked it up and a soft and sexy voice said, "Hello."

"Who is this?" I asked.

"This is Nadine Bluecrest. Is this Detective Myles Sivad?"

"Yeah. Hi, Nadine. How are you?"

She lit right into me. "Well, Mr. Detective, when a girl gives you her phone number, she expects you to call and say something. I'm quite sure you have enough women that are keeping you from having any free time to call a new piece. But, damn, you could call and say thanks, but no thanks."

I was a bit lost for words. The Bluecrest girl was quite aggressive. I really didn't know whether to move forward or take a step back and ease out of her offensive. "I've been very busy working a case, and I haven't had a chance to relax and take a break," I stalled. "Anyway, how did you get my home phone number?"

"I got connections in the police department," she sneered. "You don't need a badge to get information. I've been thinking about you. I want to know if and when we can get together for a drink and a few laughs."

I didn't know what to say. I didn't want to appear to be square and not know how to handle her approach, but I've always been sort of introverted when it came to the ladies. I finally responded with the line, "Oh, sweetie, that's all I been waiting to hear you say." I couldn't believe what I said; the words just leaped off my lips.

There was a brief silence and then she responded, "I know of a nice little bar on 65th and Halsted called J's Pub."

I knew of it too. It's a copper's bar where all of my old friends from the "Wood" hang out. There was nothing quiet about J's Pub. It was ideal for the situation because there would be a lot of people who I knew, so I wouldn't feel cornered by an aggressive, yet attractive, young woman. We planned the date for Wednesday night, which was just a couple of days away. I told her I still had her number and I would call her around 7 p.m.

I hung the phone up; before I could take a step, it rang again. I figured it was Nadine calling back because she had forgotten to mention something.

When I answered another warm and sensuous voice tickled my eardrum. It was Francine Williams. "Hi, Myles, this is Francine."

I felt like a creep. I couldn't find the appropriate words since I had just made a date with another woman.

It took a few seconds before I was able to sneak past my guilt. "Francine, I was planning on calling you as soon as I got home, but I received a phone call before I got the opportunity. I'm glad you beat me to it."

She sounded so charmed; she made me feel her excitement. She said, "I really miss you, and I was hoping we could spend some time together before the weekend was over."

"We must be sharing some kind of clairvoyant connection field. My reason for wanting to call you today was to see if you would have some time this weekend, too."

We both found sheer excitement in our desire to be together. We made plans for Friday night.

"We have made some progress in our investigation and we might be making an arrest soon." I thought I'd bring Francine up-to-date on the progress of our murder investigation.

"Oh, Myles, I don't want to sound uninterested, but every time you talk about the investigation I experience some emotion. I get a pit in my stomach and a pain in my heart. Don't misunderstand me, I want my brother's murderers brought to justice, but I'm having a difficult time living with this experience."

"I understand. I'll keep the details of the investigation to myself. I'll never bring it up until an arrest is made."

"Thanks so much. I hope you understand."

"Of course I do. I'll see you Friday."

When I hung up the phone I felt disturbed, but I really didn't understand why. I knew that I had played one phone call after the other and both Nadine and Francine were beautiful women, but I couldn't understand why I felt contrite. It was time to resolve my conflict.

I was not committed to a relationship with either Nadine or Francine, yet I had developed sincere feelings for Francine. I liked her a lot and wanted to get involved with her. I knew that the continuation of our relationship could very well lead to some unexpected demands for my time. On the other hand, there was no need for me to be in conflict over Nadine. She was aggressive and looking to party. I could live with that. Hopefully, she would remain that way and not be interested in starting up a serious relationship. The big questions were right in front of me: am I going to see Nadine on Wednesday and see what happens, or will I be foul and blow off the date with some bullshit excuse? I couldn't decide right then what I was going to do, and the knot in my stomach told me to "can the conflict" and find something to alleviate the distress.

The suspense that I entertained before I opened the refrigerator was quickly dispelled as my eyes scoured the freezer to find my old-faithful Swanson TV dinners stacked neatly together. I took out a few to choose from and decided on Salisbury steak and potatoes with green peas—a bachelor's delight. After dinner, I found a spot in front of the TV and settled in for a program before bed. I just caught the end of "Police Story" when my phone rang. It was DoubleA. "Yo, Miles, get your hat!" he ordered. "I'll be by in fifteen minutes. We got to roll!"

He didn't give me time to ask what was up before he hung up the phone. I took a quick look at the clock in my kitchen. It was almost eight-thirty. I grabbed my jacket and walked out the front door. Ten minutes later DoubleA pulled up in my parking lot and I jumped in the squad car.

"What's up?" I inquired as DoubleA sped out of the parking lot and south on Cornell to 55th Street.

"The Stones are having a big meeting at the church on 64th and Woodlawn, tonight. Our unit is going to hit 'em hard. We're looking to recover a cache of weapons and pick up several members wanted on felony arrest warrants. I talked to the lieutenant a little while ago. He told me there's an arrest warrant out for Black Sonny for illegal flight to avoid prosecution from Indiana. Apparently he's wanted for a murder in Gary. They think he might be at this meeting.

"Intelligence reported that the Stones have been using First Presbyterian for the past six years," DoubleA continued. "A Presbyterian priest, Father Fraye, allows them to hold meetings, discipline members, and hide drugs and weapons in the church. Rumor has it that two teens were murdered there and their bodies were burned in the coal furnace.

"Our unit got instructions to meet with a taskforce from the Indiana and Illinois State Police and a team of detectives from Gary. Word is that the Stones are going to ship a load of weapons to Gary tonight and a faction of Stones from Gary will be in Chicago to pick them up. Investigators from Gary have indicated that Black Sonny has been in Gary setting up new territory. He's believed to be involved in a murder that occurred there two weeks ago."

DoubleA drove us to Area 1 headquarters at 51st and Wentworth where we had all met for a briefing. Lt. Nugent was in command and he gave out the orders. "All Gang Intelligence Units will be assisted by four squads from Special Operations. The manpower will be divided into five teams consisting of one sergeant and ten detectives and police officers. The teams from Indiana and the Illinois State Police will be integrated with the Gang Intelligence teams. The intelligence gathered indicates that there may be over one hundred weapons, including automatic and semi-automatic assault weapons and handguns."

The roll call room in Area 1 was packed. Officers sat tensely as Lt. Nugent gave out assignments. We were shown mug shots of wanted suspects, and Lt. Nugent gave orders that every walking ass was to be taken into custody.

We left Area 1 in a caravan totaling over thirty-four vehicles. When we arrived at the target location, we surrounded the church and rushed the building. Once inside, the assault was on. There were at least fifty gang members present. We could see several gang leaders seated in the front, while the rank and file sat listening to their message. When they realized what was happening, they jumped from their seats and attempted to flee.

For approximately twenty minutes the situation was out of control; however, surprisingly, there were no shots fired. Police officers used every other tactic to bring subjects under control. There was gang members attempting to overpower the taskforce, only to find their attempts met with a hail of batons, slappers, and sap gloves. The melee caused injuries to both police and gang members; as a result, several ambulances and additional police were summoned to the scene. In the front of the church were the three reputed gang leaders, in custody—Jake Fontaine, Ivory Gilcrist, and Edney Bayels.

Fontaine was dressed in an Army fatigue jacket with a black tam and dark glasses. He had a trickle of blood coming from his nose and he was clearly enraged. Two detectives from the unit who knew Fontaine immediately took him out of the church in handcuffs. Once the leaders were removed, the rest of the gang members settled down and became orderly. Black Sonny tried to pass off under an alias, but the detectives from Gary were right on top of him and took him into custody. He was complaining that he was struck in the head by a white cop and he was going to sue.

One of the dicks from Gary told him, quite sarcastically, "Yeah, while you're at it, be sure you let your lawyer know about the murder you committed in Gary last month!"

The raid was a big success. We recovered twenty-eight weapons, twelve of which had been reported stolen, and a crate of .45-caliber ammunition stolen from the U.S. Armory on 55th and Cottage Grove two years ago. All of the suspects taken into custody were arrested and charged with a variety of charges—eighteen had miscellaneous warrants, ranging from simple traffic violations to burglary. Black Sonny was taken directly to 26th and California where he was processed and held for extradition. Jake Fontaine was charged with mob action and unlawful use of a weapon.

While we were securing all prisoners and removing the recovered contraband, a white man, a priest, entered the basement and demanded to know what was happening. "Why are you abusing these children? I'm going to complain to the Mayor!" He threatened.

In the midst of his tirade a voice called out from the crowd of uniformed police officers: "Yo Padre! Before you complain to the Mayor, visit the graves of the countless black boys who have met early deaths at the hands of the humble and faithful brethren gathered here in this basement tonight! Tell their mothers that their sons are not dead! Tell them that these vicious cocksuckers arrested here tonight were here doing God's work."

Father Fraye dropped his head in shame as he turned and walked toward the stairwell.

Lt. Nugent actually commended the unknown officer who had poignantly disturbed the conscience of the keeper of death, Father Fraye, and shamed his presence from our view. A copy of the search warrant was left on a table in the church basement. We deliberately forgot to present it when we entered the church basement. Our contention was in direct appreciation of the scriptures written over the stage in the church basement, which read, "Come, All ye are Welcome."

We followed the two detectives that had our prime suspect, Black Sonny, down to 26th and California to begin extradition procedures and see what type of murder case Gary had against him. Black Sonny was placed in segregated detention until all the paperwork could be completed. This process would take several weeks if he refused to agree to extradition, but right now we were only interested in finding out what type of evidence they had against him. He was in custody, and we knew where he would be until the extradition order was approved. The case was reviewed by the State's Attorney's office and set for a hearing the next morning. We completed our inquiry and called it a night. I volunteered to attend the hearing the next morning and submit a report to our lieutenant on the outcome.

CHAPTER 17

The extradition hearing was the first case on the court call and the detectives from Gary, Indiana—Jeremy Johnson and C.T. Edwards—presented the murder warrant for Ivory Gilcrist. The warrant named Ivory Gilcrist, aka Black Sonny, as the offender wanted for the murder of Tyree Eberhart—who was shot and killed while attending the funeral of Melvin Warner, a known criminal in the Gary community.

Gary, Indiana was experiencing a wave of gang violence due to the Blackstone Rangers attempting to move in and take control of the bustling steel town. Black Sonny was sent there to get things organized; however, he ran into some trouble with one of the local street gangs who called themselves the "Family Street Gang." The Stones had moved to Hammond, Indiana into a small public housing complex. They were trying to branch out into Gary. Peterman, the leader of the group, and his boys objected to this takeover attempt and thus the violence between them erupted.

I was able to take a look at the file. They had a weak case, no weapon and a bad witness. The witness was another notorious Gary gang member who was in very critical condition from a different shooting that took place a week after the murder of Tyree Eberhart.

While the hearing was still in progress, Black Sonny's lawyer, Sam Adamski, one of the best criminal lawyers in the state, entered the courtroom and approached the bench. It hadn't taken the Stones long to get Black Sonny some legal representation.

Sam Adamski defended high-powered clients. He was one of the best. He immediately approached the bench. "Your honor," he said, "my name is Sam

Adamski and I'm representing Mr. Ivory Gilcrist. My client has advised me to waive extradition and send him to the state of Indiana."

The judge responded, "If the state has no objections, extradition will be waived and the defendant, Ivory Gilcrist, is hereby remanded to the state of Indiana. Are there any representatives from the state of Indiana to take custody of the prisoner?"

Detectives Johnson and Edwards approached the bench. "Your honor, I'm Detective Jeremy Johnson and this is my partner, C.T. Edwards. We're here to represent the city of Gary, Indiana. With the court's permission we would like the prisoner turned over to us for transportation back to the State of Indiana."

The judge signed the order and directed the court to prepare to release the prisoner into the custody of the detectives. I went directly to the police room and called my office to let the lieutenant know what was happening. Lt. Nugent picked up the phone and I relayed the information to him. He wasn't surprised. "Myles, I just got a call from a clerk friend at 26th Street. He told me Adamski was in the building heading toward the extradition courtroom. Submit your supplemental report and indicate the facts in the narrative."

I arrived at headquarters at 11:30 a.m. and met with DoubleA and Lt. Nugent. They were quite relieved about the proceedings, knowing that Black Sonny would be in custody and that he still had no idea we were working hard to piece together a case against him.

Lt. Nugent expressed contempt for Gilcrist; he knew Gilcrist's past. He said, "Black Sonny is merciless. He has an undying contempt for the police and he has no respect for life. The original Gang Intelligence Unit knew his hatred for the police was unending. I believe Black Sonny was involved in the Alfona murder, but, unfortunately, the probe couldn't tie him to the crime."

We left headquarters and took our usual route to the southside. It was a warm day, with the temperature expected to reach the upper 80s by midday. As I drove down the State Street corridor, DoubleA began to reminisce about State Street after the Projects were built. "Myles, look at these buildings," he sighed. "There can be no more injurious sin heaped on a race of people than the living conditions in these buildings. From 22nd to 53rd street, from State to Federal, thousands of families suffer," he said wearily.

"Initially the Projects were built for working-class people who had a history of family and stability. Good-paying jobs and moral respect for each other was a virtue most of them possessed, but a turnaround occurred in the '70s, and many hard-working families fled. Second-generation residents who grew up in the Projects began to have families of their own, and they raised these families in the same projects. Many of them failed to assimilate into the outer communities, so they continued to live in the projects and raise their new families under the same conditions they were accustomed to.

"Countless tenants in this new group lost the values and morals that their parents hailed. They were faced with a future of helplessness and despair; as a result, a cycle of government dependency for a new generation of families emerged. The city did absolutely nothing to address this disease, so the generations who lived there grew up in conditions that would deplete them of their will to command decency."

After staring out the window, he turned and said, "Now, Myles, I'm not saying that everyone who lived in the projects was a heathen. What I'm saying is there was no structure for those types of close living conditions. People must have collective characteristics if they are to survive in an environment that does not provide support for their survival. Violence and ignorance killed their desire to improve their lot, and the cycle began for the wave of dependency. We have not yet seen the worst of the depravity and the level of violence that is to come. DoubleA was very solemn as he continued his analysis.

"'The Hiltons' was a moniker hung on the projects by members assigned to the old 005th District at 48th and Wabash. Hiltons was short for 'Congo Hiltons' because we believed that the pernicious and abhorrent behaviors exhibited in those buildings shamed the Black race—just like the insidious behavior that occurred in the Congo during its struggle for independence. And don't let us forget the behavior of the Jews and the Irish who were trapped in the ghettos of Europe. The behaviors they exhibited under like circumstances are almost identical to the behaviors of the Black progeny who have been economically and socially deprived."

I acknowledged DoubleA's analysis of the conditions that existed in the projects. He'd actually made me feel his pain. The long-standing conditions he described that plagued poor Black families was really the outcome of poor planning and the lack of understanding of political suffrage. He never mentioned that the arrival of these conditions surprised the city politicians; yet, they did nothing to improve the quality of life for the residents who were trapped by the effects of poverty and ignorance. I knew that the people living in the Robert Taylor Homes and the Harold Ickes housing projects represented a large, democratic voting block and that efforts were made to keep the voting power under control. It didn't matter to our greedy politicians that the price of comfort and security meant investing resources and scholarly wisdom to advance this group forward.

All they were concerned about was winning elections and power. Damn the price of blood.

DoubleA's spin about the projects was convincing, but he failed to mention another reason why the projects were built along the "State Street corridor." I said, "That's a very good analysis, DoubleA, but in my generation we saw it another way."

"What's that, Myles? How do you see it?"

"My analysis of the problem is advanced by the evidence I uncovered during my studies. For instance, if you've studied American history you'll recall the Federal Aid Highway Act of 1956, which provided funding for the interstate highway construction. This Act established funding for the programs that would connect all of the states and allow for the commercial transportation of goods across interstate highways. It also allowed for the rapid deployment of military personnel to any segment of the country.

"When the country began building housing projects for Black citizens the idea of building them near interstate highways was a concept to protect against insurgency in case of a Black revolt. These concepts were all part of government-planned strategies. Students of American history could easily link this suspicion to the historical fear of a slave revolt."

"Good assumption, Myles, but I see it as a sociological failure. You see it as a conspiracy. We differ greatly, but, in the end, what difference does it really make? The shit is real, right here and right now!"

As we approached 55th and State Street, DoubleA asked me to drop him off at his home. "Myles, I'm going to take a break and leave work early. If you don't have something we need to attend to, I'll see you at roll call in the morning."

I drove him to his apartment on 81st and Champlain. He lived in a three-flat on the third floor. I'd never been inside, but I knew that his sister and his nephew lived in the same building.

It was early afternoon, so I decided to stop by the bank and surprise Francine for lunch. I arrived a little before 1pm, only to find that she had already gone to lunch. I headed home to take a nap instead. I had forgotten what my apartment looked like during the early afternoon. Just twenty minutes after my arrival, I was in a deep slumber.

My phone woke me at about four-thirty. "Myles, this is Nadine. I was hoping you'd be home. I have a class tonight. If we're still going out, I can meet you at J's Pub at eight. That way you won't have to come all the way out to my house to get me."

"Okay, Nadine, that'd be fine. I'll be there when you get there." I hung up the phone and went back to sleep.

My dreams had me thinking the phone was ringing in my sleep. As I awakened, I realized the phone was ringing, again. I dreaded who it could be, praying that it wasn't DoubleA with another murder.

This time it was Francine calling. "Hi, Myles, I'm sorry I missed you."

I was glad to hear from her and said, "I just stopped by to take you to lunch since I left work early."

"That was thoughtful of you. I wish I'd been there when you came by. I can't wait to see you."

I looked at the clock next to my bed and it was after six. I knew that I had to get showered and dressed. "I'll see you at six-thirty on Friday, and we can find something interesting to do," I said, trying to end the conversation.

"I can't wait!" She replied.

I looked in my closet for a nice combination to wear. I wanted to dress sharp and hip to make a good impression. I decided to wear my black sports jacket, a pair of hounds-tooth trousers, and my black suede shoes. The cologne would be Royal Copenhagen because it stayed with you all night. I jumped in the shower and was ready to leave at six-fifty. J's Pub was about fifteen minutes from my apartment. I decided to fix a Jack and Seven before I headed out. The Jack went down quick, so I made another one and headed out the door. As I cruised westbound down Marquette Road, I had a light buzz going. I arrived shortly after seven and parked on Halsted Street.

J's Pub was a large bar and restaurant. It was about 2,500 sq. feet with a large dance floor, a long bar, and plenty of tables and booths. As soon as I entered the front door, I saw two old chess masters seated at a table near the front. Bob Lemon, who everybody calls Papion, and Berry Slappy. These guys were the chess kings of Englewood. They took on all willing challengers in a match of chess skills that, oftentimes, attacked the psyche of their competitors while attempting to destroy their confidence. Bob Lemon was skillful and witty. He talked a big game to his challengers, and when checkmate became inevitable he'd demean his opponent with insults and profanity. Berry Slappy was loud and masterful in his game. He would school his opponents as he destroyed their defenses, often shouting out his moves prior to checkmate: "White to play and mate in two moves!"

As I approached the two jousters, Berry reached out to shake my hand without ever looking up to greet me. "Sivad, my brother. What be with you?"

I returned the greeting and added my comment, "Looks like Papion is close to checkmate in two moves."

"Not here, pal. No man unseats the king of concentration and pawn deception."

I walked toward the bar to say hello to J.W. Williams, the owner of the club, and before I could get to the bar he lifted his hand with a glass. "You still downing Jack and Seven?" He asked as he extended his empty hand for a handshake.

"You know it! I guess you still remember some of the nights me and Jack were tripping and in need of some assistance."

"You can bet on it, Myles Sivad. It's been awhile. How've you been? I was just talking about you the other day."

"Nothing, Jay. I'm still caught up trying to be a detective. I'm supposed to meet a dame here tonight when she gets out of class. I guess she'll be here soon."

Although it was still early, the bar had a nice-size crowd already. Every Wednesday night the police from the 007th District had a "set" and women from all over the city would attend. Every player who had a badge made it through on Wednesdays.

I took a seat in the corner of the bar so I could watch the front door and observe the crowd. It was a force of habit; police officers were accustomed to putting their backs to the wall whenever they were in public. Even when the place was filled with police, I never gave it a second thought.

The set was contemporary; the music was bopping for folks who knew the moves. The disk jockey was playing, "That's the Way Nature Planned It" by the Four Tops, a smashing tune that brought people to the dance floor as the tempo of the set stepped up and people started to relax and get loose. It was approaching eight o'clock and Nadine hadn't arrived yet. I was working on my third drink.

I moved my seat from the bar and took a seat at the table with Barry Slappy and Bob Lemon. They'd just finished their chess game and were having a cold one. They were talking about the match, which Slappy had won. Papion could not escape the trap laid by Slappy; he went down in defeat with utter disgust.

They both seemed to be in high spirits, as usual, with Papion never relinquishing the floor to allow Slappy to discuss the strategy leading to his defeat. I admired both of these men because they had taught me a great deal about policing. Both had worked on the westside and they knew the behavior of people and the street. Lemon—pronounced Leymone—was a fast talker, and if you didn't listen carefully, you'd miss what he was saying. He carried himself well, bringing a presence of confidence and knowledge to the arena and a shrewd appreciation for life and people in the world. Barry Slappy was cunning and perceptive. He wore a big natural hairstyle, but he wasn't hung up on militancy. He took his policing seriously and worked alone.

We all sat back and watched the crowd, commenting on the big asses and chesty women. The place was almost at capacity now, and the music was non-stop. I had almost forgotten about Nadine. It was now nearly nine-thirty, and she still had not arrived. I walked to the bar to order another round when I saw this tall beautiful woman enter the front door. She had the full package. She immediately caught me staring at her. I was fixated, and I couldn't stop looking.

The Jack Daniels was in full control, so I walked straight over to her, introduced myself, and asked her name.

"Lawanda Mason," she replied.

"Lawanda, can I buy you a drink?"

"Yes you can. I'll have a glass of white wine, please."

We walked to the bar and I pulled her up a seat. Lawanda had this angelic bright smile, and she was soft and warm in her demeanor. We were having a general conversation when the disk jockey played a cruiser's song, "Summer Breeze," by the Isley Brothers. I wanted to take her into my arms and feel that long, sensuous body.

"Would you like to dance?" I asked, lowering the sound of my voice.

"Why not," she replied. "I like that song. It makes you want to dance."

I took her to the dance floor and put my arms around her and held her close to me. I noticed that she was a smooth dancer as we glided across the dance floor, pressed chest to chest. She felt good in my arms; my hands searched her back for contours and curves. When the music stopped, Lawanda turned cold. She acted like she didn't want to be near me anymore, as if I had gotten too fresh and offended her. She walked away without any explanation. I felt like an idiot. I didn't know what I did to turn her off so suddenly. I was embarrassed.

"Damn, you idiot. You can't hold your liquor," the voice in my head scolded. "Jack Daniels' Rules—you should know that by now!"

I walked back to my seat, not feeling any pain. However, I was disturbed by Lawanda's behavior and I felt ashamed of myself, even though I had no idea what happened between us. I had completely forgotten about Nadine Bluecrest. I just said goodbye in a rather sordid manner to the people standing close to me and I left.

When I arrived home I went straight to bed. I didn't even wash my face. My head was spinning and that king-sized bed was a welcoming sight. No time elapsed before I closed out the real world and began my travels into my Jack Daniels' influenced dreams.

The sound of a ringing telephone was heard in the distance. There was this feeling that the phone was walking from its stand toward the bed, ringing louder and louder as if it was making sure I understood that the call was for me. I kept hoping, while still in my state of repose, that someone would hurry up and answer the fucking phone.

After experiencing a sense of irritability and languor, I realized that it was my phone ringing and not a nightmare. I dreaded answering the phone—seeing that it was only four-thirty in the morning, and the call was undoubtedly work-related. Picking up the receiver, I prayed that the voice on the other end would not be DoubleA, but that hope was short-lived. No sooner than my grumpy and disturbed-sounding greeting was transmitted across the wires, his voice shot back:

"Yo, Miles, DoubleA here. I just got a call from Detective Banahan. Our boy Felix Hamilton is in Cook County Hospital in critical condition. He got stabbed numerous times in an attempt on his life."

My first reaction was to ask who stabbed him. "I thought they went to sleep in the county jail at 10 p.m. Did his cellmate do him?"

"No. This apparently happened during a staged fight in the dining area around 5:30 p.m. We didn't find out until about an hour ago. I just wanted to tell you I'm going over to the Area to meet with Detective Banahan. We'll be looking into this incident further. I won't be at roll call in the morning, so don't look for me. And, by the way, you sound like shit. What did you fall into last night?"

"Man, you don't want to know. I'll see you sometime tomorrow."

I hung the phone up, relieved that I didn't have to get dressed and go to work. I unplugged the phone and immediately prepared to return to the land of ten thousand sheep crossing the heavens.

CHAPTER 18

Roll call the next morning was buzzing with new assignments pertaining to the incident that occurred at the county jail the day before. The word was spreading that the Blackstone Rangers were experiencing an internal struggle involving a break between Fontaine's faction and Bull Hardison. It was clear that factions were hell-bent on confrontation. Although Hardison was in jail for murder, he was still in control of an elite group within the organization. Two members had been shot during a conflict at the gang's headquarters in the basement of the Presbyterian Church. This was not reported to the police at the scene. When the victims arrived at the emergency room, they told the staff at the University of Chicago Hospital that they were victims of a drive-by shooting. When the police arrived to make a formal report, the two victims couldn't remember what their assailants looked like.

The victims, Donald Shotter and Demetrize Brown, were two ranking members of the Stones—even though each was committed to different factions of the group. Both had been to prison in their late twenties and had extensive histories in crime and gang violence. Apparently there was a riff among current members over the split of lucrative drug profits and territory. Usually these types of conflicts involved two separate groups, but with drugs becoming so popular and greed so prevalent, intra-gang conflicts began to emerge and could only be settled by eliminating unsuspecting fellow gang members.

Gang violence in the city was exhausting police resources. We found ourselves moving Gang Intelligence officers from the westside to the southside to spread the workload evenly. Southside and westside gang leaders were experiencing friction because drug profits were so lucrative. Neither side could agree to terms that would divide the earnings fairly. They failed to realize the potential for unlimited profits and that there was more than enough to share.

The new tasks of the day overwhelmed me. I almost forgot to call Francine and remind her of our date. The incident at J's Pub last night knocked me for a loop, but I didn't get down on myself for drinking too much. I didn't call Nadine either to question her about standing me up last night. I wasn't upset about it, but she could have called me with some kind of explanation. I wasn't going to make an issue about it because I knew she was "cocksure" and I would be hearing from her soon.

After attending several briefings, I sat down at my desk and began to prepare reports detailing our investigation and our next move. DoubleA reported to headquarters at 9:15 a.m. He came over to our desk and took a seat. "Myles, our boy is in bad shape. They wouldn't let me see him earlier this morning. I think we should go back over to the prisoner's section of the County Hospital later to see if we can interview him. He's still listed in serious condition."

We arrived at the hospital and met with the guard who was stationed outside of Felix's room. We identified ourselves and he allowed us to enter. Felix was heavily sedated and couldn't keep his eyes open. It was no use trying to get any information from him, so we decided to go over to the jail to read some of the reports and interview some of the guards who could provide us with some information about what happened to Felix.

We learned that Felix was having dinner when a fight broke out behind him. He attempted to get clear of the scene, but he was grabbed from behind and stabbed in the back three times. One of the guards, who witnessed the incident and nabbed the offender, told us the offender was a known Blackstone Ranger who was probably operating under orders to whack Felix for killing Artie the Brute.

Things were really getting away from us. Our primary investigation was full of curves and frustrations. Gang violence was becoming more epidemic and nothing new seemed to provide us with any hope of solving the murder of Franklin Williams. I found myself frustrated. Nothing seemed clear. I was uptight and I really didn't know how to keep myself from being overwhelmed with this slow-moving investigation.

On the other hand, my partner never flexed. He never showed one sign of frustration. He was laid back, too cool, like steel—unemotional and detached. I often wondered why Aristotle Ashford was so composed and in control all of the time. He had a unique history, and I always felt it forced him to distrust people. He always seemed to be protecting himself from others, as if he was hiding something about himself. There was something he would not share with me. I figured that the experiences he encountered after coming from Mississippi hardened him, made him distance his feelings, and made him isolated and uncompassionate. I didn't dare snoop around and ask anybody any questions about the best detective in the Chicago Police Department. I had too much respect and admiration for him to do that; but the thought of finding out what motivated him was very tempting.

It was Friday, approaching three-thirty in the afternoon. We decided we'd knock off early and not report off duty from headquarters. DoubleA drove me to Hyde Park and promised to pick me up in the morning.

When I got home, and before I could take off my cap, the phone rang. It was Detective Ramone Smoothe. "Yo, Myles, Detective Smoothe here. I left a message at your office for you or Detective Ashford to contact me. I got some information for you guys. Have you got a minute? I need to meet with you and discuss some particulars."

"Sure," I replied.

"Where do you want to meet?" He asked.

"Are you thirsty? How about a cold beer? We can meet at Bennie's in an hour." I suggested.

"Sounds good to me."

"I'll see if I can catch up with DoubleA and have him meet us, too." I looked at the clock. It was almost four-thirty. I called South Shore Bank to tell Francine I'd pick her up a little after seven for dinner.

She answered the phone. "Myles, are you at home? I want to come by as soon as I get off work."

"Yeah, I'm home, but I have to meet a detective in twenty minutes. I'll be back here around seven."

I knew she would be disappointed, but that was the best I could do.

"Oh, that's okay. I can wait. She said. "I'll come at seven-thirty, if that's okay with you."

I hesitated because I wanted to go to dinner, but, since she insisted on coming to my place, I found no need to argue the point. I took the mail out of the mailbox and sorted through my bills. It was a quarter after five, and I figured that I could get to Bennie's in ten minutes. I hustled up my mail and left my apartment.

On a Friday, Bennie's 357 Club has a good crowd. Coppers, railroad workers, postal workers, and nearby residents fill the barstools and tables. I saw Detective Smoothe sitting at a table near the bathroom. I immediately signed to him that I was going to use the phone. I had forgotten to call DoubleA before I left home. When I dialed his number I got no answer.

I moved over to Detective Smoothe's table and he stood up and greeted me.

I said, "Man, I couldn't reach DoubleA."

He didn't seem disappointed as he called for the barmaid to come over to our table. "That's not a problem. You can fill him in later."

Detective Smoothe was a classy guy. His nails were polished and his hair and mustache were neatly trimmed. His appearance was clever and he presented himself with an aura that was all his own. "Myles, you look well. How's the job been treating you?" he asked.

I thought it interesting that he would ask that question in light of all the frustrations I had been experiencing lately. "I've been a little disappointed in how slow our case is developing, but I'm holding steady and hoping for a break."

"Well, I hope what I have to tell you will cheer you up and help clear this case before you suffer further disappointment. I have news about your mysterious junkman, William Oliver. He's coming back to Chicago next Monday for two days. I don't think his superiors are going to notify the department that he'll be in town. I think they're planning to keep it a secret and get him right out of town as soon as his mission is accomplished. If you can get a grand jury subpoena and hand it to him at the airport, he'd have to appear and answer all pertinent questions about what he saw in that hotel when your victim was murdered."

Ramone's evaluation of the conflict between both agencies was good. I couldn't believe what I was hearing, though. The excitement flushed through my body. I couldn't hide my joy as I raised my right hand subconsciously begging for a "high-five signature," signifying my elated approval.

The barmaid arrived at our little table and asked us what we were drinking. Ramone ordered a scotch and soda. I had my usual Jack and Seven. I felt like celebrating. The news was a great relief and a long-awaited break in our case. Ramone noticed my jubilation and smiled with satisfaction, but he reminded me that our plan had to work. "Serving Agent Williams with a subpoena will be a task and we can't tip our hand. The Superintendent is already aware of our plans and he's quite anxious. I think you should let DoubleA know as soon as possible. We need to sit down together and map out the steps we need to take to insure that our intentions are not leaked to the 'G.'"

I looked at my watch; it was approaching seven. I jumped up and finished my drink. I told Detective Smoothe I would brief DoubleA in the morning. I explained that I didn't want to be late for an important date. Then I rushed out of Bennie's and sped home.

I arrived home ten minutes later, and as soon as I entered the parking lot I saw Francine sitting in her car awaiting my arrival. She exited her car with a small shopping bag in her arms and hurriedly walked toward me. Her face was aglow, like a person who was very excited. She greeted me with a gentle kiss on my cheek.

"What's in the bag?" I asked, while peeking inside like an excited little boy.

"Dinner," she replied. "If you don't mind, I'd like to prepare you a special meal." Before I could respond, she quickly added, "I just want to spend a quiet evening with you, if it's okay."

"Of course it's okay, and it's thoughtful of you to surprise me like this." I took the bag and directed her to follow me to my apartment. As we walked up the short flight of steps, I prayed that my apartment was presentable and that I wouldn't have to ask her to wait outside while I tossed some things around. The kitchen was clean, while the living room was cluttered; but I wasn't embarrassed. Francine went directly to the kitchen and told me not to spy on her while she was cooking. My kitchen was really a half or a quarter of a kitchen. There was no kitchen table, only a counter between the refrigerator and the sink.

While she prepared dinner, I rustled through some jazz albums searching for some music that would complement a romantic evening. The aroma of down-home country cooking infiltrated my apartment. I told myself to prepare for some good eating, cause that girl in the kitchen was breaking ground toward the path to my heart.

Francine prepared smothered chicken, rice, gravy, and spinach. I didn't have a dining room table either, so we dined on the cocktail table in the living room. The sound of Dexter Gordon's "Around Midnight" filled the air, as we sat together in the shadows of two fragrant candles that completed the occasion. A bottle of dark Muculan Marchesante Merlot, an Italian wine I had been saving for a special occasion, reflected the glow of the candles as we dined in my fantasy—an atmosphere that reminded me of a four-star restaurant.

After dinner, we sat on the couch close to each other and talked about our fears, our frustrations, and ourselves. Francine was a beautiful person, and I could feel her wanting to get close to me. I respected her a lot and wanted to make a move, but I didn't want to right then because I didn't think the time was ideal. Although it was a Friday night, Francine had to work the next day. As a matter of fact, so did I. We held hands and swapped some tormenting kisses, but I held firm and did not allow my excitement to embarrass me. Too quickly it was almost ten and my battle with temptation was withering.

Francine was having a difficult time, too. Several times during the evening she had to break away from my clutches and go to the bathroom. It was getting late, and I didn't want her to stay any longer and have to travel home alone, so I hinted around about the time. She offered to do the dishes, but I wouldn't let her. Finally she agreed to leave and I walked her to her car. She thanked me for a wonderful evening and gave me a big lusty kiss good night. I promised her I would call the next day after I got off work.

I went back to my flat and began the task of cleaning the kitchen. The venerating sound of jazz continued to play as I reviewed the night and confirmed just how much I really cared for Francine Williams. She was a beautiful surprise.

It was almost 11 p.m. when my phone rang. I dreaded answering it. I turned down the music before I picked up the receiver and waited. A sexy voice called my name. At first I thought it was Francine calling to let me know she had arrived home safely, but after a moment I realized that it was Nadine Bluecrest.

"Myles, this is Nadine. I'm so sorry for standing you up the other night. I had car trouble after class and I had to have my car towed. I hope you're not angry with me for not showing up and waiting until now to call you."

I paused for a moment before I responded. "No, Nadine, I'm not angry with you. I figured you got tied up and were unable to make it. I stuck around J's Pub for awhile. There were a lot of people there that I knew and J's was a place I used to frequent often when I worked in the 'Wood'. After you didn't show up by nine-thirty, I kind of knew you probably weren't coming. I had a good time mixing with some of my old friends." Did you get your car fixed? I asked.

Nadine didn't sound like she was really listening to me. She kept asking me what I was doing right then, as if she had a plan.

"I'm about get in bed. I got to hit it in the morning."

"Myles, I want to see you. I'll call you tomorrow."

"Sure, I'll be home after six."

I hung up the phone and jumped in the sack. Sleep was on me before the first sheep jumped over the moon.

CHAPTER 19

DoubleA called at 8 a.m. to let me know he would be out front in fifteen minutes. I had just got out of shower and was examining my face to see if I could go another day without shaving. The weather forecast for the day was bright and sunny. "Sunny." That word stuck in my craw. I just couldn't imagine it meaning anything other than the death of another Black child. It was nearing time for confrontation. I knew when we got to work we would be meeting with the Superintendent and key members of his staff to address the department's plan concerning our mysterious eyewitness, Sampson.

We took a different route to headquarters. The morning air was refreshing and people were already out walking the streets. As we traveled, I noted the area. Forty-seventh Street is a historical avenue in the Black community. It was well-known throughout the country for its bustling reputation and animated tempo. Its been said that if you are from 47th Street you can be identified by the way you dress and walk. Everybody and everything moves fast. It is renowned for its legends and the people who made it what it is. Pimps, whores, hustlers, players, and thieves filter up and down 47th Street, daily. If you can survive the environment here, you can survive anywhere in the world.

As we approached State Street, we observed a large crowd just north of 47th. The crowd was watching a street fight between two men in a vacant lot. We curbed our squad car and approached the scene. I immediately moved to break up the melee, but my partner blocked my advancement and motioned for me to be cool. He asked one of the onlookers what the two men were fighting about. A heavyset Black woman told him that the two men were brothers and their mother had just died.

The fight was fierce. It looked like one of the brothers was about to enter the zone of unconsciousness. DoubleA walked back to the squad and turned on the siren and the crowd turned and looked in his direction. "All y'all can get to hopping. The entertainment's over. Anybody want to make a contribution to the show, just place it on the hood of this here police car."

The crowd started breaking up and the two men got up off the ground and started walking away. DoubleA called out and signaled for them to come toward him. "I understand you two boys just lost your mother. You think she would be happy to know that her two sons are out in the street fighting just like two dogs who ain't never had no training? Whatever you two are fighting about, toss it, and get on with laying your mother to rest."

The brothers looked at each other, then one of them reached and placed his arm around the other's neck and they walked away.

We continued on to headquarters and arrived just after roll call had started. Lt. Nugent was disseminating information when we walked in the room. "I guess you two dicks are working in a different time zone. Roll call was scheduled for 9:00 a.m. this week. Don't you guys read the C.O.'s book?" He teased, adding, "I need to see both of you after roll call."

Lt. Nugent continued reading off crime statistics and giving out assignments.

Murder in Chicago was still king. We were at the end of April. The murder rate was continuing at a record pace. There were 68 murders committed in April, bringing the total to 299 with 2 days left in the month. The rage of fratricide in the Black community was becoming endemic. Black children started believing they would surrender to a prophecy and their life expectancy would not go beyond age thirty. The stress of this type of life suspense had devastated the fragile minds of many young Black boys and forced many mothers to fear for their children who were trapped by gang warfare and violence.

After roll call, we followed Lt. Nugent into his office. "Boys, you're due in the Superintendent's office for a round-table with his exempt staff and the State's Attorney at ten-thirty this morning. Your coveted witness will be arriving in town on Monday. I know you may be surprised, but the "G" has not contacted us and, in all probability, they won't. Our counter plan is to serve Agent Oliver with a grand jury summons when he gets off the plane. There will be no getting around the subpoena. If we can get in front of him, he'll have to accept the summons and appear. Our main concern is keeping the plan confidential."

We had about an hour to kill, so I took a seat at my desk and made a phone call over to Cook County Hospital to see how our suspect, Felix Hamilton, was doing. I learned he was still a patient and his wounds were slow healing, but that he'd be returned to the jail hospital in a few more days. DoubleA sat down at his desk across from me and dialed Area 1 on the Pax line. He was looking for Detective Cole or Banahan to get an update on their investigation. Felix had been charged, but there was no confession and no eyewitnesses. We knew lacking that type of evidence would make it extremely difficult to get a conviction. Detective Cole and Banahan were off for the weekend and not scheduled to return until Monday.

I finished my call and thought of Francine. I decided to give her a call and say hello. I knew she would enjoy hearing from me so soon. The bank opened for half a day on Saturdays and Francine worked in customer service. I had to beg the operator to connect me with her because they only took direct calls in customer service on Saturdays.

Finally, I was able to reach her extension. "Good morning, Ms. Williams. This is your favorite admirer calling."

"Myles, why do you sound so sexy this morning? Are you at work now?"

"Yeah. I got a few minutes to kill before I go downstairs for a meeting. I just wanted to say hello early because I don't know what the day will bring, and I might not get a chance to talk to you before I get off. I'll call you back, if I don't get tied up."

"All right, I'll wait for your call. And, Myles, I have a surprise for you. Don't ask what it is. I'll tell you about it when I see you. Maybe we can see each other later tonight?"

"That'd be fine with me. I'll call you later."

This Saturday morning the whole headquarters building was buzzing as the Police Exempts scheduled to attend the meeting filed in. We got a call from the Superintendent's office telling us it was "show time." When the three of us entered the crime lab auditorium located on the fifth floor, seated at the table with the Superintendent was Deputy Superintendent Spiotro from Investigative Services, Chief of Detectives Stibby, Detective Ramone Smoothe, and Assistant State's Attorney Sullivan.

The Superintendent informed us that Agent William Oliver was not on any scheduled flight coming into Chicago on Monday. As he gave out this disturbing news, he had a grin on his face that gave way to his next statement. "Now, gentleman, what do you find suspicious about that statement?"

Heads turned. It looked like everybody in the room was stumped, except for DoubleA, who immediately blurted out, "'Scheduled' is the key word here. What do you have for us, boss?"

The Superintendent laid out the information. "I've received confidential information that Oliver will be arriving at Midway Airport on Monday at 10:20 a.m. on a military flight from Texas. He's scheduled to meet with the Assistant U.S. Attorney for the Northern District at the Dirksen Federal Building. Let me remind you, the passengers on those military flights have to use the Central Avenue entry and exit gate. Once they leave the plane, they usually have a vehicle that will take them to their destination.

"We have all of our plans in order. We will have a marked squad car at the exit. It will stop the vehicle at the gate. The commander from the 008th police district will be given instructions at 8 a.m. on Monday. If everything goes as planned, Agent Oliver will be in front of a grand jury on Tuesday morning."

When the Superintendent finished his briefing, chatter filled the room. He immediately reminded us that everything discussed in this room must not be discussed with anyone.

It was almost noon when we left headquarters. DoubleA said, "Look here, Myles, I need to stop by and see Peachazz. I want to check on her. I haven't seen her but once since she came home from the Hospital. Besides, she might have some additional information for us. You know, Peachazz is moody; sometimes she won't call me when she has information for me. She does shit like that—just sit on something and wait to see how long it'll take before I come calling with my hat in my hand."

I pulled up in front of the complex and DoubleA jumped out of the squad car saying, "Give me thirty minutes to soften her up and lay something on her."

I drove off and headed to the South Town YMCA to kill some time and chat with some of the guys at the businessmen's club. The club was bustling at that time of the day. Some of the members were finishing up their workout, others just starting. I looked at the schedule for racquetball and signed up for a court for 5 p.m. I was just about ready to leave when one of my old partners, Billy Lumpkin, came out of the sauna and shouted, "Yo, Myles, you got time for a game?"

I was glad to see Billy. We hadn't seen each other in a long time. He wanted to sit and chat. I told him I was on duty and had to get back and pick up my partner in a few minutes.

"I signed up for a court at five today. If you want to play, you can meet me back then."

"All right, I'm off today. I'll try to be back here later." We agreed to meet on the court at five.

I looked at my watch. I had been gone about twenty-five minutes. I hurried to the squad car and raced to pick up DoubleA. As I approached, I saw him standing at the curb. When he got into the car he had a slight grin on his face. I knew DoubleA had something to tell me, but I hesitated to ask. I now knew he would share whatever information he had received—I just had to let him do it at his own pace. We headed east and I pulled into an empty parking space under the el. We went into Daley's Diner for lunch.

DoubleA was intriguing when he had something exciting to say. He would ask you a lot of questions to see if you were as investigative and analytical as he. The questions he would challenge you with frequently examined your skills and required you to sometimes look beyond the evidence and think outside the box.

After coffee was served, he began to disclose the information he had received from Peachazz. "Well, my friend, if you have never heard this before, cloak this as a cerebral secret. A whore is a police officer's best source of information. Peachazz told me she has a childhood friend named Naomi who is a lifelong friend of Black Sonny's sister. She also told me our dearly departed friend, Artie the Brute, spent many an hour in the front seat of his Cadillac with Naomi 'bobbin the post.' On the day Franklin Williams was murdered, Naomi saw Black Sonny, Artie the Brute, and guess-who dragging the Williams kid out of the trunk of Artie's Cadillac, kicking and flailing? Franklin's hands were tied behind his back and he had a gag in his mouth. The mysterious third person was none other than...you got it...Jake Fontaine! And, Myles, just to make things smooth, Naomi has a case and is willing to deal for a break. How sweet it is, Holmes! But she's scared shitless of those gang niggas. She'll cooperate, but she wants some guarantees."

"What's that?" I asked.

"She wants protection, and she said she ain't going to be paraded to no witness stand. One day, one testimony! Now, Peachazz has been sitting on this information for over a week. She told me I stayed away too long, and she was never going to call me and tell me what she had. That bitch is stubborn—but sweet as she can be."

After lunch we drove to the old South-Moor Hotel to look around. The city was working feverishly to seal off the building, but every time they would secure it the Stones would break back in and conduct gang business. The building was condemned. Leaking water, rats, unstable flooring, and the chronic smell of death filled the air. Gang symbols, old gym shoes, beer bottles, drug paraphernalia, and spent rounds cluttered the floors.

The building's architecture and decayed ornamentation still captivated my attention. As we walked through the vestiges of what was once a renowned attraction on the city's southside, I envisioned the crowds of young college fraternity members hosting affairs that attracted Chicago's blue-veined and middle-class Negroes during the late '40s through the '60s. Just before its demise, the South-Moor Hotel had over two hundred tenants and sixty employees. It was once known as the Jewel of Woodlawn, but the Stones moved into the neighborhood forcing decent residents to flee after being victimized through muggings and thefts. The gang then moved its headquarters into the building, refused to pay rent, and terrorized the community.

We couldn't find any new evidence, but just walking through the scene made me feel more determined to solve the murder and take a vicious killer out of the community.

We returned to the squad car and drove to Area 1 to review some files and use the phone. I looked at some of the murder investigations that were on file in the Area, and it was clear that there were not enough detectives to handle the increasing number of homicides that were occurring. After spending several hours looking through files, we decided to call it a day and end our tour of duty. I drove DoubleA home and headed to the South Town YMCA.

When I got there my ex-partner, Billy Lumpkin, was all dressed and ready. "Myles, I'll be on the court when you get dressed."

Billy was a fierce competitor; he had great knowledge of the sport and the athletic skills to complement his game. Racquetball requires stamina, strength, and agility. We played three games and I lost all three, but the workout was energizing and the whirlpool, steam, and sauna prepped me for an expedition in dreamland on the sofa in front of the Club's television.

I slept for an hour or so, woke up at eight-fifteen, showered, and headed home. While driving home I thought about Francine. HOLY SHIT! I forgot to call her after work and make arrangements for us to see each other. Got-damnit, how could I forget that.

As soon as I got through the front door, I called her. "Francine, please forgive me. This is not my style; somehow, I completely forgot about you. I'm so embarrassed. I don't know what to say."

"It's okay, Myles, I understand. I thought something happened."

"No, no, nothing happened. I played a few games of racquetball and took a nap. I just plain forgot to call."

"That's okay. We have plenty of time to make it up. I'm sure you had every intention of seeing me, so let's get past this. Myles, I trust you and that's all that matters."

"Francine you are priceless. I want you to know that. I'll make this up to you the very first opportunity I get. Please forgive me."

"I do, Myles, I do. I'll call you tomorrow evening, okay?"

"Good!"

I knew the next time I saw Francine, I wanted to wake up in the morning and look right into her beautiful brown eyes.

I turned on my record player and relaxed listening to Dexter Gordon's "The Shadow of Your Smile" while resisting an impulse to have a visit with Jack Daniels.

Chapter 20

Monday morning didn't take long to arrive. My phone rang at 5:45 a.m. It was DoubleA making sure that I would be ready when he arrived at 6:30.

He pulled the squad car into the parking lot just as I reached the pavement. He was a bit excited, and that was unusual for him. He boasted, "Today is a day of reckoning! The number-one law enforcement agency in the country will be tested. Tomorrow the Chicago Police Department will be regarded as unfaithful sons-of-bitches who challenged the authority of the federal government and flaunted a hometown subpoena under the guise of local authority."

When we arrived at headquarters that morning, Lt. Nugent ordered us to make haste out to Midway Airport and go to the Central Avenue gate. There we would stand by and wait for the Superintendent and his entourage. We hopped on the Stevenson Expressway, exiting at Cicero Avenue and driving south to 55th Street. We entered the Central Avenue gate just south of 55th Street and waited. The commander of the 008th District, Robert McCurry, was already there with three lieutenants and four sergeants, awaiting the arrival of the Superintendent.

I remembered Commander McCurry from my first assignment as a police officer. I was assigned to the 008th District as a recruit, fresh out of the police academy. Commander McCurry was a tough-looking gentleman who reminded you of W.C. Fields. The only thing missing was the stogie sticking out of his mouth. He was dressed in full uniform and appeared anxious to get his assignment accomplished. When we parked our squad, he sent a sergeant over to have us come to his vehicle.

"Good morning, officers. I'm Robert McCurry, Commander of the 008th District." His voice was a little petulant; he even sounded like Fields.

I immediately reminded him that I started my career under his command. "Sir, my name is Detective Myles Sivad. I worked under your command immediately after I graduated from the police academy. I enjoyed working under your leadership."

He quickly responded, "Don't hand me that bullshit, Sivad. You didn't stay in the 008th long enough to appreciate the shit I was doing. But don't get me wrong, I was glad to see a young officer demonstrate his motivation and move on to a more challenging assignment."

I was surprised that Commander McCurry remembered me. I had forgotten that he was known as the old bulldog with an elephant's recall. Back in the late '50s he was a feared detective who carried a pearl-handled, five-shot, snub-nosed revolver. His reputation as a marksman was known all over the Department. During our annual firearm qualifications, he used that snub-nose while most of us fired a 357 or a .38-revolver.

While we were standing outside of our squad cars reminiscing with several officers, we observed two, unmarked, black Ford Galaxies approaching the Central Avenue gate. It was clear to us that Superintendent Rochard was making this assignment his personal responsibility. He was accompanied by Deputy Superintendent Spiottro. Chief of Detectives Stibby was chauffeured by Detective Ramone Smoothe. They were all dressed in civilian attire, but each had his identification and police star in clear view.

The Superintendent gave all of us our instructions. We left the area and regrouped in a parking lot a few blocks away—where we would await instructions and information on the arrival of military flight # NAR74501 from Texas.

The flight landed at 10:10 a.m. A dark-colored Ford Galaxy pulled through the gate about half a block ahead of us. We moved down Central at a slow pace to allow the plane to taxi and clear the runway. We could see several males exit the plane and get into the Ford. Just as the vehicle attempted to exit, we had a marked, blue-and-white squad car block its path. When we approached the vehicle we could see that all of the passengers were white. Agent Oliver was not in the vehicle.

A sudden feeling of panic swept over us, as we all stood there speechless and bewildered. Detective Smoothe then whispered something in the ear of Chief Stibby who quickly looked in the direction of the military plane, noting that it was just sitting there without making any effort to clear the tarmac. Stibby motioned for two cars to pull onto the track and block the path of the plane.

DoubleA and I joined the quest and, as we exited our squad car, we could hear Chief Stibby tell Detective Smoothe to remain in his vehicle, emphasizing that we didn't have to flaunt who helped us get the secret information on Oliver's arrival. We boarded the plane and there was Agent Oliver, sitting with a copy of the *Wall Street Journal* in his lap.

Chief Stibby called out, "Agent William Oliver."

And he, without hesitation, responded, "Yes."

"I'm John Stibby, Chief of Detectives for the Chicago Police Department. I'm serving you with a subpoena." He politely handed Agent Oliver a copy of the subpoena directing him to appear in front of the grand jury on Tuesday, April 30, 1974.

We all felt gratified as we left the plane and headed back to our squads. Chief Stibby informed the Superintendent that we had made contact with Agent Oliver and the subpoena had been served. The suspense was now over and our murder investigation, hopefully, would soon be coming to a successful conclusion. The drive back to headquarters was a time to celebrate our efforts and a time for retrospection. I thought of a number of scenarios in which our case would end. The testimony of Agent Oliver could be the one factor that would put Black Sonny behind bars for a long time. Because our victim was kidnapped and murdered, Black Sonny could face two serious charges, each with a maximum penalty, and the possibility of connecting Fontaine with the murder could become evidence discovered during the trial.

When we arrived at headquarters, we contacted the Gary Police Department to determine when their case was set for trial. We learned that Attorney Sam Adamski had appeared in court this morning demanding that his client be released immediately for lack of sufficient evidence to sustain the charges. We knew when Black Sonny was arrested at the First Presbyterian Church the murder case against him was dependent on the survival of the only witness, who was, at that time, in critical condition. We now learned the witness had succumbed to his wounds and died shortly after Black Sonny was arrested. That witness was the strength of the Gary Police Department's case, so we could see no reason for Attorney Adamski's request to be denied. We informed them that when, and if, the judge's decision was handed down, we needed them to hold Black Sonny and not release him until the Chicago Police arrived. Our next task was to head straight to 26th and California and have the pre-written warrant for the arrest of Ivory Gilcrist signed by a judge.

En route we received a radio message from the dispatcher telling us to call Lt. Nugent as soon as possible. I pulled into a gas station and DoubleA hopped out of the squad car to use a pay phone. When he returned, he told me the lieutenant had instructed us to go to Branch 27, the courtroom of the Honorable Judge

Anthony Urso. Judge Urso was a good friend of the lieutenant and a friend of all police officers. We knew we could get the arrest warrant signed without any unnecessary waiting. The warrant only needed a date added to the body of the complaint.

As soon as we entered the courtroom, Judge Urso waved us to the front and instructed the Assistant State's Attorney to review our warrant and bring one of us up to the bench to be sworn in. The process didn't take twenty minutes before we were finished.

We gassed up our squad car at the Area 4 garage on Kedzie and Harrison. It was 12:40 p.m. We headed to Gary, Indiana to pick up our prized suspect. The trip took about fifty-five minutes in mild traffic. We pulled up in the parking lot of the police station and went inside. We identified ourselves, and we were directed to the Detective Division.

A sergeant named Bob Jones met us and presented us with some temporary, but discouraging, news: "You guys will have to go to the County Court House in Crown Point, Indiana, and you'd better hurry. Gilcrist's lawyer is there now, and he's demanding that his client be released or made eligible for bond."

We were not familiar with the location of the County Court, but knew Crown Point was a good distance away. This was unpleasant news, but not nearly as unpleasant as the sergeant's next statement. He reviewed our arrest warrant and made a copy of it for their records. While reviewing the warrant, I noticed a puzzled look on his face. "Where are the extradition papers? Don't you guys know about the extradition agreement that the state of Indiana has with the state of Illinois?"

Extradition was a process under state law that allows the accused to voluntarily agree to return to the state that is accusing him or her of committing a crime. If the accused fails to waive extradition, then the state must grant the accused a hearing and this could take some time. This was a shocker because, in our haste and excitement to get to the end of this investigation, we totally forgot about extradition. Gilcrist's lawyer had appeared in court in Chicago earlier and advised us that he would be preparing a defense against extradition to Indiana; but he never did. We totally forgot about it. If Gilcrist didn't want to go back to Chicago under our arrest warrant, he didn't have to go without demanding a hearing; obviously, that could take some time. We were stumped. We completely overlooked the extradition laws and now it appeared to be too late. My only issue was how we could neglect something so important. I wondered if Attorney Adamski was being misleading when he fed us the line about preparing a defense against extradition, when he knew he wouldn't do it. We were confronted with a dilemma that we hadn't prepared for. It looked like we made the drive to Gary for naught.

I huddled up with DoubleA in the corner of the hallway, and we quickly went through an emergency management session. We knew Attorney Adamski was in Crown Point to facilitate Black Sonny's release from custody. If he gained that release, Gilcrist would more than likely come back to Chicago with Adamski.

Suddenly, I thought of something. "We should wait around, stay out of sight, and see if Black Sonny would be released. If so, we could tail them back to Chicago and, once they enter the city limits, we could have them stopped, present the arrest warrant, and wham—so much for extradition laws."

DoubleA's face lit up like a neon sign. "Sivad, you amaze me. That's thinking outside the box. You learn fast, my-boy. Let's get after it!"

We went back into Sgt. Jones' office and explained our plan to him. He, too, thought it was clever, and he told us he could help us hang low and keep us informed. Sgt. Jones also reminded us that if Adamski obtained a release of his client, it would be hours before he would be discharged. "The best thing you can do now is find a spot close to the courthouse and wait for some movement by the lawyer and the client," he advised. "Once you find a place to settle, I'll keep in contact with you and let you know what your next move should be."

Sgt. Jones directed us to a restaurant in Lake County, Indiana, about a mile away from the Crown Point courthouse. There we settled for some lunch, and waited on our suspect's next move. DoubleA went to the pay phone and called our office to let Lt. Nugent know what we were up to. I could see that DoubleA was taking some heat from the expression on his face; however, the conversation did not last long.

"What's the lieutenant's beef?" I asked. "I could see a little concern in your face while you were talking to him."

"It's okay, man. He was down on himself; a little frustrated for not remembering the law after working in extradition for over twelve years. But he was real happy with our recovery. He complimented you for your quick assessment and management of the situation."

After lunch, we hung around the restaurant, waiting until we got a call from Sgt. Jones informing us that our suspect had been freed and that he and his lawyer were leaving the jail, walking toward the parking lot. "They're in a '74 dark blue Lincoln, Illinois license number ZR194. You can pick up their trail at the entry to Interstate 65 and stay on 'em to Interstate 94 westbound to Chicago," Jones suggested.

We didn't hesitate getting into position on time so we could execute our strategy according to plan. Attorney Adamski entered Route 30, heading toward Interstate 65 north to Interstate 94. We followed him, making sure he didn't pick up our tail. About twenty-eight miles down the road, we were able to pick up communications with Chicago and request a blue-and-white squad car to position itself on Interstate 94 at 115th Street and wait at the bottom of the entry ramp until we contacted them. We decided to have a marked squad car stop the attorney's vehicle and then we would drive up and make our move.

When we got to 130th Street we again contacted the dispatcher and inquired about the position of the marked squad car. We heard, "Beat 6812B, your squad is in position."

I responded, "Squad, we want that blue-and-white to stop a 1974 dark blue Lincoln bearing Illinois license number Zebra-Robert 194. Instruct them to hold the occupants until we arrive on the scene."

"6812B, we copied and we have relayed that information to the Unit." The dispatcher said.

The Lincoln was stopped just north of 111th Street. We pulled in behind the squad car and approached the vehicle. Attorney Adamski was standing outside talking to the uniformed officer as we walked up. We identified ourselves to Attorney Adamski and presented him with the arrest warrant for Ivory Gilcrist.

He quickly reviewed the warrant and slammed the paper to his side. "Where the fuck did this come from? I just got this man released from jail in Crown Point, Indiana, for some bullshit murder charge and, before we could barely get into the state of Illinois, here you guys come with some more bullshit. What the fuck is this, a get Ivory Gilcrist campaign?"

DoubleA ignored the attorney's rumblings and went straight to the passenger door and ordered Black Sonny out of the vehicle. "We have a warrant for your arrest for the murder of Franklin Williams. Step out of the car and place your hands behind your back!"

Black Sonny looked a bit contemptuous and he challenged us the moment he realized what was taking place. "You motherfuckers don't let up, do you? Anything to keep a nigga under attack. Can one of you two Toms tell me what the fuck is going on here?"

I didn't say shit to him because I knew the master of self-redemption would be undressing him with a daunting attack.

Sure enough, DoubleA lit into him. "Hey, Nigga, who the fuck do you think you're talking to? It's niggas like you who have overwhelmed the race with behaviors that have tarnished our efforts toward progress. Your murderous acts in the community have caused many young men to die. You flaunt your gang affiliation and gang coercion like armor, depressing the value of life and property in the Woodlawn community. My brother, you have reached your closing stage. Life as you have been accustomed to will no longer be yours to enjoy. I pray that our democratic system of justice recognizes your deeds as attacks on humanity and you are gravely punished."

Those were kind remarks considering who made them and for what reason. However, I knew DoubleA had more in reserve and I was sure, during our long evening of prisoner processing, Black Sonny would realize that there was one particular Black crusader who would not retire until killers like him had been removed from society.

We took our prisoner to Area 2 Detective Division headquarters. He was processed and a 005th district squadrol was called to transport him to Central Detention at police headquarters. There he would be transported to the county court building for arraignment the next morning.

After processing the prisoner, I decided to call our office and let the lieutenant know of our success. He wasn't in; however, there was a message from a Mr. Oliver requesting that we contact him as soon as possible. I took the phone number from the desk officer. It was 7:32 p.m.

"DoubleA, we have a message from a Mr. Oliver. He wants us to call him as soon as possible."

We were both intrigued with the name, suspecting that it was our phantom junkman. I dialed the number and after two rings a male voice answered the phone. I identified myself and was greeted with, "Detective Sivad, this is Agent William Oliver. I want to sit down and have a conversation with you before I go in front of the grand jury. Is there some place we can meet? I need to talk to you, but only on one condition."

"What's that?'

"I want you to promise that you'll just listen and not ask any questions."

"Okay, man. You have my word."

I thought we could meet at Bennie's since it was a Monday night and, even though Bennie's was known as the Big Drink Saloon, it was a good place to have a beer while discussing important issues. I gave Agent Oliver the address; he said he could be there by 8:00 p.m. We finished up our reports and dropped them in the police mail. We had about eighteen minutes to make it over to Bennie's.

When we entered we noticed a young man sitting at the bar having a beer. We were sure it was Oliver so we walked over and identified ourselves. He greeted us with a kind of reverence and a noticeable degree of admiration. We took a seat at a table in the corner and ordered three more beers.

Agent Oliver began the conversation: "First of all, I want to apologize to you for the conflict that has erupted between the Chicago Police Department and the Federal Bureau of Investigation."

DoubleA interrupted, "Don't fret that issue, son. Clashes between government organizations are perpetual. What we want to do is get a vicious killer off the street. But let me commend you, Agent Oliver, for having the balls to sit down with us and share your knowledge of the incident before giving testimony tomorrow."

Oliver began his story: "On the day of the murder I was on covert assignment for the Bureau. We were working an extended investigation of the Blackstone Rangers. We had tons of data on their drug operation and gun smuggling. They were spreading their criminal activities throughout the city and even across state lines. Shipments of heroin and automatic weapons were being made at an alarming rate. Our intelligence told us the abandoned hotel had a 24-hour operation—with negotiations, transactions, and deliveries taking place at every entrance to the building." Taking a sip of his beer, Oliver continued:

"I had just entered the building under the disguise of a scavenger. I was really looking for a place I could set up some listening devices. I heard the sound of people coming up the stairs. They got on top of me so quickly, I didn't get a chance to find a secure hiding place. I jumped behind some old raggedy curtains that hung from the windows. I could see through the assortment of holes in the curtains that there were four Black males; one was younger—he was gagged and his hands were bound behind his back. I recognized two of the adult males, Arthur Shelby and Jake Fontaine, but I didn't know the name of the third guy. I believe you know him as Ivory Gilcrist. I must say to you guys right here and now that I don't know at this moment if the third suspect I saw was the one known to you as Ivory Gilcrist; but he was the shooter." DoubleA looked at me with a glow in his eyes.

"Jake Fontaine was berating the kid, threatening to harm his family if he didn't tell them where his two friends were. Fontaine then whispered something in the ear of Arthur Shelby and left. The unidentified person grabbed the boy by the throat and pushed his head down while discharging the weapon, which was pointed at the back of the kid's head. I could feel the splatter of blood and brain fragments hit the curtains that I was hiding behind." Oliver seemed shaken.

"I stood there, helpless to do anything. My soul cringed. I told myself I didn't join the Bureau to allow something like this to happen right in front of me, while

I stood by powerless. I suffered with internal conflict and I really didn't know what to do. My superiors convinced me that I had to maintain the secrecy of our investigation, and that I could present this evidence after our investigation was completed.

"I wanted to meet you guys and personally apologize. More important than that, I wanted you to know that I grew up in this city. I came through the gang struggle. I changed schools and routes to school to avoid the gangs. I knew of their brutality, and I lost several schoolmates to gangs. I hated them and that's why I volunteered for this assignment. I wanted to come back to Chicago and make some contribution to their destruction."

DoubleA interrupted the young agent again, saying "Man, I regret to inform you, but we have an impending emergency. Your statement has revealed a pressing problem that has to be addressed before you sit in front of the grand jury tomorrow morning. You just mentioned that you knew Ivory Gilcrist was our prime suspect, but you can't testify that he's the man you saw shoot young Franklin Williams in the head. The only way you can do that is you must identify him in a police lineup before you sit in front of the Grand Jury."

This revelation caused us to again test our readiness and come up with a quick solution to this very significant problem. We concluded that Agent Oliver would need to view a lineup as soon as possible. I raced from our table to call the Area 2 Detective Division to determine if Black Sonny had been transported to headquarters. The desk officer told me the prisoner van was in the lot and our prisoner would be downtown within the hour. A sigh of relief eased past me as I told him to hold the transportation. I asked him to call in a homicide detective team and prepare for a full lineup. I told him we'd be in with a witness in thirty minutes. DoubleA paid our tab and we rushed to our squad car.

When we arrived at Area 2, the homicide team of Refro and Wiley had five suspects ready to stand in a lineup with our prime suspect. Agent Oliver picked Black Sonny out without any hesitation. We were set for tomorrow. We had completed a long day; tomorrow would be a day of certainty. A finding of probable cause at the arraignment and a true bill at the grand jury would be a fitting closure to our murder investigation and would remove a predator who had terrorized the Woodlawn community. We felt confident that Black Sonny would be incarcerated, and, with the public outcry against gang violence, we could rest assured that there would be no bond for his offense.

Monday, April 29, 1974, would be a day that I would always remember. We collided with the unexpected on two separate occasions, and each time we were fortunate enough to escape calamity. However, in the final review, we both knew we could not breathe any sigh of relief until the mallet of justice had imposed a verdict of guilty.

It was approaching midnight by the time all of the final paper work was completed. We'd put in a long day but, in the final analysis, it was a day of accomplishment. We left Area 2 and drove Agent Oliver back to his vehicle at Bennie's. I was exhausted. I wanted to get home and get to bed. DoubleA must have been reading my mind when he told me he would take the squad car and drop me off at my apartment. What a relief. I was almost asleep when he pulled up in the parking lot. He reminded me that we would had an early start tomorrow and that he would pick me up at 7:30 a.m.

It didn't take me long to fall asleep. I caught up with one of my interrupted dreams as soon as my head hit the pillow.

CHAPTER 21

We reached headquarters the next morning at 7:55 a.m. As we stepped off of the elevator on the way to our office, Lt. Nugent was standing in the hallway. He quickly hurried us into his office. He told us to have a seat as he poured three cups of fresh coffee.

The lieutenant had a big smile on his face as he lavished us with approbation. "Detectives, you men did a great job. You guys are two of the best detectives I have working for me and, gentlemen, I truly mean that."

We thanked the lieutenant for his kind words and gave him a complete rundown of our efforts and what we needed to do to close out the investigation. We knew Black Sonny would face a double fate this morning. He would be arraigned in Branch 44, Felony Court. If probable cause is determined, he will be bound over to the grand jury. We also knew that at the grand jury, a true bill could be obtained and, consequently, Black Sonny would be indicted for murder. This two-tier attack guaranteed that he would no longer be walking the streets of Woodlawn.

We decided to leave our office and ride through the Woodlawn community—do a little aggressive patrol and wait until the news of the court and grand jury actions filtered out to our office. When we approached 51st Street, I decided to go into the Area and look for Detectives Banahan and Cole. I was interested in how Felix Hamilton was recovering, and I wanted to know if they'd made any headway in breaking him down—in getting him to confess to the murder of Artie the Brute.

Detective Banahan was busy at his desk typing a report. When he looked up and saw us, he gave us a big-old Irish smile. "Boys, I know you guys will be happy to hear that old Felix has been asking about you. He wants to know more about the deal DoubleA offered him. I do believe he's wised up.

It sounded like Felix was ready to deal and, realistically, he could draw a light sentence if his lawyer could convince a jury that Felix was actually in fear for his life. Judging from Artie's history of violence and murder, I would say that it was a reasonable conclusion that Felix was in fear for his life when he made a preemptive move against Artie.

Time seemed to drag as we waited to find out what decisions had been made over at the county court building. It was approaching noon and still there was no word on the arraignment or the grand jury proceedings regarding Ivory Gilcrist. We drove around the southeast side, stopping here and there, talking to people we knew.

We were parked at the curb on 63rd Street, just east of Cottage Grove, when we saw Peachazz being escorted from Walgreen's by two uniformed police officers. She was handcuffed, and there was no doubt that she was on her way to jail. DoubleA seemed a bit concerned judging from the expression on his face. He got out of the squad car, walked over to the store, and went inside. I waited in the car. I saw him come out and motion for one of the officers to come back in. Several moments later the officer came out and went to the rear door of the paddy wagon. He opened it and took Peachazz back into the drug store. The officer then returned to the wagon and drove off.

Peachazz came out of the drug store and walked southbound on the Grove. DoubleA came back to our vehicle and sat behind the wheel. He didn't say anything for a moment. Then he opened up. "That bitch, Peachazz, was caught shoplifting toiletries. I had to talk the store manager out of signing a complaint. He wouldn't do it until I offered to pay for the items she was attempting to steal."

We continued to circle 63rd Street from Cottage Grove to the lakefront, driving around to kill a little time. DoubleA began to reminisce about life in the city as he remembered it: "When I came to Chicago from down south, 63rd Street was the hub of business on the southside. Every inch of serviceable rental space from Cottage Grove to the lakefront was occupied—stores, shops, bars, theaters, banks, and Johnny Conlon's Gym. People were not afraid to move about in the community. Then these niggas upped with terror. Gunshots, murders, robberies, heroin, and gang violence permeated the area. People were afraid to walk. The businesses began to disappear, replaced by empty storefronts and property decline. Overnight, it seemed that the community was under siege and everything that Woodlawn stood for was being dismantled. Property values declined and people began to flee to safer areas—away from the scourge of gang violence and property apocalypse."

I could feel the pain in his voice as he described the death of a bustling community that once enjoyed neighborhood stability and pride.

"You see, Myles, I hate these niggas! I was born in the south, and I know the struggle that our parents and grandparents and their parents and grandparents had to go through. The hard life of trying to survive in a country where they lied to you and told you that you were free, but then refused to give to you the 'means to be.' Trying to survive with dignity and respect for yourself and your family was difficult, but they survived." He was really getting angry.

"Generation after generation following slavery, they progressed to the next stage. We proved as a race of people, under the worse circumstances, we could survive. Now come these unloved, unlearned sons-of-bitches successfully dismantling the progress of the people who lived and invested in this community. Woodlawn has been under siege, suffering from continued divestments and neighborhood decline. Arsonists, community organizations, churches, and the academe all jostled for the redistribution of the coveted land that was surrendered. These gang niggas were the tools used to pry landowners and businesses away. The fear of death and violence was a psychological weapon that spearheaded their fright. Myles, take a look at this street. It looks like a ghost town, planets away from what I experienced as a boy."

That was another of the many lessons I learned, working with the best damn detective in the department. I could feel his anger. He was proud and stately. These were characteristics he more than likely developed growing up in Mississippi. He held on to those qualities and often exhibited them when discussing issues about the Black race. I had great love and respect for Detective Aristotle Ashford; he was my mentor, partner, and friend.

It was approaching two-thirty in the afternoon when we received a notification over the police radio to contact Detective Banahan at his Area 1 office. We drove to the other side of Cottage Grove. I went into Akins' Pool Room to make the call.

Detective Banahan answered the phone. "Area 1 Detective Division, Detective Daniel Banahan speaking."

When I identified myself he began his message. "Yo, Myles, you guys got a true bill from the grand jury on Ivory Gilcrist. He was indicted for murder. His attorney, Sam Adamski, asked the court for a continuance at the preliminary hearing on the warrant so that he could prepare for the case. He also petitioned the court for a bond, but that was denied. The judge, apparently weighted by the pressures from the public about the violence in the city, chose not to be the target of protest groups who're suddenly clamoring for a stop to the violence."

After I finished talking to Detective Banahan, a man sitting in the pool hall wearing a black durag yelled out to me, "Thanks for helping me out a while back."

I didn't recognize him, until he reminded me who he was. It was Rodney Fletcher, the guy who played double agent and rat during the Alfona trial. I nodded my acknowledgement and left the pool hall. I didn't dare mention to DoubleA who I just saw, for fear that he'd go into the pool hall and finish kicking the shit out of Rodney. I did tell DoubleA that Black Sonny was indicted and his attorney attempted to get a bond hearing, but the bond was denied. Black Sonny was ordered held without bond until a trial date could be set.

The news coming from the criminal court's building was unusually slow that day. For some reason, everything seemed to move at a slow pace. We were thrilled about Black Sonny being indicted, yet the realization that our case was winding to a close interrupted our magnetic flow of energy and made us feel anxious.

We were driving southbound on Stony Island when the dispatcher put out a simulcast of two men shot at 62nd and Greenwood. A description of a dark blue Ford heading southbound on Greenwood with two male Black occupants was given over the radio. We were approaching Marquette Road when the call came out so we headed westbound on Marquette hoping to catch the fleeing vehicle. As we approached Greenwood, we saw a late-model dark blue Ford turn off of Greenwood heading westbound on Marquette Road toward Cottage Grove. The vehicle was moving at a high rate of speed and it disregarded a red light at Cottage and ran into a dump truck that was moving north on Cottage Grove.

The impact of the crash threw a passenger out of the vehicle as it continued on to slam into a paper stand on the west side of the street. The passenger was thrown about twenty-five feet from the point of impact. He was lying motionless on the sidewalk, and it looked like he was bleeding profusely from all parts of his body. The driver was trapped inside the vehicle. We stopped our squad car and ran to the crashed vehicle. Our guns were drawn as we ordered the driver to exit the vehicle. He did not respond.

We approached the vehicle cautiously and observed the driver bleeding from the head. He was not moving. DoubleA told me to cover him as he approached. He stuck his hand inside the shattered window and placed it on the driver's carotid artery to determine if he was alive. DoubleA looked in my direction and indicated that there was no sign of life.

A fire department ambulance arrived on the scene and removed the deceased driver from the vehicle. We were then able to conduct a search of the vehicle. We found a .45-caliber semi-automatic handgun on the floor. DoubleA took his pen and removed the weapon from the vehicle and secured it in our squad until the assigned unit could recover it. Another passenger was also removed from the scene by the fire department. His condition was critical.

We later learned that the three occupants of the vehicle were members of the Devil's Disciples, the Blackstone Rangers' biggest rival. They were doing a drive-by shooting on the Rangers' turf. Oddly enough, they sustained more injury than the two Blackstone Rangers they shot.

Our tour of duty was just about over. We gave the reporting unit all of the necessary information regarding the incident.

I realized today was the last day of April. The smell of springtime was in the air as we returned to the station. Traditionally, the police department measures crime statistics by quarters. The month of March was the end of the 1st quarter and, if the forecast was accurate, the City of Chicago was in for some turbulent times based on the estimate of criminal activity expected to occur during the remainder of the year.

When we reported to our office, I requested compensatory time off for the next two days to go along with my three-day weekend off. Lt. Nugent granted my request and I looked forward to a relaxing five days off. Not having to report for duty until Monday was a much-needed relief.

En route to my apartment, DoubleA warned me not to get too relaxed. "Look here, man, remember you're a cop twenty-four hours a day. Don't be surprised if duty calls while you are anticipating respite."

I nodded my head, noting my understanding and respect for duty; but, under my breath, I told myself this would be one time when Myles Sivad came first.

DoubleA dropped me off in front of my flat and said, "Enjoy your good fortune. I'll see you on Monday."

It was just after six when I walked into my apartment. Within the next five minutes I heard a faint knock on my door. I opened it and there stood Nadine Bluecrest. I was a bit startled, but I invited her to come in. She had a cute little gift bag with a red ribbon tied around a bottle of Jack Daniels.

"Myles Sivad, you are a difficult person to contact. I've been calling you here and at work. I can never catch up with you. I hope it's all right for me to drop in on you like this."

"Sure it's okay. I just got in from work. I was going to relax and listen to some sounds, maybe order a pizza."

She presented me with the bottle of Jack Daniels and offered me a big hug. I accepted.

"Would you like me to pour you a drink?" I asked.

"Yes, please. I'll have mine the same way you prefer yours."

She took a seat on the sofa while I went into the kitchen to fix us a couple of drinks. A sudden flash of her appearance struck me. Nadine Bluecrest was a beautiful woman. Her long black hair complemented her olive complexion. Her voice was sensuous and captivating. She was wearing a pair of stiletto-heeled shoes, a black satin jacket, and a black dress that revealed her long legs and high, perky breasts. I felt weird remembering all those details, in such a brief moment. Any man would work extra hard to capture her, but to me she seemed to bypass formalities with her aggressive style. I found myself a bit slow accepting her offensive posturing.

We listened to the sounds of the Jazz Crusaders and sipped the Jack. After a while I found myself slipping off into the magic of the music. I closed my eyes slightly to project my emotions into the music while, simultaneously, analyzing my thoughts vis-à-vis this sexy woman sitting in my living room. I peeked out of one eye, closely examining the beauty of her legs, ending at tapered ankles that were accentuated by those high-heeled shoes.

While I was subconsciously submerged in the music, Nadine asked me where my bathroom was. I opened my eyes and pointed. I slipped back into my appreciation of the melody and again closed my eyes, still marveling at her impulsive appearance at my door. Suddenly, I felt a soft and lacy-like fabric drop gently on my face. I opened my eyes and discovered that it was a pair of red panties—yikes! I immediately looked in her direction, stammering and stumbling. I couldn't figure out what to say.

Under normal circumstances I might have retreated, but the Jack was making its approach, and I had all the courage I needed to confront the moment. I reached out for her to come close to me and she moved in, devilishly touching my face with both hands and bringing her body intensely close to mine. I placed my hands around her waist and pulled her into me. Our lips met as my hands moved down to sample her body and search for the moist surprise that she anxiously offered me. Her body felt commanding, as I struggled with my enthused emotions and body gyrations.

I took her by the hand and led her into my bedroom. I was attempting to move closer to the bed when she stopped me and said, "Myles, I hope you don't think I'm some kind of tramp. I know I've been very aggressive. If you knew me better, you'd know I go after what I want. All my life, guys have marveled at me. Yet those who were not afraid to approach me, I never liked, and the ones that I did like, they never approached. So, you see, I learned to skip the wait and move toward the things I liked. I was attracted to you the moment I saw you. You are good-looking, intelligent, and personable. I like that in a man. So here I am, Myles, all yours, right here, and right now."

The music in the background complemented our emotions as we passionately kissed and I struggled to undress. Dizzy Gillespie's "Lady Be Good" appropriately played softly in the background. Recklessly we fell on the bed, groping frantically, searching each other's body in a fierce exchange of passion and lust. Nadine was a sensuous woman. Climbing on top, she spread herself open and mounted me. In a matter of minutes, I realized that this was a woman who did not hesitate to demonstrate how she could shower a man with the kind of sex he would enjoy.

When I woke up, I discovered that Nadine had gotten out of the bed. I put on my robe and went into the bathroom. There I found her combing her hair. She stood at the mirror with only those red panties on. The sight of her standing there half-dressed, dark nipples standing at attention, aroused me intensely. I put my arms around her, attempting to draw her closer to me. Suddenly, she put her hands on my chest and slightly impeded my effort to caress her. She kissed me lightly and whispered, "Hold on, cowboy. The next time you sample my love will be when you make an effort to see me again. I've shown you that I want you. Now you must show me that this wasn't a one-night stand."

I felt a little perplexed, but I understood. "Nadine, you are an extraordinary woman and you really made me appreciate you."

She continued combing her hair and began putting on her clothes. When she finished dressing, she put on her jacket and walked toward me. "Myles, I truly enjoyed the evening. I'll be looking forward to seeing you soon."

As I opened the door she kissed me; this time with a lot more intensity. I held her tight in my arms realizing, as I experienced the warmth of her body, that she was a genuine heartbreaker.

I closed the door gently and took a seat on the couch. I sat there trying to paste together the events of the night. Nadine was sexually satisfying, beautiful, and intelligent. I knew I wasn't going to let her aggressive style chase me away. I took a long hot shower and jumped back in the bed. I felt satisfied and refreshed.

Chapter 22

The next morning I was up and out the door, heading to Volois for a hardy breakfast. Sausage, eggs over easy, cooked on a hot grill, with potatoes, toast and jelly would satisfy my appetite. It was another spring day and I was off duty. It was time for me to enjoy myself and do some of the things I had been longing to do.

After breakfast I went to the South Town YMCA for a brisk workout—swimming, steam and sauna, and a good rub down. I passed out on the masseuse's table. He woke me up and directed me to lie down on the couch. I slept for several hours. When I woke up, it was after one p.m. I got dressed, stopped at a nearby newsstand to pick up a daily newspaper, and then headed home. I had a great morning; I was feeling refreshed and high-spirited. The sun was shining bright and the fresh air was invigorating. Taking time off from work was just what I needed.

I settled down in the living room and turned on the radio. Daddy-O-Daley was busy with his afternoon jazz show. He was playing one of my favorite tunes," Take the A Train," written by Billy Strayhorn for Duke Ellington while he was taking the A Train to a scheduled interview with the Duke. I poured myself a beer and settled back on the couch in my favorite position. Ellington's big band sound was captivating; his music was for jazz lovers all over the world.

I had just started to do my own improvisation when my phone rang. I dreaded answering it, but I had to. The voice on the other end was Francine Williams'. When I recognized her voice, I had a guilt attack. I felt like shit. I guess I wasn't made up like most brothers I knew. For many of my friends, noncommittal sex was all a part of being a single male. A player, unattached, and free to do what you wanted and with whom. But with me, I suffered from "morality conflicts"—too much Catholic schooling.

"Myles, I called you at work and they told me you took the day off. Is everything okay?"

"Yes, Francine. I'm fine. I was going to call you later. I took the day off so I could just relax and enjoy myself. I've been working too hard and I needed to relax. How are you?"

I really didn't know what else to say, especially after last night, but I faked innocence.

We talked for a short while. I told her I'd call her back after she got off work that evening. When I hung up the phone, I could feel those awkward feelings returning, so I hurriedly turned my attention toward the music and I picked up the newspaper to see what was being reported today. The headlines in both the *Chicago Sun-Times* and the *Chicago Defender* reported the arrest of seven people in the Zebra Murders that occurred in San Francisco. Apparently, members of the Angels of Death, a terrorist cult, murdered twelve people.

While scanning the *Chicago Defender,* I stumbled on the editorial page, which featured an editorial titled "Black Police Percentage." It described a recent survey conducted by the Washington Police Foundation, a research arm of the Ford Foundation, which revealed a dismal picture of the low percentage of Black policeman in principal urban municipalities. The survey showed that only six percent of the nation's police departments were Black. This was compared with the estimated seventeen percent minority representation in the country's population as a whole.

I also found an amusing article on the same editorial page. It was a response to a recent column written by Stu Fitzgerald. According to Fitzgerald, the widespread use of the term "black" was destroying the family unit. The older generation would not relinquish what was dear and true a generation ago. There now seemed to be a conflict between the generations, with the younger generation refusing to return to the stagnation of the past and recognizing that times are different. New methods must be established and accepted. I could tell that Stu Fitzgerald was suffering from self-hate. He had been taught to call someone black when he meant to demean or impugn that person's character. He couldn't accept being called Black without being ashamed.

After I finished the paper, my day suddenly got slow. There was nothing interesting on television and I began to get bored. Time was moving slowly and I needed to find something to do. I decided I would walk over to the lakefront and relax.

Lake Michigan was quiet; the water was still and the wind was low. I looked across the water, gazing stoically at the horizon. I began to think about the job, the problems in the city, and my life. I was proud of the accomplishments I made in such a short time, but I knew I was lucky. Politicians, corruption, and racism influenced the department and prevented equal opportunity for the majority of Black police officers. This needed to be changed. The department was currently facing a court decree, which ordered it to redress past discriminatory practices. The mayor and the City Council refused. The federal court sanctioned the city and froze $76 million of federal revenue-sharing funds. Mayor Daley and the City Council voted to borrow $55 million from a local bank to balance the city's budget rather than comply with the federal decree. What I found so disturbing was that all of the Black City Council members voted in favor of this loan—rather than stand up and protest the city's anti-affirmative-action position. Meanwhile, the increase in murder threatened to topple all records, and the department had no strategy to combat gang violence.

I sat there on the lakefront experiencing feelings that I'd never encountered. I thought about Francine and how much I enjoyed her company. I knew she had values and morals that were consistent with mine, but I was not absolutely sure I wanted to make that kind of a commitment. That troubled me, but it was my life and I didn't want to make the wrong decision.

Somehow time crept by and I tired of daydreaming. I walked back to my apartment, still feeling unsatisfied with my emotions. When I arrived home, I still couldn't find the right temperament. Something was stuck in my consciousness, and I couldn't figure out what it was. I decided to go out for a few drinks and fellowship with the men who helped me early in my career. It was Wednesday. The officers assigned to the 007th District had their weekly set at J's Pub. I sat around my apartment until eight and then headed over there.

When I entered, it was just like the last time I was there. Bob Lemon (Pappion) and Barry Slappy were perched at the front door engaged in battle. As usual, Bob was doing a lot of fast-talking and being aggressive. He was truly in his own heaven when playing chess. "Check," He shouted in a demeaning voice, threatening Slappy with a trapping attack. Barry Slappy, in his usual calm and confident response, moved out of danger to contemplate his defenses. Neither looked up as I entered until I spoke. "Gentlemen of the shield, greetings," I said, acknowledging their presence.

Still neither looked up from the game, but both responded almost simultaneously, "Sivad, what it be like, my brother?"

I moved toward the bar, greeting police officers that I knew and had not seen in a while. The pub was rocking; there was a good crowd and the music was jamming. I took a seat at the bar and ordered my usual. Wendy was working the bar and she poured me a drink.

"Myles, there's a woman here looking for you."

I instantly thought it was Nadine, but the description she gave me did not match. I took a sip of my drink and sat back and watched the crowd on the dance floor searching for the woman Wendy had mentioned. While I was enjoying the crowd, a voice behind me whispered my name. Turning to see who it was, I found the young lady who left me standing on the dance floor the last time I was here. All I could remember from that night was that we were dancing and she felt good in my arms; that I was feeling pretty good, and that I might have gotten fresh with her and she took offense to my actions. I said hello, not clearly remembering her name. Then I began to apologize for my actions the last time we met.

She immediately stopped me. "No, no. I should be the one to apologize."

"I don't understand. I thought I had offended you the last time we met."

"No. I offended you. That night was my first time here. I had no idea that the sponsors of this set were police officers assigned to the 007th District. When we were dancing, I felt the weapon on your side and it frightened me. I had no idea you were a police officer. While riding home with my girlfriend, I told her what had happened. She laughed and told me you were probably a police officer. I came back here several times to apologize. Finally, that bar maid told me your name."

I felt relieved and offered to buy her a drink, but she said she was with a friend. Suddenly, sitting there at the bar watching the crowd no longer interested me. I actually realized I didn't want to be there. I sucked down my drink and headed toward the front door. Nobody seemed to notice my early exit. I was glad, because I didn't feel like explaining.

As I exited the front door I saw a blue-and-white squad double-parked in front. I peeked through the passenger's window and recognized the driver, "The Tyrannosaurus," Antonio Francis, sitting behind the steering wheel. He waved me closer. "Sivad, you still hanging out in that punk-ass joint? I thought after you made detective you would rise above them silly bitches. You ain't learned yet, have you? All you gon' get from them ho's is the clap. If you gon' be a man, you need to learn how to associate with some women of substance—women that got money and a good job. Them young bitches in there, all they got is babies and needs. Straighten up, my boy. I like you. You a good cop and a good dude. I gotta go now. I'll catch you on the rebound." He drove off with his mars lights flashing.

I learned some good lessons from El Antonio. He was unusual—an extremely hard and tough man. He reminded me of a ferocious-looking rabbit caricature, always unshaven with long strands of hair growing out of his ears; but he knew the fundamentals of policing. He taught me how to improve my observation skills and how to conduct a burglary investigation in the "Wood."

I remember my first lesson. We were on aggressive patrol when we saw a guy walking out of an alley. Tony touched me on the leg and said, "Hey, Myles, watch this dude. When you're working a high crime neighborhood, where everybody's got a gun, nine out of ten will make that familiar move to insure that the weapon is secure when they first notice the police. That typical motion of clenching the waist with the elbow to make sure that their weapon is secure is a dead giveaway." Sure enough, that guy made the move and we stopped him. He had a .38 long-barrel on his hip.

Tony was extremely proud of the way he policed, but to me it was reverential over-zealousness. The second lesson I got from him was burglary investigation. I recalled the lesson: "Myles, remember, whenever you conduct a burglary investigation the offender is usually not some guy walking through the neighborhood ringing doorbells to see if anybody is at home. He's typically somebody who lives upstairs or across the hall, downstairs or across the street, a friend or a relative."

Tony always worked 10-99 (solo). His marquee signature was his right hand clenched on the steering wheel and his left hand, sporting a black leather glove, gripping the window well on the driver's side. In the passenger seat, there was Mrs. Remington, a twelve-gauge pump shotgun with four rounds in the tube and one in the chamber. I always believed Tony's mission statement was an overhand right to the jaw. Everybody had the same name if he didn't know you. "Pal" was the last thing an unsuspecting offender would remember before his lights went out. Tony truly believed that his assignment in life was to wear the police uniform and to knock somebody out…every single day.

I headed to Bennie's 357 Club. After I parked my car, I noticed another blue-and-white squad double-parked in front. As I went inside I saw the beat officers had a subject in custody. I asked one of the regulars, an old-timer, what happened.

"Looks like Bennie had to get his baseball bat for a guy he told to leave the bar," the old-timer said, shaking his head. "These young Negroes never learn." Then he asked, "Young fella, what are you drinking?"

"Jack and Seven."

We sat together at the bar and started talking about the city and the neighborhood.

"My name is Ted, Ted Blackwell. I'm a retired public school teacher. What's your name, son?"

"Myles Sivad," I replied.

"What kind of work do you do?"

When I told him I was a detective he seemed surprised.

"You kind of young to be a detective, son. You must be pretty bright?"

I didn't know what to say.

We started exchanging views about contemporary topics when we settled on the gang violence in the city. Mr. Blackwell was very insightful and knew the history of the city and its neighborhoods. He spoke with a sophisticated voice, accompanied by some street vernacular that accentuated his use of the King's English. "You know, I used to teach a lot of those Blackstone Rangers at Hyde Park High School. Many of those boys came up from the south in the late '50s and early '60s. Coming to Chicago from the south and adjusting to the environment was difficult for most of them. They lacked the education and skills to survive in the big city. The youths here rejected them and labeled them as being 'country and stupid.' Academically, many of them were two, maybe three years behind their age group, so the system put them in classes with students much younger. They were written off as not 'educate-able' or socialized.

"Rejection hardened those boys, forcing them to seek friendship from each other. Suffering from rejection, isolation, and hopelessness they formed their own culture, a street gang. That fulfilled their need for belonging and family. Their resentment grew with their feelings of being unwanted and criticized, so they turned to the weapon, the handgun, and violence. This immediately earned them the distinction of attention, fear, and respect. Terror was their manner of recognition, and it spread rapidly throughout Woodlawn."

I sat there amazed at Mr. Blackwell's knowledge and his characterization of this urban problem. He demonstrated his vast knowledge of the Black youth's struggle to assimilate into the existing culture of the Woodlawn community. I was impressed. I felt comfortable talking with Mr. Blackwell and ordered two more drinks. I wanted to know how he felt about the conflict between the police and the Blackstone Rangers.

"Mr. Blackwell, what's your opinion of the police and how we addressed these issues?" I asked.

He looked surprised at my question. Then he looked at me, reached for his drink, and took a sip. He asked, "Son, do you honestly want me to answer that question or do you want me to give you an honest answer? I can give it to you two ways."

"I prefer an honest answer," I replied.

"Well, son, I don't approve of the way the police department is handling the gang crisis. I've spent a great deal of time in the Woodlawn community. I've seen the assault the police have launched against the gangs. I know these boys have given the term 'street gang' a new meaning, but they weren't always that way. The police have been extremely brutal in their tactics and strategies. Because of these attacks, the youths have grown to despise the police. Just several years ago, the police couldn't drive a squad car down east 63rd Street without taking in gunfire.

"This type of combat taking place on urban streets in 1971 was alarming. The police department's response to it was to suppress the gangs, keep them under attack. They disregarded all constitutional liberties and kept a foot in them niggas' necks! That didn't work. Then that White detective was killed behind the South-Moor Hotel and we really saw the mentality of the Department." He said with disdain.

"No, my friend, those misguided Black boys merely adapted to their environment. They fought back with more hatred. Thus, you have the conditions that exist right now."

While I sat there listening to Mr. Blackwell, I could not keep from thinking back to what Captain Bluecrest had said about the problem. The Chicago Police Department failed to appropriately address the situation and, consequently, it was exacerbated far beyond their capacity to control it. They failed to view the gang problem as a sociological conflict that required research and input from the academic community. To put the Blackstone Rangers on a chalkboard and dissect their affinities was considered soft-peddling the issue. The police, instead, believed they had to confront this violent group with equal brutality.

Our conversation was unforgettable. I gained a great deal of insight from Mr. Blackwell: I let him know that I agreed with his analysis of the conflict.

"Thank you, sir, for sharing your views. Can I buy you another drink?"

"No thank you, Detective Sivad. I hope I didn't offend you with my opinion. It certainly was a pleasure talking with you."

I left the bar and headed home. It was almost 11:30 p.m. and, although I didn't have anything important to do for the next few days, I felt like calling it a night. While driving home I thought about our conversation. It was very clear to me that Mr. Blackwell and Captain Bluecrest shared similar views. They both clearly accused the department of being numb to the root cause of the gang problem and making the situation worse with the excessive use of police brutality.

Captain Bluecrest and Mr. Blackwell were very experienced and intelligent Black men and I learned from their conservation. Just for a moment my thoughts fell upon the "what ifs." What if the department had developed a different approach to the gang problem? What if some of the Black police officers had done more to confront these issues? What if the community had been more welcoming to a generation of southern youths who were uprooted from the south and brought to Chicago during a time when Black people were demanding civil rights? Coming to Chicago from the south with limited social skills and education made their adjustment too difficult. Their success was contingent on their ability to assimilate into a new culture. This new culture rejected them because they were from the south and exhibited simple country ways—another example of the intra-race conflict. I wondered how this story would ever be told.

CHAPTER 23

My phone rang early the next morning. It was Francine.

"Myles, I called you several times last night. I thought you were going to call me yesterday. It seems like you have a difficult time doing what you say. I'm starting to wonder if you're truly interested."

I had forgotten to call her again and it sounded like she was pretty upset.

In a hurried ramble, I pleaded my case: "Please forgive me, Francine. I'm having some difficulty right now. It doesn't involve you, but I can't explain it. Work has been pressing and I needed to take some time off. Yesterday I took advantage of being off and I found so many things to keep me busy I just forgot. I'm sorry."

"Myles, we need to talk. I'm having a hard time understanding what direction you want to go in. If this is too much for you, I'll understand. Just don't string me along."

"Okay. Okay. Let's figure out when we can talk. Maybe it will do us both some good."

"Can you pick me up after work? I get off at four-thirty."

"I'll be there."

I laid there in the bed for a moment, realizing that being off work without any plans could be very boring. I knew the next time I took off, I would have something to do. I spent the rest of the morning cleaning and reorganizing furniture and closet space. I thought about what we could do after Francine got off work. A surprise dinner at a nice restaurant would be fitting. Maybe we could see some moonlight entertainment. My thoughts about Francine became more intense. I sat in my living room looking out of my large picture window, amusing myself with questions about our relationship.

I was very attracted to Francine, even though we had never been intimate. She had been warm and compassionate; moreover, I was attracted to her vigor. But today she showed a different side. Maybe it was because I had been unreliable and she started to question my intentions. My feelings toward her were confusing. Part of me said I should move in and establish a relationship; the other part said no. I was experiencing an approach/avoidance conflict, and I could not decide which direction to take. I guess I found myself really wanting to make a commitment, but I was afraid to surrender.

It was almost noon when my phone rang again. It was DoubleA.

"Yo, Homeboy, what're you doing with all that time off? Black Sonny's case is set for trial in two weeks. The Assistant State's Attorney's office called to say our key witness, Agent Oliver, won't be needed until the trial begins. One other thing, Felix Hamilton has a lawyer and he's going to plead not guilty to the charge of murder."

"Thanks for the phone call, DoubleA. I'm enjoying my time off. I'll see you Monday morning roll call."

I got dressed and headed to the old Woodlawn Hospital for lunch. As usual, the lunchroom was filled and, of course, the police officers outnumbered the hospital staff.

After lunch I hurried home to take a little nap. I wanted to be fresh for my date with Francine.

I awoke just after three-thirty, took a hot shower and got dressed. It was about four-fifteen when I left my apartment. When I pulled up in front of the bank, Francine was standing outside. When she saw me, a big smile covered her face as she swiftly walked to my car and got in. "Myles, you're very punctual. I admire that in you. I've been so excited. The girls at work have been teasing me all day. I told them that you were going to pick me up after work. They all wanted to know what we were going to do."

"Let's have dinner. While we are eating, we can think of something exciting to do afterwards." I put a little emphasis on "exciting."

She smiled. "Whatever you want to do is fine."

We dined at Army & Lou's, a small neighborhood restaurant with a big reputation—very popular among Chicago's south-side residents. The food was a mixture of soul food and contemporary dishes. If you wanted cocktails with your meal, they offered a variety. We took a seat in a booth in the dining room and prepared to order our meal. A young waitress came to our table, introduced herself, and offered to take our order.

"What would you like?" she asked.

"I'll have a bowl of soup and a salad. What about you, Myles?"

"I'd like a T-bone steak, a baked potato, and two glasses of white wine, please."

The waitress brought us a beautiful candle to complement our table. Stanley Turrentine's "Pieces of a Dream" filled the room, as flickers from the candle reflected off of Francine's silver earrings.

We both knew this evening would be decisive. We knew something had to be accomplished tonight. We had been nibbling at a relationship for several weeks and now it was time to convince one another that we really wanted to be together. I could tell that Francine was waiting for me to confront the issue; she was being very coy about it.

I took the initiative: "Francine, tell me what is your honest opinion of me?" It was a forward approach; I knew she would have a hard time being frank, but her kind spirit would help her through the anxiety.

"Myles, do you remember the first time we met? We were in the police station."

"Yes, I do. I know, you already told me you 'felt' me coming up the stairs.'

"I didn't see you or know what you looked like. My faith told me to look toward the stairwell and you appeared."

"Yes. What about it?"

"Now, Myles, don't be afraid that I'm some type of religious zealot who has swayed God to deliver me a man. Contrary to my religious beliefs, I'm still a woman who has needs and desires. You are my desire. If you don't feel that you can be with me, commit to me—that you can only 'be with me'—I hope you let me know tonight. I promise I'll not be offended and will understand. I realize that you're a single man and you're enjoying your life. What I'm trying to say, Myles, is that I'd like an opportunity to be in your life for however long that may be."

While Francine was talking, the flicker from the candle created an atmosphere that made her conversation more heart wrenching. I realized that sitting across from me was a woman who was sincere, loving, and beautiful. She was a woman who wanted to be with me. I also realized I was in a tough spot. Francine was sincere and I knew I had to be straightforward in return. I reached across the table for her hands and held them tightly. I was stumbling for words, hoping that the right ones would surface.

"Francine you're a real prize. Any man would be lucky to have a woman like you. But I must be truthful. I can't sit here and commit to a relationship. I have to find myself gradually, experiencing all the happiness and affections that make a man say to himself 'this is the one.' Francine, I wouldn't be truthful with you right now if I agreed to commit to a relationship. All I know at this moment is that you are someone special to me."

Francine didn't waver one second. "Myles, if you give me a chance, I won't disappoint you. I promise I'll not take anything said tonight to mean we are now dedicated to establishing a relationship. I'll let that happen on its own."

I got up from my seat across from her and sat next to her. I kissed her slightly on the cheek. "We can see more of each other, and, over time, we'll find out if our meeting each other was indeed a Divine Providence."

The food was great. The steak was cooked to order, and Francine enjoyed Army & Lou's gumbo soup. I ordered a cocktail and another glass of wine for Francine, just as the six o'clock news came on the TV over the bar. The feature story was a report of a police officer shot during a robbery attempt. I was a bit concerned about the incident but wasn't going to let it interfere with my evening. Then the news reporter, Fahey Flynn, returned to the air, saying, "Veteran police detective Aristotle Ashford was seriously wounded during an armed robbery attempt outside of the Parkway Gardens housing complex on South Martin Luther King Drive this afternoon, as he attempted to get into an unmarked police car."

I jumped up from my seat. "We have to get out of here," I told Francine.

I went to the phone and called my unit. The desk officer told me DoubleA was being treated at the University of Chicago's Bernard Mitchell Hospital. I was overcome with anxiety, fearing the worst about the condition of my partner.

When we arrived at the hospital, Francine didn't know what was expected of her so she offered to wait in the car. "Hell no. Come with me, please!"

As we entered the emergency room, I saw Detective Banahan talking on the phone at the nurse's station. When he looked up and saw me, he put the phone down and rushed over. He had a troubled look on his face. He gave me a big hug.

"DoubleA is in surgery," he said. "He took two bullets in the back. Myles, this wasn't no fucking robbery attempt!"

I felt an immense surge of anger and pain as detective Banahan began to tell me exactly what happened. "All we know is DoubleA had just left the Parkway Gardens when he was approached from behind by two men who opened fire without saying a word. He was able to call in the shooting from his squad car radio. Myles, he never got a look at the cocksuckers."

Just as Banahan was finishing his statement, his partner was coming from the other end of the emergency room along with a uniformed officer. They both looked dejected. They had DoubleA's weapon; it had never been fired.

I had all kinds of feelings racing through my body. I just couldn't stop my emotions from clashing. Who shot DoubleA and why were the questions that needed to be answered. I took a seat in the corner and put my head in my hands. I was crying inside. The rage that was surfacing would soon be uncontrollable.

Detective Bananhan came over to me and put his hand on my shoulder. "Myles, this looks like a hit! The first car that responded to the scene found DoubleaA crouched down in the front seat. Blood was all over the seat, as well as on the ground outside of his squad car. The area was crowded with pedestrians, as cars from all over converged on the scene. Right now nothing is getting through while we scour the area for evidence."

I looked up at Banahan and suddenly my rage erupted. I screamed at the top of my voice, "Why! Why couldn't I have been there with him? If I'd been there, this wouldn't have happened!"

As I continued to rave, a young Asian doctor approached the family waiting room and asked, "Are there any family members present?"

My heart stopped beating. Just then Lt. Nugent entered the room with a woman I had never seen before, but I knew it had to be DoubleA's sister. She was a petite little woman about thirty-six years old. Her hands were trembling and she held the lieutenant's hand. Her eyes were swollen as tears continued to slide down her face.

Lt. Nugent introduced her to us. "Men, this is Anastasia Ashford, DoubleA's sister."

I gained my composure and approached her. "Ma'am, I'm Myles Sivad, DoubleA's partner. I'm so sorry this had to happen. I just hope that he pulls through."

"Myles, DoubleA talks about you all the time. I feel like I know you."

While we were occupied with Anastasia, the Asian doctor interrupted us again. He spoke with a Japanese accent, but his English was very fluent. He folded his hands and asked again, very calmly, if any family members were present.

Lt. Nugent spoke up. "Yes doctor. This young lady is the patient's sister."

"Miss, I'd like to discuss your brother's condition. Will you please come with me for a moment?" He asked.

"No. No, doctor. Everyone here is family, and everyone here wants to know what my brother's condition is."

"Yes, ma'am, if you wish. The patient is still unconscious. We removed two large-caliber bullets from his back. He has some damage to his right lung and kidney. We can't tell how extensive it is right now. He has lost a lot of blood. We had to give him two transfusions during surgery. Right now, all we can do is wait and see how he recovers. He has a fighting chance, but we won't know anything for the next twenty-four hours."

We all stood there, silent, allowing the information to sink in. Lt Nugent then suggested we all join hands and recite the Lord's Prayer. As we stood there joined hand-in-hand, the Superintendent of Police and the Chief of Detectives entered the room and joined hands with us. More and more police brass continued to stop by the family waiting room to check on DoubleA's condition. Our vigilance persisted through the night, as we continued to pray for DoubleA to pull through.

I had completely forgotten about Francine. She stood near the emergency room entranceway, away from us, as if she was not supposed to hear anything we talked about. I sought her attention and asked her to come with me. I found us a comfortable spot down the hall, away from the crowded family waiting area. Francine was close to a tragedy she seemed ill-prepared to understand. It's difficult for anyone to understand what we police officers feel when one of us goes down.

I offered to take her home but, to my surprise, she refused. "Myles, I want to be here for you and DoubleA. I know the police officers here are a comfort, but I want to be here, too. So if you don't mind, I'd rather stay here with you.

The doctor, Dr. Masuti, returned to the waiting area and informed us that DoubleA was still unconscious and we would not be able to visit him until the morning. "Ms. Ashford, your brother's vitals are stable, but he has not regained consciousness. Hopefully, we will know more within the next twenty-four hours."

I awoke at four-thirty in the morning from a tug on my arm. It was Detective Banahan. "Myles," he said, "I thought I should let you know, we got a tip on DoubleA's shooters. We just finished a briefing and we're headed out to make the arrest. My commander doesn't think you should go along, but he didn't say you couldn't. If you want to, let's get with it. I'll brief you on the way."

I leaned toward Francine to tell her what was happening, and I discovered she was already awake and listening to our conversation. "I'll see that you get home. I gotta leave, now," I said.

She nodded her head and said, "Myles, be careful."

We took the elevator to the main floor and jumped in the squad car. There were two detectives waiting as we entered the vehicle. I immediately noticed they were "loaded for bear." There were two pump shotguns in the back seat. Detective Banahan began briefing me about the situation as we sped away.

"My office got a tip around midnight," he began. "The caller said, 'If you want to get those niggers that shot the cop in the back, you can find them at 7337 S. Shore Drive, apartment 1107.' The informant also gave us their names. We ran them through the hot desk and both came back with gang-affiliated arrest histories associated with the Blackstone Rangers: Mark Driscoll and Napoleon Jones, both ex-cons with extensive backgrounds. We got a detective in the building to check the layout. He informed us it's going to be tough getting through the door, but we're prepared." Banahan continued soberly, "Myles, I don't know how you feel about this, but I have to tell you right now, if we take any gunfire, we ain't taking no prisoners!"

I reflected briefly on what he'd just said. Through gritted teeth, I responded, "I'm in!"

The apartment building was located on the lakefront, a high-rise apartment complex with over two hundred apartments. We entered an underground garage and were met by two detectives who were staking the location out. There were six squads with a total of sixteen detectives. A detective on the scene, Tom Buchanan, was standing in the garage attendant's office with the overnight attendant.

Tom approached us, bringing the attendant along with him. "We can't trust this guy. If we leave him here alone, he might call upstairs and warn the suspects," Tom said.

"Good thinking, Tom," Banahan countered. "We'll take his ass with us."

"Just a minute," I responded. "Let me ask him a question. Do you know who lives in apartment 1107?"

"Yes. The guy that drives that dark blue Olds over there, the attendant answered.

"Do you have a contact number for him?"

"Yeah, we have to have a number for all the tenants who park down here."

"How about having this guy call the apartment," I said to Banahan, "and tell the guy up there that something fell on his car and he needs to come down here to see about it. We can be waiting right outside the apartment when the call is made. That should make it easier to take him."

"That sounds good to me. Let's move out," Banahan ordered.

We made our move, all sixteen of us. Once in place we relayed the information downstairs and the call was made, but there was no answer. We decided to take the door down and go in. With one hit from the Ram the door came down and we rushed in. There was no one there.

"Fuck, where are those son-of-bitches?" one of the detectives shouted while holding his pump shotgun. We searched the apartment but couldn't find any evidence. Finally, we headed back to the garage and loaded up to leave. Just as we all were about to pull out from the parking stalls, a dark-colored Chevy pulled into the garage. There were three occupants.

"Holy Fuck," the driver of our squad shouted, "that's them."

We got out of our squad car and approached the suspect car as it was backing into a parking stall, but before we could announce ourselves, the passenger made us and alerted the driver who shifted gears and attempted to drive away. A squad car blocked his path and he crashed into it. Gunfire erupted as the suspects fled the auto and separated in the garage. The lighting was dim and there were over a hundred cars parked in the garage. It was pure pandemonium as the suspects, heavily armed, returned fire toward one of our units. There were three officers in the squad and they took intense fire. People were scurrying for cover as one of the suspects went down after being struck in the back.

I moved quickly around the parked car and fired several rounds in the direction of two suspects who were taking cover behind a van. The door to the van was open and it appeared that the suspect was attempting to get inside. I heard the engine start up and the van lurched forward, peeling rubber and moving erratically. Detective Banahan stepped in front of it and emptied his .45, forcing the driver to lose control and crash into several parked vehicles.

The police broadcast could be heard throughout the garage, as squad cars were left with their engines running and doors open. In the minutes that passed, there was a hailstorm of gunfire exchanged between the police and the suspects. The driver of the van slumped down over the steering wheel. There was no movement. Additional units rushed to the scene, but were delayed entry due to the failure of the overhead door to open automatically. There were two suspects shot. The third suspect was somewhere hiding in the garage. I found a blood trail and carefully tracked it, only to discover a police officer shot in the stomach. I shouted for assistance and several detectives hurried to my side to help get the wounded officer some medical attention.

Suddenly, an eerie quiet fell over the area and only the crackling sounds of the police radios could be heard. Then several shots were heard coming from the northeast corner of the garage. Detective Banahan called out to the rest of the officers in the garage to determine if anyone else had been hit. I could see him crouched down behind a vehicle covered with a tarp. He signaled for me to stay down. A police canine unit was on the scene and several more were in route. We had a confirmation that two of the suspects had been shot, but we were unable to determine who they were. The whereabouts of the third suspect kept us on edge, not knowing if he intended to shoot it out, surrender, or make good his escape.

Once the team of canine officers and their dogs arrived, all police officers were ordered to the exits and instructed to remain behind the doors until the suspect was located. They were also instructed to be extremely cautious. While we were waiting, there was suddenly a loud burst, followed by rapidly spreading flames, coming from a car several feet away. Another explosion occurred as the fire began to rage in the northeast corner of the parking garage. We had to evacuate immediately and abandon our attempt to capture the third suspect. The fire department had been summoned for the wounded officer and the two suspects. All police personnel were instructed to maintain observation of all exits from the garage. The third suspect was still believed to be in the garage.

The fire department arrived on the scene and immediately began rushing the fire with large hoses and axes. The blaze had damaged a number of vehicles. Many more had to be towed to eliminate the threat of more explosions. The fire waged for several hours before it was extinguished. Only then could we continue our search. The third suspect had escaped. When the Fire Marshall examined the scene, he determined that the fire originated from the fuel tank of one of the parked vehicles. He was unable to establish at that time whether the fire was a deliberate act or the result of gunfire striking a gas tank.

The scene was taped off and several additional detectives were summoned to conduct the crime scene investigation. We had two suspects and one police detective critically wounded. The identification of the suspects would take some added time, but it was obvious that Mark Driscoll was not one of them. Napoleon Jones was believed to be one of the wounded suspects. We had no idea who the other suspect was.

It was 10:30 a.m. when we arrived at the Area to complete our reports and statements. The building was filled with high-ranking Exempt Police personnel, along with the Assistant State's Attorney assigned to the investigation. It would take the remainder of the day to complete all interviews and statements.

I was exhausted, but my concern for my partner kept me going and I hurried back to the hospital to see about him. When I got off the elevator, I saw Francine and Anastasia standing in the hallway. I couldn't believe Francine was still at the hospital.

"Francine, you're still here?"

"Yes. I thought I'd stay here with Anastasia. She needed someone here with her. We were just preparing to leave. There's a squad car waiting to take us home."

"What's DoubleA's condition?'

"The doctor just left. He told us DoubleA was still unconscious, but his vitals are good. However, the doctor had some concern about paralysis from the trauma near DoubleA's spine. He said he would know more after further examination of the x-rays, but he expects DoubleA to pull through."

"That's a relief. I couldn't help thinking about him all morning. We had a hell of a confrontation with three suspects. One officer was seriously wounded and two suspects were shot and taken into custody."

I rode down the elevator with them and volunteered to take them home. Anastasia was still very quiet. I asked, "Anastasia, are you okay? I know this is difficult for you, but I want you to know I'm here for you."

"Myles, I don't know how I'm feeling. I'm very tired and concerned about my brother. DoubleA and my son are all I have. This has been a very difficult experience for me. I just keep praying he'll be all right."

"Don't worry, Anastasia. DoubleA is strong; he'll pull through."

I drove Anastasia home. Before she got out of the car, she turned to me and said, "Myles, you and Francine have been so helpful. I don't know how I would have handled this without you. Lt. Nugent gave me a number to call when I need to return to the hospital. Doctor Masuti said he would have his staff contact me if there is any change in DoubleA's condition."

The drive to Francine's house was filled with emotion. I was so impressed with her compassion and support, especially since she had just met Anastasia. "Francine, you're special," I told her. "You don't meet a person like you often in life. I have the utmost respect for you. You've been so supportive during this difficult time. Your spirit shines. You must be a soldier for the lord."

"That's awfully kind of you, Myles. I just wanted to be of help to Anastasia—and to you. During times like this, most help usually comes from those you least expect. So I'm just glad I was here to help."

When we arrived at her door, she leaned over and kissed me passionately. I could feel her emotion in my body and I attempted to make her feel mine too. I promised I would call her as soon as I knew of any developments in DoubleA's condition.

"You promise, Myles? You know how busy you can get."

"Yes, I promise. You'll know as soon as I get the news."

It had been a long day and there were still several questions that needed to be answered. Why was an attempt made on DoubleA's life? Was there an attempt planned for me? I knew our investigation of the murder of Franklin Williams and the members of his crew put a high-ranking member of the Stones in custody, but was this retaliation? Was this an undeclared war? I desperately wanted some answers.

I drove over to Area 1 to see Detective Banahan. I wanted to know how much he had found out in his investigation. If my life was in danger too, I needed to practice keeping my head up at all times.

When I arrived at the Area, I found Detective Banahan in conference with several other detectives. They had a chart on the board with several names on it. When I entered the room, Banahan began erasing the information on the board. "Myles, glad you stopped in," he said. "We were just attempting to identify the wounded suspects. I know for sure that one of them is Napoleon Jones. We just got a call from the county hospital. He didn't make it. He had bond slip in his shirt pocket, according to the coroner's office. Plus, one of the detectives identified him at the morgue. We're waiting for his prints to come back for a confirmation."

I was glad the son-of-a-bitch died, but my questions still weren't answered. I motioned to Banahan to come out into the hallway. I needed to ask him some questions. Too much was going on too fast; I was starting to feel overwhelmed.

For the first time, I felt that my confidence in the department was shattering. I wanted to find out as much as I could before I went home. When Banahan stepped out into the corridor, I took it right to him. "Man, I need some answers. What the fuck is going on? Are those motherfuckers this brazen? If I have to step outside of my sworn oath to survive, I don't have a problem with it. Somebody is responsible and I want to know who."

"Take it easy, Myles. We don't have all the answers right now. We did get a little bit of information from one of our CI's. He said Black Sonny put it out that you and DoubleA assaulted him on the expressway shortly after he crossed the state line. We don't have enough evidence to put the entire picture together, but in a few days, as things shape up, we'll know the whole story."

"I sure as hell hope so! But in the meantime I gotta walk soft and keep my head up. Oh, by the way, I just left the hospital and DoubleA's doctor is concerned about some type of paralysis that may affect DoubleA. Man, I need some answers."

"Don't worry so much, Myles. We'll find those answers for you. Right now it's touch and go, but I can guarantee you we'll put an end to these assholes' dreams. Myles, I live by this creed: There are two types of animals that don't live long: *dogs that chase cars and people that fuck with the police!*"

I cancelled the remaining two days of my scheduled four days off and attended roll call the next morning. It was Saturday and the building was buzzing with unit members and Area detectives scheduled to attend an early-morning briefing. Lt. Nugent was already in the Chief of Detective's office and he wanted to meet with all Gang Intelligence members, as soon as possible.

I grabbed a cup of coffee and took a seat in the rear of the squad room. Sergeant Angelo was trying to answer a volley of questions from all over the room, but suddenly decided to defer them to the lieutenant.

"Okay, boys," he said, "hold off all your questions. The lieutenant will address them at the briefing at 0830. I just want to give you the status on detectives Ashford and Collins. Ashford is still unconscious, but his prognosis is good. Detective Collins sustained a gunshot wound to the abdomen; fortunately, no vital organs were damaged. He's doing well after four hours of surgery."

After roll call we all sat around waiting for Lt. Nugent to begin his briefing. He arrived shortly after nine o'clock and started talking as he entered the room: "Men we have a serious situation brewing. It appears that the Stones are determined to kill another police officer. The word on the street is 'Off another pig!' Apparently there is some dispute between ranking members. Some are for the attack and others would rather continue benefiting from their lucrative drug activities. We can't determine what else they have planned, but I want all of you to be alert. Every assignment, every call, is potentially life threatening, so be extremely cautious. We have several detectives conducting interrogations of three gang members at this moment. We may gain some further insight into the problem.

"Another note of interest is the identity of the third suspect wounded in the gunfight yesterday. The arrestee is Stanley Ketchum, a homosexual who was incarcerated with Driscoll some years ago. Apparently they were coming home to have a little fun before all hell broke loose in the garage."

A voice from the back of the room yelled out, "I guess they were going to have a little 'ménage a trois.'" The room filled with laughter, as another detective shouted, "You know all that time behind bars, the only kind of pussy they know is boy pussy." The laughter continued.

I spent the rest of my tour reviewing reports. Then I headed back to the hospital. It was just past 3 p.m. when I approached the patient information desk and asked to see my partner. "I'm sorry, sir," the receptionist said. "This patient is still in intensive care and only family members are allowed to visit. Are you a member of his family?"

I pondered for a second. Then I said, "Yes. He's my brother."

She gave me a visitor's pass and I took the elevator to the 4th floor. I entered the room and Anastasia greeted me.

"Hi, Myles. I'm glad you came by. DoubleA is still unconscious, but the doctor said his vitals are stable. It's just a matter of time before he wakes up. The doctor also mentioned that there is still some concern about paralysis, but he felt that it would only be temporary."

"That's good news. I had to lie to the receptionist downstairs to get a pass. I told her DoubleA was my brother."

She laughed," Myles, you are his brother. He told me that some time ago."

For a moment I stood there watching DoubleA with all that hospital equipment surrounding him. He had a tube in his mouth, an IV in his arm, and an EKG monitoring his heart rate. He didn't look comfortable, but who was I to judge. The doctor said he would be fine and that was good enough for me.

I sat there with Anastasia for awhile, just chatting about DoubleA and her. I didn't want to probe, so I let her do all the talking. Finally, I remembered she had a son and I wondered how he was handling the situation, so I asked, "How is Alex? Is he okay?"

Anastasia didn't hesitate, "Oh, I haven't told him yet. He's only eight and I think this would be too disturbing for him. I'll wait until DoubleA recovers, then I'll let him tell Alex if he wants to."

I agreed with her. Why should she burden a small child with such drama? We talked for several more minutes, until I started getting fatigued. I had just experienced one of the most harrowing times of my life. My energy level was extremely low. It was four-thirty in the afternoon. I was tired and hungry. I gave Anastasia a big hug and promised to return every day, until DoubleA recovered.

"Thanks so much, Myles," she said, hugging me back. "You're truly a good friend to have."

I headed home to rest. When I arrived, I found a note on my door. It was from Nadine Blucrest instructing me to call her as soon as I got home. I figured she was interested in DoubleA's condition, but I decided to call Francine first. When I couldn't reach Francine at work or at home, I made the call to Nadine. She answered after the second ring.

"Nadine, this is Myles. I got your note."

"Oh, Myles, I'm so sorry about DoubleA. I tried to see him, but they were only letting family in. Is he going to be all right?"

"Well the doctor said his vitals are good and that he will pull through."

"Oh, I hope so. My father is upset. He can't believe those bastards would do something like this. He's been on the phone all day, insisting that every retired police officer speak out against the gang violence."

I assured her we were doing everything we could to get to the bottom of this murder attempt, and I would keep her and her dad informed. We ended our brief conversation with a promise to meet when things settled down.

Right then I needed to find a bite to eat and get some rest. I made a visit to the freezer and took out one of my trusty TV dinners: Salisbury steak and potatoes. I added a coke. It wasn't a hungry man's delight, but it was enough to satisfy my hunger.

Then I laid across my bed and pondered the entire ordeal. There were so many things taking place, I couldn't keep focused on the important issues. I knew that my partner and I had been targeted for a hit and the Stones were behind it. But, Black Sonny's lie about being assaulted by us was not enough to warrant murder. There had to be more to it than his arrest.

Finally, after all the confusion had dissipated, sleep sped upon me. Before I knew it, the alarm clock was ringing. It was time for another day of drama.

CHAPTER 24

I dressed and prepared to leave for work when I thought about Francine. I hadn't talked to her since I dropped her at home Friday. I figured she would be home on Sunday morning. I dialed her number, but again there was no answer. I headed for work, stopping along the way at the newsstand on 53rd and Lake Park. I picked up a *Tribune* and a *Defender* and tossed them on the rear seat. That morning I had a new motto to live by: "Beware of danger at all times and protect yourself from harm." I knew I had to be concerned about my safety, and, from this day forward, I would be suspicious of everything and everybody.

I parked the squad car in the lot and entered headquarters through the rear door. When I got off the elevator, I saw Lt. Nugent walking into his office. I followed him and knocked on the glass window. He motioned for me to come in.

"Myles, good to see you this morning. I have good news. I just received a report from the hospital on DoubleA's condition. He's conscious, but I'm not going to release that information to everyone yet. They don't want a lot of visitors. His sister is there with him now. I had a car pick her up at five-thirty this morning. He's still groggy. He'll need some time to rest and recover. You should get over there as soon as you can. There isn't much to do around here today; so, if you want, you can take that day off like you originally planned before this shit happened. I'll see you at roll call tomorrow."

"Thanks, Lou, I appreciate this. I'll see you in the morning."

I left headquarters and drove over to Bernard Mitchell Hospital. When I entered the room, I saw Anastasia standing on the side of DoubleA's bed and, to my surprise, I saw Francine standing on the other side. DoubleA was sitting up, but he looked a bit tired. I walked into the room and greeted everyone. But the greeting I shared with DoubleA was pure emotion.

When he looked up and recognized me, a big smile appeared on his face. He spoke in a weak and scratchy voice. "Myles, my man, I guess you think I can't take care of myself without you, huh? I don't know why, of all the people out there today, this had to happen to me. Why would a nigga come fuc...," he stopped himself abruptly realizing that ladies were present. He cleaned it up, saying, "...come mess with the Crow! I couldn't even get to my Browning. The bitch shot me in the back twice."

I walked over to his bedside and gave him a big hug, and surprisingly DoubleA held on tightly.

Then he spoke again: "Myles, thanks for rushing here to see me. It makes me proud that you're concerned about my welfare. I really appreciate you, man. You are a good cop and a good person, and I love you for being that way."

I almost burst out in tears. We had forgotten about Francine and Anastasia; they just stood there silently watching us.

When DoubleA finally noticed Francine he excused himself for not greeting her sooner. "Ms. Williams, I'm sorry I didn't speak to you earlier. As you can see, I've been having a bad time. How's your mother?"

Francine smiled, "My mother was disappointed that you didn't show up for dinner and she wants to prepare another dinner for you soon."

DoubleA smiled back and said, "Tell your mother I'll not disappoint her again."

"Man, I'm relieved that you're okay," I said, emotionally. "I won't stay long because they told me you need to rest. I'll be back tomorrow."

"No. No, don't go anywhere. I need to talk to with you. I need to know who did this and why."

"Don't worry now, DoubleA. Tomorrow, I'll tell you everything I know."

"Okay, man, and I promise I'll take better precautions next time. I'll see you at work in the morning."

"At work? At work?" I responded. I was perplexed by his eagerness to return to work. As I laughed to let him know that he would not be recovered by then, he quickly reminded me that he was the senior officer.

"Slow down, Sherlock, those two bullets in the back ain't enough to stop a warrior like me."

I gave Anastasia a hug and reached for Francine's hand and lead her into the hallway. She always seemed to amaze me. I wanted to tell her again how much I appreciated the things she did.

"Francine, how did you get here so soon? I didn't expect to see you here this morning."

"Anastasia called me right after she heard from Lt. Nugent. She asked me to come with her. She said she had a squad car on the way and they could stop by and pick me up, too. How could I tell her I had something better to do?"

"I understand, but what are you doing when you leave here?"

"I'm going home to rest. I didn't plan on getting up at five-thirty this morning. I need to get home and see about mother. Why?"

"Oh, I thought we could spend a little time together. Have some breakfast. I've been feeling you, so much lately. I'm feeling you right now. The sudden events of the past few days took the excitement out of our night. I had planned for us to do something exciting after dinner, but we've lost a few days."

"I know, but can we make it up? Not next weekend, but the weekend after next?

"Why not next weekend? I don't know if I can wait that long."

"Next Friday mother and I are going to North Chicago to visit her sister. We'll be there for the weekend. Why, what's on your mind, Myles? Wait that long for what?" She queried.

"For me and you. I want to see you now—today! Can't we make some time for each other?"

"Myles, I'm sorry, but I can't. I need to get home. I see you are having some anxiety. What's the matter?"

"I don't rightly know. All I know is I'm sunk for you. I can only dream of you close to me, cheek to cheek, breath to breath. What more need I say."

"Myles, it's Sunday morning. I've been up since five-thirty. Can't we wait for a more opportune time?"

"If you say so. I'm just feeling you right now. I thought we could spend some time together today."

"Sorry. I really wish I could, but…"

I didn't let her finish. "Okay, Francine, I understand."

I was disappointed. I wanted her now and she was not feeling me. I wasn't sure if she had an issue with going to a man's house on a Sunday morning, something that conflicted with her principles, or if she really needed to get home. One thing was for sure; there would be no carousing this Sunday morning.

I drove Francine home and promised her I would call. She gave me a kiss good morning and I walked her to her hallway. There she kissed me again, this time more sensuously than before.

I headed home, feeling both lustful and disappointed. I arrived home and took the newspapers from the back seat. Once inside, I sat on the couch and opened the *Defender*. I began to browse through the sections. On the fourth page, I noticed a small article that alarmed me. It reported that a body was found in a car destroyed by fire. It went on to describe how a body, burned beyond recognition, was discovered in a car fire outside a lakefront apartment complex. The article described a 1954 Ford Thunderbird, in mint condition, destroyed by the fire. It further stated that the coroner was conducting an investigation. It said the police department was awaiting the results of the coroner's ruling.

The article distressed me. I knew it had to have some connection to the shoot-out that took place in the garage. My suspicions began to increase as I recalled the incident. My principal concern was the victim. I also wondered who in the police department would be conducting the investigation and what the cause of death was.

The suspense overwhelmed me; I couldn't continue to sit at home without knowing the answers. I headed back to the hospital. When I arrived, I found Lt. Nugent and Detective Banahan in DoubleA's room. As soon as I entered, they all looked up in surprise. It appeared that they changed the conversation. Detective Banahan looked uncomfortable, his color suddenly disappeared and he looked pallid.

Lt. Nugent was the first to speak, "Myles, you back so soon? DoubleA here said you just left."

"Yeah, Boss, I had a couple things I wanted to share with the Crow and I couldn't because there were women in the room."

"Oh, I see, son. Well, Danny and I were just filling DoubleA in on the shooting and giving him an update on the investigation. I think we've given him all the information we have, so maybe we'll let you two dicks chat. We'll get back with him later."

"Great, Lieutenant. I'll see you in the morning."

They left the room and headed toward the elevator.

I could tell immediately DoubleA was back to his old self and knew exactly why I came back to his room. "Okay, Holmes, what's eatin' you?"

"What's eatin' me? I'll tell you what's eatin' me: Like the lieutenant always says, 'something stinks in Denmark.' That's what's plaguing me. What the fuck's going on?"

"Settle down, my boy. Hold on there. You got something on your mind, get it off. I'm listening. Getting all hot-headed ain't explaining what you're feeling. I want to know what you're feeling."

"All right. All right. You get shot in the back, we get involved in a shootout, and two people come up dead. One at the scene and another mysteriously comes up dead in a burned-out car. I'm betting my paycheck the mysterious victim is Mark Driscoll, the main shooter in the attempt on your life."

"So you're saying the police killed Driscoll?"

"You fucking right I'm saying it! There was a lot of shooting going on in that garage and people were scattered all around. The lighting was bad and the only way Driscoll got out of that garage was the way they found him. Who's doing the death investigation? Banahan and the dicks from Area 1?"

"Myles, I don't know how to tell you this, and perhaps I should let you figure out what you're going to do, but them niggas are serious. Killing one of us don't mean shit to them. They already proved that. As far as I'm concerned, we got to play by the same rules they do—and that is no rules at all."

"So you're telling me we can commit murder anytime we feel like it? Fuck this! I didn't take this assignment to become a murderer. I'm out' a here, man!"

I left the room in a huff. When I exited the main floor, I saw Lt Nugent's driver parked inconspicuously on the north side of the building. That meant the lieutenant was still in the hospital and probably waiting for me to leave before going back to DoubleA's room. The rage in me kept me from thinking rationally. I couldn't accept what I believed was happening. I desperately needed some answers. I drove off, leaving my zeal to be a police officer in the hospital parking lot.

CHAPTER 25

Monday was another day of suspense. Although it was another beautiful spring morning, I couldn't resolve my conflict. The sun was up, and judging from my bedroom window, which faced the lakefront, the sky was clear. I knew it was going to be a lovely day, but not for Myles Sivad. It was almost eight o'clock. While contemplating the events of the past few days, I thought of my grandparents, Homer and Mattie Sivad. They lived in Chicago for almost forty years, but they grew tired of the bustle of the city and moved to a small house in Union Pier, Michigan. I hadn't seen them in awhile. I thought it would be a good idea to give them a call to see how they were managing in the woods.

My grandmother answered the phone. She was so happy to hear from me. I wished I could have told her how I was feeling, but I dared not trouble the sweetest person in my life with such problems.

"Myles, is that you? Sho' is good to hear from my favorite grandchild this morning. What made you think to call us today?"

"Well, Grandma, I was just about to get up, so I thought I'd give you guys a call."

"I sho' preciate your thoughtfulness. Your grandpa is up and gon'. Been gon' since daylight. I don't know which place he's at; he gets restless most everyday. I just let him carry on. He comes back home befo' noon and has his lunch."

Just listening to my grandmother, I felt an overwhelming need to see them. "You know, Grandma, I'm thinking about coming up there to see you. I was wondering if you could stand a guest for a few days."

Grandma was overjoyed. "Boy, you ain't foolin' me? Are you really thinking 'bout comin' to see us?"

"Yes, ma'am, I can't think of nothing more important than making the trip to see you."

"Myles, your grandfather will be so happy to see you. I know he will. Sometimes he gets kinda lonely up here, but he's handlin' it well."

I hung up the phone and two minutes later it rang again. Her familiar whispering voice was barely audible. "Myles, what time you 'spect you gon' be here?"

"I'll be there before noon."

"Don't have my food getting cold on the table. I sho' hope you can get here befo' Homer gits back. It would do his old heart good to see you sittin' at his kitchen table when he gits home."

I called the station and asked to talk with Lt. Nugent. When he came to the phone I didn't make small talk. I had no desire to report for duty. "Lieutenant, this is Detective Sivad. I'm requesting to take some emergency compensatory time. I need to get away to see my grandparents in Michigan."

The lieutenant, suspecting my conflict and his own dilemma, was very accommodating. "Myles, you take as much time as you need. I'll have the time keeper put you in the books for comp-time for the next seven days. If you need more, just rattle my cage."

I got dressed and headed to the gas station. I filled up my tank and I was on my way. Interstate 94 would take me all the way into Union Pier. It didn't take me an hour to get there traveling at this time of the morning. I drove straight to my grandparent's house and parked in the back so my grandfather wouldn't see my car. I knocked on the door and my grandmother answered.

She opened the door wide and stepped back, as if she was admiring a statesman. "Boy, don't you look like some young politician on vacation." She came out on the porch and gave me a big hug and a kiss. She took me by the hand and brought me inside the house. The stove had a flame under three burners and the dining room table was set for three.

Grandma was a small-figured woman, barely five feet tall, but she had a direct line with God. She always seemed to glow, and that made her seem larger than she actually was. I sat down at the table and she began serving lunch. The menu included smothered pork chops, rice and gravy, cabbage and candied sweet potatoes. I didn't want to ask where Grampa was, but I had to.

She didn't even look my way when she said, "He'll be here befo' you can pick up yo' fork."

I chuckled, but she was right. As soon as I took my first bite, he was in the front door singing a down-home tune and dancing a jig like he had just won a number from the policy wheel. Before I could stand up to greet him, he rushed over to hug me,.

"Myles, I saw that car out back with all those police stickers on it and I knew you must be here. I thought 'bout you just this morning. It's funny how your thoughts turn into reality in just a short while."

He took a seat at the table and grandma served him. My grandfather was an extraordinary man. He had experienced a lot of trials in his travels from Georgia to Chicago. Hell, I learned a great deal from his lectures on what it would take to survive in America. I put that knowledge and wisdom to work for me. All of his lessons were designed to make me a better man. I learned discipline, self-respect, and love from him. He was my mentor; from the very first day I learned the importance of family.

After lunch, we took a seat on the rear porch. Their little house sat just off the lake. It had a beautiful view. You could sit there and watch the boats and planes as they crossed the lake. I remembered all the fishing trips and journeys down the lake as a child, the wonderful people we met and the stories he told. For a moment, I found myself making one of those journeys in my mind before my grandfather interrupted my thoughts.

"Myles, what made you decide to visit us on a Monday? Are things all right with you back home?" He inquired.

"Naw, Gramps, things couldn't be any worse. I don't know how I'm going to get through this."

"Tell me something, grandson, do you want to talk about it now?"

"I don't know what I want to do. This is some troublesome shit. I'm not sure if I can get past this."

"Let me tell you something, son—something I'm feeling right now. I know you probably wanted to come and see us today, but I really think you wanted to talk to somebody 'bout how you're feeling. Whatever troublin' you, you need to address it. It looks like you came all the way up here to talk to me 'bout it. Sooo, let's get wit' it!"

"Gramps, I got a bad situation at work. Some gang members almost killed my partner and it looks like they might be looking to do me some harm, too. But that ain't what's disturbing me. A day after the shooting we got into a shootout with the suspects and two were captured. The third suspect was not captured, but two days later I read in the *Defender* that a body was found in a burned-out auto. It was a car that was in the garage where the shootout took place. Now, I don't have all the facts, but I'm betting that body was the third suspect—and he was murdered in the garage by the police."

"Now hold on, son, you said murdered. Not 'kilt in the shootout?"

"That's exactly what I said. I suspect that one of the detectives in the garage discovered him hiding in an auto and blasted him. I haven't done all of my homework, but if I could take a look at the pathology report, I'm sure I'd find out what else happened to the body, besides being burned beyond recognition."

"Now, I have just one more question, Myles."

"What's that?"

"Why do you believe this is the way it happened?"

"Well, if he had gotten shot in an exchange of gunfire, why didn't someone admit they exchanged gunfire with him and make it a part of the incident? They were shooting back, trying to kill us and escape. There was all kinds of chaos during that exchange. We couldn't see very well, people were scattered throughout the garage, then a fire broke out forcing us to leave the area until the fire was extinguished. I believe the fire was a cover-up to hide the murder. Who knows what a policeman is thinking when he confronts a suspect who just shot a police officer.

"Finally, after reading about the body in the paper, I kept hearing the voice of one of the detectives before we headed to the garage. He said if we take any gunfire we won't be taking no prisoners. Gramps, what am I supposed to do with that?"

"Myles, you got a serious dilemma. If you speaks out you may be puttin' yo'self out of favor. If you ain't planning on leavin', you need to develop a plan, one that will help you make your mind up 'bout yo' mess, boy. Now do you have a plan?"

"Nope, not right now. But before I get back home, I'll have one."

"Good. Let's make some plans for the water in the mornin'. Fishin' is good this time of year; it'll do your mind some good. Hell, I ain't been out in the boat this season. Remember now, we rise here at 0400 hours."

"I gotcha. I'll be ready."

We spent the remaining evening sitting around reminiscing about old times. My grandmother enjoyed preparing dinner and listening to us distort the past. Occasionally she would interrupt and say, "Now, Homer, you ought not tell that boy all those lies," and we would all laugh. It was the comfort I needed. After awhile, I forgot about my problems and just relaxed and enjoyed the presence of my family.

At four-twenty in the morning, we were heading down the lake searching for trout, perch, and bass. My anxiety had faded, and I felt free from worry. We spent six hours on the lake, downing some cold beers and napping in the boat. It reminded me of my youth when my grandfather and I would sneak out early in the morning and return at dusk. We both caught a few fish and, of course, they made the menu for the evening. After dinner, I told my grandparents I would be heading back into the city the next day.

My thoughts were clear. It didn't matter how they tried to palliate the situation. I was sure DoubleA, Lt. Nugent, and Detective Banahan knew what happened and they were probably waiting to see if I was willing to go along with it. My position was simple: whatever comes out in the wash is between the coroner's office and the investigating unit. I still suspected that the cause of death would not be death by fire, but death as a result of a gunshot wound.

I didn't give my plan any further thought. I already knew what I had to do. One thing was for sure. I wouldn't be resigning from the department, and, whatever information I got, I would not turn against the man I had faith in.

Wednesday morning, Grandma prepared a real southern breakfast: fried chicken, rice, and homemade biscuits—my favorite. I ate so much I had to lie down after eating. I didn't wake until noon, and Grandma was in the kitchen working on lunch. I didn't have much of an appetite, but southern folks don't allow you to turn down a meal. I nibbled on some baked ham and sweet potatoes, with a small side of collards.

"Grandma, if I lived here with y'all, I'd be big as a house. You folks eat too well for me. I couldn't take this every day."

She smiled and said, "Myles, I wouldn't make you suffer like this ever'day. I just want to make sure you eat well whiles you here with us, 'cos I know you ain't eatin' right at home. 'Specially with all those TV dinners you always talkin' 'bout."

After lunch, Gramps and I took a seat on the rear porch. I knew he had something else to say about my situation at work. "Look here, grandson, you done made up your mind 'bout what you gon' do? I hope you done devised a workable plan. I hate to see you go back unprepared."

"Yeah, I got a plan all right. I know I can't go back singing like a canary and disclose what I know to the media. I'm not thinking like that. The way I see it, every one of us involved in that shooting incident is a suspect. When, and if, the investigation begins, I'll defend my actions. I didn't kill the guy. Whoever did will have to avoid prosecution."

"That's what I was hopin' you'd say. You'll be all right. Now git yourself in gear. I 'spect they'll be watching you to see which direction you take. Keep you head up, boy, and watch yo'self."

CHAPTER 26

I really needed the time I spent in Michigan with my grandparents. It brought some tradition and excitement to their lives for a few days, and some clarity and good food for me. I realized how much the visit matured me. I was suffering from a form of cognitive dissonance, and I needed to decide if I was going to approach or avoid the conflict. I chose to avoid it. Fuck it, let the chips fall where they may.

Wednesday night I was rolling down Interstate 94 westbound, heading home. The traffic was light so there wasn't much to concentrate on except highway signs. I thought about my grandfather and all the conversations we had while I was growing up. He taught me a lot about life, America, being Black, and religion. His acumen spanned the world. We would sit on his front porch and listen to baseball games, and he would tell me stories about his life in the south. Grandpa wasn't bitter. He was mindful of our condition as a people, and he always reminded me to be a good judge of people. He often told me, "In life there will always be persons greater and lesser than thyself." I live by that creed, today.

My trip to Michigan had been short. I wanted to stay longer, but I knew I had to get back home. My grandmother was a little disappointed, but I promised her I'd return soon and she'd settled for that.

I was due back at work on Monday morning. I knew the routine of being a gang crime investigator would be back upon me by then. But, in the meantime, I still had four more days to prepare. I knew they would be waiting to see which road I would travel; I was prepared to keep them in suspense. However, the first thing I had planned to do upon my return was talk to DoubleA. Once I talked with him, I knew everyone would ease up on their suspicions and not consider me a threat.

I arrived home at a little after eight in the evening to find a note on my door. It was from Francine. She must have been furious. The note read, "If you really cared about me, you would have thought enough of me to let me know you were leaving town. Please don't bother to call me. I don't care to ever see you again!"

I stared at the note for a moment and then I tossed it over the railing. I had had my fill of conflict. I could think of nothing more painful than having to explain to her my feelings, what I had been experiencing, and why. I gathered my mail and opened my front door. I didn't give her a single thought before I went to bed.

The next morning when I awoke, I grabbed the telephone to call the hospital. I was given DoubleA's room. He had been changed to a private room on the 2nd floor. When he answered the phone, his voice was strapping and rejuvenated.

"DoubleA, man, you sound well. What's the prognosis on your recovery?"

"Myles, my boy, everything is going good. The doctor was a little worried about some delayed paralysis, but the bullets didn't do as much damage as they thought. I'm doing fine and ready to go home. How was your trip? Grandma and Grandpa doing okay?"

"They're fine. We enjoyed each other. Me and Gramps got some good fishing in."

"I'm glad to hear from you. I'll be out of here in a couple more days; the damage to my lungs and kidney was not as bad as they first thought. The surgery was minor. My biggest problem was I lost a lot of blood."

"Listen, I'd like to come see you. There are a few things I need to discuss with you before I go back to work."

"Sure, man. I'm glad you feel that way. I ain't got no place to go. I'll be waiting on you."

I got dressed and prepared to leave when my phone rang. It was Detective Banahan. "Myles," he said, "I took a chance on calling you today. I didn't know if you were back in town yet. Listen, I need to talk to you. Can you stop by the Area sometime today? We need to chat."

"Sure, Danny, I'm leaving the house right now. I'll be there in ten minutes."

I was suspicious of his desire to talk, but I knew I had to play the role and not make him think I would be a threat.

When I arrived, Banahan was in his office. He had a cup of coffee in one hand and a large Danish in the other. As soon as he saw me he waved me inside. Just as I was about to take a seat, he greeted me and stepped out into the outer office to talk with a detective. His phone rang and he motioned for me to answer it. I picked up the phone. "Banahan's off…"

Before I could complete the identification the voice on the line said, "This is the coroner's office. You need to send an investigator down here. We have the report on the body found in that burned-out auto. Somebody needs to discuss this with us before we release these findings."

I didn't know what to say, so I said, "Sure, no problem. I'll send a detective right over."

Banahan came back into the office and asked me who was on the phone. I lied and said it was the district desk looking for a records division number for an old case. I told him that I switched the call to the front desk.

"Take a seat, Myles. How was your trip? DoubleA told me you had to go to Michigan to see your folks. I hope everything is all right."

"Yeah, fine. I just went up to relax and visit with them. I haven't seen them this year. What's on your mind?"

"Oh, nothing in particular. I just wanted you to review the report from the shooting incident." He then gave me a copy of the report. "You don't have to read it now. Look it over when you get a chance and give me a call later."

"Sure. I'll call you this afternoon."

I left his office and headed to the coroner's office located in the Cook County Morgue at Polk and Wood Streets. My body was tense; I was filled with concern about what I might find in the pathologist's report. When I arrived at the coroner's office, I met an assistant who asked to see my identification. He told me his name was Al Winston. He had me sign in before he took me to the pathologist's office. There I met another assistant—a man named Howard Friedstein who took me into the lab. He showed me some x-rays and then he carefully described the examination of the corpse pulled from the burned-out vehicle.

"Detective, I didn't want to get into this over the phone," he said, "but I found some interesting evidence when I examined the body. At first I thought what I was dealing with was a routine fire victim, but when I examined the nasal passages, esophagus, and lungs, I found them to be intact. No signs of soot or damaged tissue. I realized that this victim did not die from the fire or smoke. I extended my examination into the torso and I found two large-caliber bullets. One embedded in the thoracic area and another one in the intestines. If you will take another look at the x-rays, you can see where they were located.

"I didn't have a scientific method for the next examination I performed, but I concluded that this victim was murdered in the vehicle or he was placed in the vehicle after he was killed. You guys will have to conduct a homicide investigation on this one. It will take us several more days before we can make identification, but the preliminary examination tells us that the victim is a male Black, approximately 34 years old, 6'1, about 190 pounds. We were able to get a good dental impression, so it shouldn't be difficult for you to find out who he is."

He gave me a copy of the report and reminded me that there must be a detective assigned within the next twenty-four hours. That was policy. He had no knowledge of the shootout in the garage and, therefore, no reason to suspect any impropriety on the part of the police.

When I left the coroner's office I didn't know which way to go. I was filled with conflicting thoughts and uncertainty. The decisions I had to make would be with me for the remainder of my career. The facts were clear, even without a positive identification of the victim. How could it be anyone other than Mark Driscoll? I thought about how I would present the information to Detective Banahan. Should I take this report right over to him and look him in the eye when I hand it to him?

No, that would be confrontational. Not unless I decide to cross the "line." I decided to put the report in the mail basket in the Area. That way they would get it when they picked up the mail. I had to make sure Banahan would not see me until after he had received the report. I had to talk to somebody quick. There was only one man who could soothe my trepidation.

I arrived at the Area shortly after noon and made a stealthy move into the building. I had to get the report in the basket on the second floor. That meant taking a chance on being seen. As fate would have it, I saw a guy who went through the police academy with me: Louis Portlock, a jovial dude who always had a wide smile and cheerful attitude. When he saw me in the hallway, he rushed to greet me.

"Myles Sivad, you som'bitch, you lucky som'bitch. How have you been? I heard you made detective. Good for you."

I returned the energy and then I asked him to do me a small favor.

"Sure, Myles, what is it?"

"I need you to take this envelope upstairs and put it in the mail basket for the detective division. Don't ask why I can't do it. I just don't want anybody up there to see me."

"No problem, man. I'm glad to see you. If you ever have time, stop by the Spanish Village on 49th and St. Lawrence. I'm in there every Friday night."

"I will, man. It was good seeing you, too."

I eased out of the building and headed for Bernard Mitchell Hospital. When I arrived, I saw Lt. Nugent's driver parked in front. I went in and used the house phone to call upstairs to DoubleA's room. When he answered the phone, I could hear laughter in the background. When he recognized it was me, he didn't respond right away. Then he greeted me, saying, "Yo, Myles, when are you coming?"

"I'm downstairs right now."

"Well come on up. What are you calling for?"

"I see the lieutenant's driver out front. I guess he's in your room now."

"So what, man, you hiding from him?'

"Nope, I just want to talk to you first."

"Okay, why don't you go to the cafeteria and have a cup of coffee and I'll get rid of him."

"Cool. I'll call back in twenty minutes." I grabbed a cup of coffee and took a seat in the cafeteria. I sat there for a moment; then the note from Francine flashed across my eyes. "Please don't bother to call me. I don't care to ever see you again!"

I thought about it and concluded that I just didn't fucking care. Shit, the problems I'm facing right now far outweigh her disappointment. I won't call her ever. On the flip side, if things don't clear up, she won't have to worry about me, anyway. This was not the time to be concerned about her anguish. I, me, that's what matters.

The twenty minutes had passed, so I called upstairs again. The lieutenant had left and I was relieved. Finally, I could get some much-needed direction. I took the stairway to the second floor. When I entered the room, DoubleA was sitting up in his bed. He looked well.

"Myles, my boy, you've been busy. Your ass has been the topic of discussion throughout the division—but don't fret. I know there's a lot on your mind, and I guess you have never been in this kind of position before. So tell me, how're you going to handle this? I promise I won't try to influence your decision. The decision you make will be yours and yours alone."

I sighed for a moment, and then I began to reveal my dilemma. "I don't know if you know it, but I read the pathologist's report on the victim discovered in the burned auto. DoubleA, he was shot two times. The coroner's office is yelling right now for a homicide investigation. I didn't become a police officer to get involved in a murder and, believe me, this is a murder. For me to consciously know that a criminal act has been committed disturbs me. I have not been able to find an acceptable resolution."

DoubleA didn't say a word. He sat there without taking his eyes off of me. Then he gazed out the window for a moment and he began his reply: "Myles, the transgression you have witnessed will always be a challenge to you, whether you remain a police officer or not. Now, the question you must ask yourself is what you will do. If you choose to cross the blue line, your career will be stained. Whatever you do, wherever you go in this department, will be unpleasant. You must make a decision now regarding which direction you will take. If they get wind of you crossing, it's over for you in your present assignment. I wish I could tell you what to do, but I can't. It's your decision, my man, only you can make it."

"Fuck! I wish I didn't have to be in this kind of predicament. What should I do?"

"Do what's best for Myles Sivad."

"I know, I know, I know. You're right. I know what I have to do."

"Good. I'm glad you've made a decision. But before you leave here, just to keep me from having any further disturbing moments, tell me which side of the blue line you'll be standing on, Holmes?"

"DoubleA, I've listened to every word you said. It's not like I haven't had those same discussions with myself. I have tossed this issue around, over and over again, and I've decided that I won't be crossing that blue line. So whichever way the wind blows on this investigation, I'm going to remain steadfast in my decision."

"I'm glad to hear you say that, Myles. In this profession, sometimes we are called on to make decisions that won't be accepted in the real world. Our oath is too demanding. Can you imagine how I feel after being bushwhacked in the back by those nothing motherfuckers. I'm not swearing I'm going to go out and seek revenge, but what I've realized for some time is that our lives don't mean shit to them. They don't give two fucks if we go home to our families every night or not. To them, police officers are supposed to be killed. Occasionally, we react in kind. That is the nature of the beast; don't ever forget it. Take pride in who you are and what you are, and remember that this country didn't get to this level of development by playing by the rules. It's a fact of life. Sometimes we uphold the law by breaking it."

CHAPTER 27

A week had passed and the Monday morning roll call was like all the others. Lt Nugent briefed all of the officers present about the incident involving DoubleA and told us that DoubleA was doing fine. He was released from the hospital on Sunday and probably would not be back to work for several more weeks. Lt. Nugent gave out the homicide statistics for the month of April and the year. Chicago was on a record-breaking pace, with close to 300 murders occurring in the first four months of the year.

He assigned me to work with Detectives Folks and Clark; they were part of the B team working exclusively on the Blackstone Rangers. When we exited the elevator, to our surprise, there stood DoubleA. I asked him what was he doing at work.

"I'm not at work, my boy, I'm just in the building. I need you to go with me to see Mr. Gilmore. He's been calling us for almost a week. I promised him that when you came back to work on Monday, we would stop by to see him."

I told Folks and Clark that I would ride with DoubleA and, when we finished, I would contact them on citywide-2 and have them meet me somewhere.

When we pulled up in front of Mr. Gilmore's house, he was sitting on the front porch. It was another beautiful spring morning, and there were several neighbors out in front. He stood up to greet us, invited us into his home, and asked us to take a seat. DoubleA and I didn't show any unusual concern, but Mr. Gilmore had never invited us into his home before. He seemed concerned, yet humbled as he began telling us what he thought was important.

"Gentlemens, I have somp'n I need to share with y'all. Now don't go thinkin' I done lost my senses. I's still in control of what come out of my head. My daddy been dead nearly fifty-somp'n years, and I ain't never dreamed about him, but last night he come to me and scolded me. I nearly jumped out the bed after his ghost appeared. He told me that I was wrong for the way I treated that boy—that I'd never loved him and my soul was in debt until I straight'n out my kinship with my grandchild. Gentlemens, I done went to see Felix and I done got him a lawdyer. I knowed that he done had a tough life, and I doubt'n if he has ever been shown love from me. I don't reckon I'll be dying tonight, but in case'n I do, I done made my peace wid him."

For some reason, Mr. Gilmore thought that he owed us an explanation for what he had done. But, on the contrary, he didn't owe us anything. His dream was his notification for redemption. He acknowledged that he had not shown love to his grandchild and that he was wrong for the way that he treated him.

DoubleA agreed. "Mr. Gilmore, your recognition of your behavior toward Felix is a true sign of a man who wants to be forgiven."

We thanked him for sharing his need for forgiveness with us, and we wished him the best in his challenge.

I made radio contact with Folks and Clark and asked them to meet us at the field house on 55th and King Drive. DoubleA was returning to his non-duty status, but I still had work to do. Our case was now in the hands of the criminal justice system. It was up to them to give Franklin Williams' family the justice they deserved. It was weird how Mr. Gilmore's words made me think about how we can always change our thinking when given a moment to step back and really reflect. For some reason, that made me think about Francine—I wondered if I would really never talk to her again.

En route to our meeting with Folks and Clark, a call was simulcast on our citywide-2 radio of a "boy shot at 64th and Ellis." I looked over at DoubleA and he just smiled. Grinning back, I acknowledged the call and raced toward the location. As we proceeded to the call, I could hear the units on the radio informing the dispatcher of their intentions: "Beat 313, going;" "Beat 6122, going;" "Beat 6812B-Boy, going;" "Beat 371, squad, we are taking that call." I realized right then that, no matter what would eventually happen with Black Sonny and the rest, this war would continue to rage on—and we would be right in the thick of it.

0-595-32167-4

Printed in the United States
59762LVS00003B/126